MW01178851

Lily of the Valley

Flowering, #1.5

Sarah Daltry

Also by Sarah Daltry

Lily of the Valley (Flowering #1.5)
By Sarah Daltry

Copyright 2013 Sarah Daltry
All rights reserved.

Cover Design by Braxton Cole
Photo Copyright Bigstockphoto.com

No part of this book may be reproduced or transmitted in any form or by any means, electronic or mechanical, including photocopying, recording, or by any information storage and retrieval system without the written permission of the author, except where permitted by law. The only exception is by a reviewer, who may quote short excerpts in a review.

This book is a work of fiction. Names, characters, places, and incidents either are products of the author's imagination or are used fictitiously. Any resemblance to actual persons, living or dead, events, or locales is entirely coincidental.

Visit Sarah online at http://www.sarahdaltry.com

Printed/Published in the United States of America
SDE Press
September 26, 2013

Acknowledgements

I make a big joke about this being harder than writing the book, but I have to admit it's challenging. I want to thank everyone, but then I worry that I will forget someone. So, if I forgot you, it's only because I am dumb and I'm probably writing this in the middle of the night!

For starters, I want to thank my friends and family, especially those who know and keep my secrets! Cindy, Megan, Pete... thanks for not outing me.

I'd also really like to thank all of my Facebook friends, because they're always the ones who motivate me when I don't feel like doing anything. If I'm wasting time, I can count on them to yell at me to get writing and I need that sometimes! I'd especially like to thank my street team, because you guys help me exist beyond my little Facebook page.

Indie writers depend a great deal on bloggers and I want to acknowledge you all for taking the time to read my books, post promos, host giveaways, and just for being all around awesome.

Again, there are a lot to name and I know I would inadvertently leave someone out, but if you've gotten the word out for me, I thank you!

Thanks to all of the writers who create a safe and supportive place to vent and to brainstorm. We all have our ups and downs, but in the end, I couldn't ask for a better group of people to experience this with!

My editors and beta readers need to be mentioned, because without them, my book would still be sitting on my laptop, way too incoherent for the public eye.

Finally, as always, I want to thank fans and readers, because you guys make this possible. Words and paper are meaningless without readers to give the story a home. Thank you for making room for *my* story.

"I almost wish we were butterflies
and liv'd but three summer days –
three such days with you
I could fill with more delight
than fifty common years could ever contain."
-    John Keats to Fanny Brawne, 1819

This book is dedicated to my husband,
for being my Lily and for giving me hope.
That horizon is so much clearer having you in my life.

Chapter 1

Well, fuck. Three games, my Xbox controller, and a can of something – probably Spaghettio's – crash down the stairs. The giant black garbage bag I used to carry everything is gaping open and I'm about to lose *Black Ops II,* which is completely unacceptable.

An incoming freshman eyes me as I try to balance the leaking bag while holding the emergency door with my foot.

"Little help?" I ask.

Apparently not, because he runs into his room and slams the door. Maybe he didn't hear me.

Another kid and his family look at me and I can see the mother reconsidering sending her precious son to a school where kids live out of trash bags. Whatever. I manage to prop the door open, salvage my stuff, and make it to my room. All the while, the family continues to stare.

"Thanks. You guys are the best," I say, as I kick the now useless bag past my doorway.

1

The mom rolls her eyes and they continue to help their kid redesign his 12" x 12" living space. For all their neatly packed boxes that they went out and bought, I saved money and time by throwing my entire collection of basic needs into three trash bags. Sure, it almost resulted in sauce and cheese raining down over the emergency stairwell, but that's okay. Home, if that's what you want to call it, is less than two hours away; I'm sure I would've survived.

I leave my door open and watch families and their kids struggle to load refrigerators, electronics, hell even full-sized furniture through the tiny doorways. They don't seem to realize that college isn't on a different planet. Wal-Mart is right down the street.

The last bag and the fugitive games are now in. I can "unpack" later. My grandmother already left, since I don't like having her on campus. She drove my bags up and we said goodbye outside. I don't know if that's weird or a dick move. Probably both. But after two years of this, neither of us has it in us to pretend we're a normal family and it's better to avoid the traditional Kodak moments as much as possible. I'll call her tonight to make sure she made it back okay and then I'll put up a poster or something. But first, I need food.

I consider going to the cafeteria. I got a prime parking spot and I don't want to lose it just because socializing sucks so much, but once I'm out in the hall again, I can't take it. My friend with the helping allergy has his door open now and is playing some shit pop music way too fucking loud. I'd last a total of eighteen minutes with these people. Maybe.

Thus, my destination ends up being work. I'm not scheduled for a few days – I was told to take some time to "adjust," as if this isn't my third year at school and as if anything needs adjusting. However, I need food and I like being at work. It's one of the few pleasant distractions I have. Since I'm already out and I'm heading in that direction, I drive to one of the other local places I know too well.

The parking lot is nearly empty, because visiting hours are almost over – and because it's a Monday. No one comes to a prison during the week. Most people do their obligatory visits on the weekends.

Sitting on my bike, I debate. I have no reason to go in; I shouldn't even be here. I don't know why I came. Some nights, I just do this. I drive here, sit in the parking lot, and tell myself just to grow up and face it. I almost always leave without going in, but something makes me try over and over again. Maybe it's just knowing it's here, that I didn't drive past without even considering stopping, that makes me pretend something will be different.

Hell, I know I'm supposed to make an effort, but the darkening sky and the ugly gray of the building just look so... uncomfortable. A barbed wire fence runs along the perimeter of the building and the lot. Six years and it's never stopped being unnerving.

I gaze at the sky; it looks like it might rain. Maybe I should head to the café in case the weather gets bad.

Stop making excuses, I tell myself, but I listen to myself as much as I listen to everyone else. Not at all.

Still, I almost make it off the bike, almost decide to say fuck it and go in, until I notice one of the other cars in the parking lot. It's my grandmother's. I shouldn't be irritated that she came here once I shooed her off campus, but I am. *She could have asked if I wanted to come.*

The thought is out, but it's a stupid thought. She visits every weekend – and I pretty much never go with her. I've only been here twice all summer. So seeing her car here shouldn't upset me, because I wasn't going to come. Regardless, though, I'm pissed.

Fuck everyone, I think, and I pull away from the prison, focused on getting as much distance between myself and the place as possible.

Riding makes me feel so much better. The prison, my home, campus – they're all behind me and there is nothing but the road ahead. It's still technically summer and it's that time of night that doesn't have a name. Pre-evening, when the sun is already past the horizon, but the echo of the day lingers. The sky is an endless stretch of fading salmon and I can almost believe that beyond the horizon is something worth riding toward.

I love school, but I hate everything else about college. I love my grandmother, but being home makes me want to hurt myself. I love nothing about the prison. It's a fucking prison. But riding? I love it. There is no qualifier for this. No one interferes and there is no direction to go but forward. It's the only time the past can be outrun.

Work isn't far from the prison; I feel like my entire life is all within this small area. Home, school, work, prison – there are at most a couple hours between any of them. I thought I was getting away, but I didn't get far. Someday, though. Someday, I will leave it all behind.

The café is fairly empty tonight even though it's dinnertime. Generally, it's always empty except for weekend brunch or in the middle of the night. Being the only open dining option for college students at 3 am after a party is an amazing way to earn business. I prefer the times like right now, though. No one raises their eyebrows when they see me. The few customers are mainly truckers passing through. As messed up as my own story is, I get the impression many of them have seen the same kind of darkness. There's a weird comfort in commiserating in our lonely brokenness.

6

Sandee's on tonight. She's the only person here who knows my story. Most know I live with my grandmother because I started working here at 16 and someone had to sign paperwork for me. However, Sandee knows why.

Tonight, she looks tired, which makes me think Liz called out again. When Liz's boyfriend Keith is in town, she suddenly grows severely ill. And then he's back out on the road, and she miraculously recovers. The guy's an asshole but we keep our mouths shut. Liz is forty and she works part time as a waitress; no one needs to make her life worse than it already is.

The customers all have their meals and Sandee leans across the counter, folding silverware. While we're on the clock, we're technically not supposed to rest, but we've all developed our tricks. Mine is searching the walk-in. You'd be amazed at how long a person can believably look for salad dressing.

"Hey," she says, as I sit at the counter. "Didn't expect to see you so soon. Weren't you moving in today?"

"I was hungry."

7

"Don't they have food up at that fancy college of yours?"

"Nothing that compares to Mal's ham on rye."

"You know better than anyone that his ham on rye monstrosity will kill you. I don't know what he puts into that thing, but it's like begging for a heart attack."

"Good. Quick and tasty death." I give her my biggest grin.

She rolls her eyes. "Besides, Mal's off tonight. We've got Carl and I wouldn't touch anything he makes."

"There's got to be something he can't screw up."

Sandee shakes her head. "Good luck finding it."

I twirl on the barstool like I'm seven. It makes her laugh, which is nice. "Working a double?"

She nods. "Liz is feeling under the weather."

"She's under something, that's for sure. I didn't know Keith's nickname was 'the weather.'"

"Oh, stop it. You're too young to know about such things."

"I'm twenty, Sandee. And I know plenty."

She gets quiet and pushes the silverware aside. "I'm worried about you, honey. It's your first night back at school. You should be spending it with kids your own age."

"You know how I feel about socializing," I reply.

"I do, but usually you fake it for the first few days of the semester. What's going on?"

"I don't know," I confess. "I just couldn't deal. For two years, it didn't get to me. Okay, well, not as much, but seeing all those kids, mom and dad smiling and hugging and everyone just so ... normal? It bugged me today."

She rests her hand over mine. "Normal is a state of mind. No one's as picture perfect as they look. Some just cover the cracks better."

"Yeah," I say but I don't look at her. I know all about faking it.

I feel so undeserving of the way Sandee treats me; it's become especially true recently. I was picking up my check one night when she came in to get hers and she had her son with her. The way she looked at him broke my heart. No one has ever looked at me that way.

"Coffee?" She moves her hand, giving me space. I nod. It's late for coffee, meaning it's probably been burning for hours, but there's something familiar about being here. It's one of the only things I know that's familiar in a good way.

"I added something special for you, Jack."

She'd get in a lot of trouble if anyone knew that she sneaks whiskey into my coffee on nights like this. Luckily, no one here actually cares. I let the burn of the scorched coffee as well as the alcohol soothe what's aching to burst from me.

Sandee drops off the checks at the few tables occupied by customers and then returns to sit next to me. She's breaking a lot of rules tonight, but no one seems to notice.

"Honey, I'm worried about you."

"You said that."

"Are you okay?"

How do I answer that? Each year, I get more hopeless than the one before. Here is this woman, ten years older than I am but with the same haunted look, trying to piece me back together. From most people, this kind of concern would make me react with rage, with bitterness. But Sandee has been there, I can tell. She hasn't told me her story, but I really don't need to hear it. I met her son, I know she's been having trouble with the school system because they refuse to address his mild autism, and I know it's just the two of them and their cats. I don't ask where her son's dad is, and she doesn't volunteer the information. Instead, we cling to companionship the only way we know how – with a little desperation and a lot of booze.

"I'm fine. I told you."

"Did you go see your Mom today?"

I nod. Before moving in, I made my regular visit to the cemetery. Nothing there ever changes. It's both a relief and a constant reminder. Even my grandmother stopped going a while ago, but I can't. I can't just not go.

"You don't have to say it," I tell Sandee. "I know she's not there."

At one point, during my father's trial, when I refused to take his side on the stand, he nearly kicked me across the lawyer's office. *"Your mother was a fucking junkie, and you meant shit to her. Asking to go up there every weekend, leaving flowers on her grave? You're wasting your time. She's dead and good riddance to her. There's nothing in that grave because, even if there is a soul, that bitch didn't have one."* The lawyers later came to work out guardianship one afternoon when I was home and shook their heads when they saw me. Was it guilt they felt? Irritation? Something else? I don't know, but fuck them. That's what I know now.

"You do what you need to do. She's there if you want her to be there."

"You know, they spelled her fucking name wrong. Right there on the tombstone. E-V-E-L-Y-N. It was Eveline, with an I-N-E. And no one bothered to fix it. I remember being led to a plastic folding chair out on the cemetery lawn, the gaping hole my last physical memory of my mother, and looking up. That fucking Y. By the time we noticed, it was done and they said it would cost us several hundred dollars to change it. Like it was our fault."

"Shit. Why didn't you tell me?"

"It doesn't matter. They couldn't really change it, even if they'd put up a new one. They did it and you can't fix something that deeply ingrained, can you? It's been dug in too far. That Y is not going anywhere, no matter if I cry, punch something, or just give up."

"Things can always be fixed." Sandee's a regular source of inspiration, but her optimism wears me down right now. I don't get how some things can be fixed.

Whenever I think of my family, either then or now, all I feel is rage. Rage at my mother for turning out like she did, rage at my father for his actions, rage at the way the world shits on your dreams, and rage sometimes at myself. For existing.

"Hey, can I get some chicken strips? And honey mustard. None of that fake ass barbecue crap."

Sandee shakes her head, realizing I'm shutting down the serious, and goes to the kitchen to place the order. I don't know why she doesn't yell it. There's almost no one left and the few who are are in the process of leaving. Still, the moment of solitude has a beautiful sting to it.

I'm not even hungry anymore; I just ordered something to change the subject. When Sandee comes back ten minutes later with my order, having left me alone to brood or whatever it is she imagines I do, I don't want to look at the chicken strips. But the look on her face tells me that she'll be devastated if I don't, as if these undercooked slabs of meat will heal me in all my broken places. I know it's the mother in her, but that phrase remains alien to me. However, I force myself to eat the chicken.

"I was thinking. That girl, Alana. Do you talk to her about these things?" Sandee asks.

I think of Alana. Beautiful Alana. Alabaster skin, dark hair, eyes that could destroy you. It's been nearly six years since I met her and I still can't believe how beautiful she is. We had our fun, our requisite, fumbling high school relationship, but it didn't work.

Alana looks like a doll and, inside, she's like a doll. Hollow. I don't mean shallow or vapid. The girl is brilliant and could challenge me academically. However, I've known her long enough, and known her in every single way, that I also know that her

14

eyes go dead after she has sex, even though it's only for a split second. It's a deadness I recognize and it terrifies me. Sometimes I think she's reflecting my own eyes back to me.

I shake my head and focus on Sandee. "We talk."

"Do you *talk* talk?"

"What kind of question is that? Yes, we talk. We talk about all kinds of things."

Like how Alana was eleven when her father started to touch her. Like how when she fucks, she's an animal, because she can't stop seeing his face. Like how she knows I know and yet she continues to sleep with me, because neither of us thinks we belong with anyone else.

"Maybe she would be good for you."

"We don't date," I say.

"Why not?"

"Well, she dated my friend, Dave. And I would rather see them work than see us fail."

"You don't know you would fail."

"I do. Besides, she only comes to visit to get laid."

15

"She comes to visit because she loves you. As much as you love her."

I eat the chicken faster, because if my mouth is full, I can ignore what Sandee said. She's right. I know how Alana feels, but I can't give her anything of myself. I hate myself when I'm with her for everything she knows about me. There's too much history between us. For some people, that makes a relationship, but when you're people like me and Alana, it destroys it.

Sandee is also correct that I love Alana. I just don't love her in the way she still hopes I will. Thinking about it only depresses me, though. Because now I feel undeserving of both Sandee and Alana.

"You know, Sandee, you really suck at cheering people up."

She looks sad for a second and I regret teasing her. What was I thinking? She's been through as much as I have, if not more, and here I am acting like I have the right to claim misery for myself.

"Well, then, finish your chicken and get the fuck out."

Is our friendship normal? No. I doubt it. But she knows how to make me feel. Feeling is good, as long as it's in small doses, and in safe places, like here - with Sandee, the truckers, my chicken, and the whiskey-soaked dregs of my coffee.

Chapter 2

Day one of school and I forgot to set the alarm. Sandee was kind enough to bring me my own bottle of whiskey, which I finished immediately upon returning to the dorm. And now, with a headache and a hangover, I run to my first class, managing somehow to get there just as the professor shuts the door.

"I do not tolerate tardiness," he says and makes a point to look directly at me. What the fuck? I was here before he shut the door. "And you will earn every last decimal of your grade. Do not come to me at midterm with a sad story about your alcoholic father and your poor abused mom and tell me that *they* are the reason *you* could not write a paper on digital design. Because I do not care for your stories, as you do not care about mine."

Part of me hates him, but another part of me respects him for being honest. I know how many kids do exactly what he said – cry to their professors at midterm and end of term, even though they wrote no papers and attended no classes. The worst part is that the professors always say yes. *Always*. Then the assholes go back to the dorm and brag to their friends about how they pretended daddy was a drunk. And two weeks later, drunk old dad shows up in his Lexus and the family rides off into the sunset, both assholes still ignorant as fuck. Meanwhile, I actually do earn every last decimal as this professor – I look down – Dr. Ahorn has suggested we do. I can't afford a school like this, but all that math homework in high school got me near perfect SATs, which then got me a nice scholarship package. It's just too bad this school is overrun by douche satchels.

I don't pay attention to class today – any of them. I can read. For some reason, we waste a day each semester reviewing everything in the syllabus. What I don't understand is why a prestigious college would use a day of learning – which equals approximately $443.75 – to ensure that we can read a piece of paper. Sometimes two pieces. Ideally, every single student here has the basic reading skills to do just that. But no, we read the paper. Four times for me today.

Sometimes, I wonder why I came here. I hate almost all of them. Living on campus can be really tough. There was the option of commuting, although it wasn't an easy drive, but I'd done almost the same commute working at the café. My grandmother makes the same commute every weekend for the prison. So it could have been done. But the scholarship came with a dorm room and it was a change of scenery. It isn't far enough, but it was something. Finishing here will mean opportunity – a chance to get farther away. I just wonder if there is anywhere far enough.

I need to get off campus, but when I get out of classes, I have a text from Alana. She wants to come see me. I sigh. I can't say no. With Dave overseas in the military, I'm all she's got. She's still stuck at home, fortunately with just her mom now, while she takes a few classes at the community college at night. I don't know where her dad went, she doesn't tell me, and neither of us cares.

I know Alana. Wanting to come see me means she sent the text when she was halfway here. There's no way to stop her when she wants to visit. I text her back that I'm looking forward to seeing her and hit the shower.

She's quick, which means she drove way too fast. I've barely made it out of the shower before she's at my door. I almost lecture her, but I can't speak as she starts pulling my clothes off, her hands moving faster over my body than my brain can process. I don't even know if she shut the door, but it's closed, so I guess she must have.

She has my shirt off and moves to my belt, and then to my pants. I should stop her. I should tell her she's better than this, but she's hungry and my cock is not listening to anything. Every time I touch Alana, I feel a hint of guilt, but then she gets ahold of my cock. Broken or not, caring or not, a beautiful woman's mouth wrapped over my shaft is not something I can say no to.

Alana's lips envelop me and Christ, she is amazing. I don't even know how I stay standing. Her fingers tease me behind my balls and I feel like I'm going to come almost instantly. Her tongue swirls around the tip of my cock and when she slides it under the head, I lose it. I grab her head and push her against me, my cock all the way down her throat. I come and she swallows, continuing to move her head slowly along the length of me while the shivers subside. When I'm coherent again, I unclench my hands in her hair and she looks up at me. She runs her tongue along her stunning lips and smiles.

"I missed you," she says.

"You missed fucking."

She stands up. "That, too."

Alana's body is amazing. There are tiny white scars reaching across her thighs from something that happened to her when she was a kid, but she's never told me what caused them. If I touch them, she shuts down, so I've learned not to touch them.

Now, she undresses, and my cock stirs again at the sight of her. Her tits are my favorite part of her. I reach out and caress them. After she steps out of her jeans, she grabs one of my hands and slips it between her legs. The wet heat of her pussy is all it takes to make me rock hard.

"How?" I ask her.

Alana always dictates how things go, the position we use, and how long it lasts. She needs to be in control of something. We tried switching roles a few times, but she can't be submissive and I can't argue with her.

"Just real. Nothing kinky. I just want to be with you. We haven't been together lately. You were so busy with packing and everything." She pouts and I hate myself a little bit more. I should break this off with her. It isn't fair and I know she doesn't think she deserves more, but she does. Yet all of my logic and emotion disappear when she pushes my fingers further into her cunt. "Touch me, Jack."

I do as she asks, bringing her body to the edge before sinking to my knees in front of her. The smell of her, the taste of her – so familiar. I slide my tongue inside of her pussy. Her fingernails dig into my scalp and I tease her clit while she pushes herself against my face. I need more than this, though, so as she starts to crest, I move away, knowing what will come next and how needy she will be.

On cue, Alana pushes me to the bed and straddles me. She slips her wet, hot pussy over my cock and it's fucking heaven. All of my reason and doubt disappear as I feel her contract around me. She rides me until we're both satisfied – and I am *extremely* satisfied.

"I wish you weren't so far away. It's so hard without you," she says after.

I stroke her hair. I know her mind races after we fuck. I've seen it when her dead eyes come back to life – the fear that it's a mistake, that things will change between us. Despite my shitty lack of self-control, I would never hurt her. She's my best friend, my only friend now that Dave's gone and left us behind with nothing.

She dozes off and I will myself to love her, to be more for her, but I can't change anything. It's weak and pathetic, but those are the traits that seem to define me.

****

Alana comes back one more time during the first week of classes, one night after I finish work at the café. It's late and I've just parked my bike when I walk up to the dorm and see her sitting on the grassy hill nearby. I join her on the hill; it's still warm and the night seems more comforting than the sterility of my dorm anyway.

"I missed you again," she says. I sense her wariness in the way she bites her lip, the way that the words don't fall from her as they should. "I needed to see you."

"I know, and I miss you, too. But you're going to spend all your money on gas."

She only works part time, between classes and dealing with her mother. It's unfortunate; she's too smart to be where she is. She could have had scholarships, too, but she didn't want to leave. I'll never understand that and it's what divides us more than anything.

"Why didn't you stay?"

We've been over this and yet we have to rehash it at least once a month during the school year. I know Alana's moods well now. This one is neediness, driven by fear of losing me, of losing *us*. We aren't an us, we haven't been an us in years, and yet she still imagines a future where there *is* an us. Every time, I try to let her down gently, but it doesn't work. And, of course, every time I end up in bed with her, and then I wonder why she believes there's a chance.

"You know I couldn't. I needed out of there. Fucking bullshit and the way they looked at me. I need this, Alana. I need something new. I need to prove that I'm not this guy, that I can be something else."

"You can do that at home."

I shake my head. "No. I can't. And you know it. What's going on?"

She lies back on the grass and I join her. She slips her hand down to my crotch, but as much as my cock says one thing, I let my brain take over this time. I move her hand back.

"I'm losing you," she says. "I can just feel it. Something is different. The air is different."

"You're being ridiculous. The air is exactly the same. And it smells like ass."

I get a laugh out of her, but the sadness returns. "I'm not enough for you."

"Don't do this."

"Why is it so hard with us, Jack?"

"Because you're my best friend, and I adore you, and I want to love you always. I can't love you always if I *have* to love you. You know I can't be in a relationship."

"You're not him," she tells me.

We've trodden over our pasts endlessly in the time since we met. I'm not him and she's not the victim she was. Either way, though, I refuse to talk about this. I need school, I need to get out, and I need not to have roots here. The farther I get away, the better. And I will never give Alana what *she* needs, which is someone to love her unconditionally. For me, everything has a condition. She's just lucky she gets the shortest list.

"You wanna go for a ride?" I don't really feel like going back out now that I'm mere yards from my room, but I also don't want to invite her back there. Some nights, there is too much promise in what's supposed to be fun.

She shakes her head. "I miss him, you know."

"Dave?"

She nods.

"Me too. Asshole never even said goodbye."

"He didn't want us to hurt if he dies. But I hurt already."

I say nothing, only hold her against me. I miss him, too. At the end of high school, we had a fallout – something stupid, my own anger at everyone tearing me away from the two friends I actually had. Although we fixed things before he left, I still imagine the day we get a telegram that he's dead and I know that guilt will destroy me for good.

"Everyone leaves me," she says.

"You're being whiny as fuck."

She smiles. "You're a shitty friend."

"The worst," I agree.

And we're okay. It's not a mood shift; it's not a sudden acceptance of anything. It's simply realizing that, for all of the ways we hurt each other, we are still better together than apart. Alana kisses me, but it's a resigned kiss. I'm not sleeping with her tonight. She's too volatile and as much as her skin sets mine on fire when her hands slide up my arms, it's dangerous to be with her like this.

"You want me to go, don't you?"

"I want you to wake up tomorrow and not hate me."

There have been a few times in our friendship, early on – after we broke up - when I didn't listen to the warnings in my head. She would have moods like this and try to solve everything with sex. And every time, I conceded. In these moods, the sex is better than it's ever been. Alana loves to prove that I need her and she gets creative when she wants to show me something.

I get hard just thinking of it, but I resist the urge to have sex with her here on the grass. In the morning, I won't be her boyfriend. And she'll feel used, like she did those other times. To outsiders, we may have a fucked up relationship, but I know the rules now and I make sure I follow them, even if Alana cannot.

"You're still a shitty friend."

"Yup. And you're still whiny as fuck."

Chapter 3

By Saturday morning, I feel like I've been back at school for the whole semester. Not having a roommate has its perks, but the biggest one is that I wake up at noon, undisturbed by anyone else. I have to work, but first I need coffee. I grab my work clothes – black pants, black shirt – except for the apron, and I get dressed before heading into the lounge.

The girl sitting on the couch looks like everyone else at this fucking school. Blonde, clean cut, dressed in clothes that probably cost more than my grandmother's house.

"Lost?" I ask.

It's her eyes that get me. I don't even know what color they are. They seem to swim across the entire palate of blues and greens, no color enough to own the eye completely. There is something else in those eyes. A strange innocence mixed with a subtle sensuality that I bet she doesn't even know she possesses. **I can't look away from her.**

"I'm waiting for my boyfriend." She gestures to the hall. I guess she's saying this boyfriend is in the bathroom or something. It figures she has a boyfriend. Something about her, though, is causing things to happen that I don't understand. The voice in my head knows how poorly this could go and I try to act cool, to distance myself from her.

"Innocent thing like you? I wouldn't let you out of my sight."

That was *not* cool and certainly not distant. I'm standing here flirting with this girl who probably thinks I'm a creep. I see in her face a wary curiosity, but girls like her think of guys like me as nothing more than a challenge. Anything that could happen after this moment would just turn out bad, likely with a lot of anger and her calling upon the aforementioned boyfriend to kick my ass. I don't even have to see him. I know his type.

She meets my gaze and her mouth turns up in a wry smile. "I'm not that innocent."

The challenge is there and I would love to test it. This girl looks like she's just one wild night away from becoming an entirely new woman. I wouldn't mind being the guy to help her out, to give her that one wild night. I'm tempted to touch her, to play with her damp hair, to see how she'd react if I kissed her right here. Her challenge would surely result in me being slapped, though.

"Sweetheart, I am sure we have very different understandings of the term."

"That wouldn't surprise me, but I don't know that I mind being your idea of innocent."

There it is. The judgment. She may have something hidden in her that's more than what she appears to be on the surface, but the superficial persona is too important to her. Fuck her and her judgments. I'm going to watch her squirm.

I step closer and lean down slightly in her direction. She smells like she just showered; her wet hair carries the scent of a strawberry field.

"I don't doubt it, but I just wonder what would happen if you let loose a little. You know, had a bit of fun."

She backs away. I can almost hear the words in her head. *Freak. Loser.* What would her parents think of her for talking to me? What would her *boyfriend* think? She's still nervous, but I can sense that our closeness makes her feel something. I just don't know that I want to test it.

"I have plenty of fun. I don't need anything else. Especially not whatever *you* have in mind."

I have to get to work. Things are hard enough without playing games like this and I go back to my coffee. She crosses her legs and I think of what's between them. I hope I made her tingle at least a little. After I finish my coffee, I smile and I see her thighs reflexively tighten. The muscle movement is hot and my cock springs to life. I need to get out of here.

In the doorway, I reconsider, thinking of her strawberry hair and her gorgeous eyes. Turning in her direction, I reiterate the challenge.

"I'm Jack. 401. If you ever want to test that theory. See what real fun is like, princess."

Back in my room, I know I need to get to work, but I'm feeling horny as hell. It's strange. She isn't even my type. I like girls like Alana – wild, bitter and angry, and willing to do it all in bed. Lounge girl is probably a virgin, a sweet and pure angel who doesn't even swear and goes to church every Sunday. Given my own experiences, I should feel some guilt about how badly I want to corrupt her, but I don't. I think of strawberries as I stroke my cock; closing my eyes, I picture slipping into her innocent pussy, the strawberry smell surrounding me as I fuck her into submission. It takes almost no time to come, and then I go to work.

I can still smell strawberry as I ride.

****

Today the café is busy, but Liz is back. Sandee has the day off, which is disappointing, but the rush is endless and I don't have time to chat anyway.

Cooking here is always a pleasant break from the elitism at school. Given everything I am and everything people think that I am, I'll never be able to make sense of the way people use college as another totem. Most of my classmates are not even functionally literate, yet tuition is over forty grand. Although I suppose I should thank them every time I need to use the library. Someone had the buy the books none of them can read.

At work, though, the people are real. Both the customers and the staff. During the busy times, we get more douchebags - mostly my classmates who probably should be in said library and not eating a hangover away.

Mal is also on this morning. He's a recovering alcoholic, a total asshole to nearly everyone, and an incredibly shitty employee in a lot of ways. But the dude can cook and when I walk in a couple minutes late with no explanation, he just shrugs and hands me an order.

"Big parties last night?"

"Huge party. I spent the night reading Dostoevsky."

"He a scientist?"

Mal flips over the largest slab of ham I have ever seen. For all the sort of dive element of this place, the food is fucking great.

"Yeah, something like that."

"Eh. Never cared for all that mumbo jumbo. Don't know any of it and I'm doing just fine."

That's something else I admire about Mal. By no one's standards is he "doing just fine." He has a tendency to fall off the wagon as soon as he approaches his ten-month anniversary – which he's been doing for longer than I've been alive. He's been married and divorced five times. He has three kids who don't speak to him. Finally, he only eats the food from the café and he lives in a motel out by the prison. Oh – and he works as a short order cook in a crappy café. But in his mind, life is "just fine." Sometimes, I think I need to get ahold of whatever it is that keeps Mal from losing his shit.

We settle into our routine, since there's very little we can talk about. I can't discuss Raskolnikov's character traits with him and Mal simply has nothing to say. So we cook in silence, but it's comfortable.

I feel a strange affinity for this place. Even thinking about leaving when I eventually get the hell out makes me a little sad. I hate that it makes me sad. I want to leave with no connections, with no strings.

I go to stick an order on the counter for Liz when I see *her*. Strawberries. She's with some dude, who's what I pictured when she mentioned her boyfriend. Broad, tan, blond, and eating like a fucking pig. I don't know what they're talking about and I can't see her face, but he loves her. It's immediately recognizable and I hate him for it. I don't know why I hate him, since at least maybe he's not as much of a dick as I would've expected. If we'd been placing bets, I would've gone with the safe assumption he had something else on the side.

I wonder if maybe she isn't as innocent as she looks. The thought makes me horny again. I don't get what's so damn attractive about this girl, but something makes me want to taste every inch of her skin.

"-not listening." I catch the end of what Liz is saying.

"Huh?"

"Right. Thought so. I need you to make this order, but they want to change every fucking thing on the damn menu."

"Bastards."

"Just make sure it's perfect so they don't fuck me out of my tip."

I look at the slip. What is it with people?

I get to work on their ridiculous order, but my eyes keep going back to that girl.

"Do you know her?" Mal looks over at me and it's strange. I think he's trying to converse, like in a real conversation.

"She lives in my dorm." Then, as an afterthought, "I think." Maybe her boyfriend lives in the dorm and she's just visiting. I haven't seen either of them around – but really they would both blend in for the most part.

"She's cute," he says.

"I guess."

He shrugs and keeps cooking. I feel something starting to stir inside my body and I don't get it. Mal calling her cute shouldn't make me jealous. But suddenly, I need a break and I finish making the order before running outside for a smoke.

It's a combination of several things that bug me. Strawberries looked at me just like everyone else always has – and she doesn't know a damn thing about me. Her boyfriend reminds me of every other asshole I've tolerated, the kind of guy who has so little awareness of other people that he walks over anyone in his way. And Mal's comment – "she's cute" – irritates me. She *is* cute. I don't do *cute*. She's just another dumb bitch whose parents pay for her to come here to pretend she's intelligent and then she'll marry her idiot boyfriend. And they'll live happily ever after, her being a housewife with a shopping addiction and him being a stockbroker. Or some stupid shit. So who cares how she looks at me?

I finish my cigarette and stab it out in the ashtray. I hate feeling fucking inferior.

Chapter 4

The best part of being back at school – outside of learning, which is actually something I enjoy - is that it means band practices are more frequent. We all try to play over the summer, but Neil lives on the other side of the country, so it's either shitty practice or some kind of crappy Skype jam session.

Week two of classes is underway and I have work to do, but the idea of practicing, of playing in general, has been gnawing at me. Neil texts me Monday afternoon about practicing the next night and I feel high leaving the academic building now that we have a schedule. I have to get to work, but I'm so focused on practicing that I get my stuff and I'm nearly out the door before I realize I forgot my damn helmet. I'm already cutting it close and this will make two times in less than a week that I've been late. It's not my style and I'm distracted when I get back downstairs.

I actually smell her before I see her. The strong scent of strawberries nearly knocks me over. Oh, wait. No – that was just her.

"Whoa, watch where you're going." The words are out before I can think and I realize I probably sound like an asshole. For some reason, I don't want her to think I'm an asshole.

"Sorry," she apologizes, but she looks right through me. I don't know what possesses me to try to engage her in conversation. Clearly, she is not interested.

"You know, princess, you never told me your name."

She glares at me like she wishes I would disappear. What the fuck?

"Not gonna, either."

She may be cute and she may smell sweetly of strawberries, but the way she is looking at me right now tells me she's no different from every other girl who thinks she's better than me. Every kid I went to high school with who thought that they had the right to torture me because my dad killed my mother. I hate her.

"Oh right. Too good for me. Little innocent princess like you."

I'm sick of the pretension and the entitlement of people like her. As if she gets to look at me like she is just because her life is fucking easy.

I grip my helmet tightly, fighting the urge to slam it into the wall. I don't know why I don't just walk away, but fuck her if she thinks she can come here and assume anything. What is she – a freshman? Fuck. I can barely see through the red haze of anger.

"Seriously, what's your problem?" She asks me as if she wants an answer, and since I haven't walked away, I decide to oblige her.

"I just see the way you look at people like me. Daddy paying for everything so you have no idea what it's really like. You think you have every right to judge."

"As a matter of fact, I'm on scholarship." She says it as if she's proud to be able to prove me wrong, but it changes very little.

"Oh great, a smart snob."

She meets my gaze and I soften, despite how angry I am. Her fucking eyes. Why are her eyes so beautiful? I check out the rest of her; she isn't anything special. Cute, yes. Maybe even pretty. But there is nothing about her that warrants how much I want to prove something to her.

I will myself not to meet her eyes this time, because I can't deal with feeling something for another person and she's making me feel something. I can't even control my emotions with her near me. I both want to hurt her and kiss her.

She sighs. "Whatever."

She pushes past me and is almost to the elevator. Rage, curiosity, and an undeniable attraction all swell inside of me and I call out, "Hey, princess."

She turns around and this time I can't help it. I look at her eyes.

"Don't forget. 401. You look wound up. I would be happy to help."

I take off and I don't look back to see if she reacts. I walk faster than I normally do, because I need to ride and I need to go to work and I need to stop thinking about her. *You're wasting your time,* I remind myself.

It takes until I'm halfway through my shift before I can breathe without feeling the ache inside my chest.

****

It figures that I don't even make it back to the dorm that night before she's there again. Of course, she walks in to me. For some reason, she's pissed about it.

"Seriously? Are you stalking me?" She looks at me like how dare I walk around on my own college campus. What a bitch.

And yet – here I stand. Like a tool.

"Yeah, because I desperately want to stalk an uptight princess who cannot even pay attention to where she's going. If you must know, I just got off work."

Why are you acknowledging her? Walk away. Walk away NOW. The logical voice is right, but my feet don't move.

Strawberries smiles and gestures vaguely into the woods. "Oh yeah. You work at that café."

Huh. She noticed?

Her snobbery disappears for a moment and her eyes actually sparkle when she smiles. Damn it. This is not going to be good for me. I contemplate applying for a dorm transfer, but as I'm thinking it, my stupid mouth moves and encourages this fucking interaction.

"I do and the fact that you know that makes me think *you* may be stalking *me*."

She smiles even broader. I don't think she knows she's flirting with me, but her body opens up. I could kiss her right now. I feel like she'd probably pass out. Sure, she has that boyfriend, but I bet she's never done anything wild.

"You wish," she says.

The comment is sweet and it's genuine, but it reminds me of the differences between us. I shut down, letting the momentary fantasy fade.

"I don't believe in wishing. Anyway, did you want something – other than to walk into me yet again?"

She moves closer and, fuck, I want to kiss her. Why does she smell like strawberries? How many fucking showers does this girl take? I don't even *like* strawberries, yet her scent clings to me and makes me stand here, waiting for her to make a move. *Walk away*, the voice repeats, but I'm not going anywhere.

"Are you going back to the dorm for the night?"

Is she suggesting we go back together? Did taunting her actually work?

"I was planning on it. Why?"

She gestures to my helmet and shrugs. "I'd love to go for a ride."

Oh, this is good. She'd probably be grounded via text message for even suggesting it.

"You? Would Daddy approve?"

The comment bites and she looks wounded. She steps even closer, though, and the way she stands up for herself just makes me think about fucking her right here in the middle of the quad.

"Look," she says, "I don't know what the problem is, but do you want to take me for a ride or not?"

Say no. SAY NO. But I say nothing. I simply turn back toward the parking lot. I don't really expect her to follow, but she does. Every time I look back at her, she gives me a determined stare. It's fucking adorable and it kills me.

"So where to?" I ask her when we get to the lot.

She says she doesn't care, so I hand her a helmet and we take off. There is seriously something wrong with this girl. Even with the wind flying past us and two helmets in the way, I can still make out the faint smell of strawberries lingering in the air between us. Damn her and her eyes and her strawberry hair. She's going to ruin me; I just know it.

I don't know where to take her, because the only places I know well are too personal. Instead, I just drive and she clings to me. I can feel the soft outline of her tits pressed to my back and it takes a lot out of me not to pull over and see just how far she wants to take this little charade. I don't, though, and after a while, I figure we should get back. I want to say something, to brush her fingers with my lips, but I keep my distance. I know what I am to her. I'm a symbol of how bad she wants to be, but I'm not anything real.

When we reach the doors to the dorm, however, I don't want to let the night end.

"Still feeling wild?"

I hope she'll say no, that this will be it, because I know I won't be able to control myself with her and I don't have anything to offer this girl.

"It's late," she says. "And I have to call my boyfriend."

Ouch. That hurts. But a part of me wonders why she's spending the night with me instead of with him. "He's crazy to let you out of his sight."

I don't know who makes the move, but suddenly our bodies are only an inch apart. She breathes deep and I wonder what goes through her head when she's near me. I know there's nothing going through mine except her eyes, strawberries, and the incredible pain I'm going to be in later tonight if she walks away right now. Already my cock is throbbing and I have to fight not to push her against the door and fuck her right here.

She leans closer to me, her lips almost against my cheek, and whispers, "I'm not that kind of girl."

Her breath tickles the hair on my neck and I lose myself. I lean down and kiss along her collarbone, feeling her body fit against mine and I pull her in to me. I don't know if this girl is a virgin or if she's more than she seems, but the things I want to do to her are certainly not in her repertoire. I move down closer to her tits, feeling them rising and falling as she breathes. I don't touch her, but I kiss her where the slight curve of her breasts reaches her upper chest and she lets out a soft flutter of pleasure.

"I'd love to know exactly what kind of girl you are," I tell her and she reacts exactly as I'd hoped and feared she would. She reaches into my jacket and runs her hands along my back. I need her desperately. Her hands move fast and I bring my lips to the edge of her breasts, kissing them as they rise to meet me. She moans, but then backs away with a gasp.

"I have a boyfriend. I can't do this." Her voice is insistent, but her hands are shaking and her eyes are burning.

I resist the urge to grab her and make her forget all about him. I don't cheat and I don't help people cheat. I refuse to be the guy who does that, no matter how carried away I'm getting. The reminder sobers me a little. Still, I'm not ready to give up completely and I reason with her. "Where is your boyfriend? You've mentioned him before, but you run into me a lot for someone who's so in love."

It's the wrong thing to say. She crosses her arms and closes herself off to me. My body is going to hate me for this when I get back to my room.

"It was an accident," she says.

Hearing it hurts. Tonight felt like something more than an accident. I know I'm wrong for her and I know we could never work, but it's insulting that she can deny what just happened. Her reaction to my mouth on her skin didn't say accident. It said she wanted this as badly as I do. It said that she was well aware that she made the choice to spend tonight with me, not with this other guy.

"Tonight was an accident?" I ask. I want to hear her confirm it, to hear her argue that the last couple hours were a lie.

Her eyes start to water and she can't speak. I feel guilty about putting her in this situation, but I also want her so fucking bad right now. When her eyes grow wet, they shine. She could ask me for anything and I would do it.

"I have a boyfriend," she says again.

I'm not fighting with her. I walk away and leave her standing outside. I hope she regrets that the moment ended, because leaving is nearly impossible to do.

When I get to my room, I slam my door and turn on music. It's angry and violent and I grab the pillow off my bed and scream. What is it with this stupid girl and her stupid hold on me? I unbutton my pants and jerk off with the music raging, my cock so desperate for her and her stupid, stupid strawberry fucking hair. When I come, I cry out but I don't even know her name. I wish I knew her goddamn name.

I fall asleep naked, dreaming of her and hating myself for it.

Chapter 5

By the time I make it to practice the next day, I'm a wreck. Yet as soon as I pick up my bass, I forget her. The music is escape.

I help Neil write a lot of the songs and they come from both of our own issues. I don't know much about what his issues even are, but we're both angry and hate everything around us, so I feel like we get each other.

The other two band members, the drummer and the guitarist, tend to fluctuate. Right now, we have Eric and Devon. This is Devon's first practice and it's a good thing he kicks ass on the drums, because Devon is one stupid ass name and I almost hate him for having it.

The newest song that Neil and I wrote last semester works well with this group and we play it a few times before taking a break.

"Here. I brought beer," Devon says and passes around a six-pack. Okay, lame name or not, this guy might be okay.

"I think I got us a gig," Neil announces while we're drinking. They're the best possible words someone can say in band practice. The only words that come close are, "Here. I brought beer."

It's a shitty opening gig, but it's a gig and that means exposure. I'm not stupid and I'm not majoring in music. I play because I need to play. I need to feel that release, that washing away of the anger and the hate that comes from creating a song. I can't deny that there's a small part of me that hopes the music could be a literal escape, as well as an emotional one. I love the idea of being on the road, of not having roots, of not settling, and of letting the road be my only friend.

Realistically, I can't even call the guys in the band my friends. I just met Devon, Eric is pretty new and we just spent the summer at home, and Neil and I don't talk much except about the band. Still, there's something pleasant about hanging out here, drinking beer, talking about a gig, and not having to be anything. There's no depth to the conversation, and I can't talk to them about things that matter, but I also don't feel trapped being around them.

"You guys want to play anything new?" I suggest, since our last gig included everything off the CD we put out. We aren't big by any means, but a lot of kids from school came to the shows we did in the spring. What's funny is that most of those people who stand in the audience would never even look at me on campus.

"Do we *have* anything new?" Neil hasn't been writing much, I know, but I live with my grandmother and I hate my life. I have endless piles of new songs.

"I worked on some things this summer," I offer.

"Cool. Let's hear 'em."

So we listen to what I put together this summer. I'm not one for being open about my feelings, but there's a part of me in my lyrics and in the melodies. I don't get too explicit in my songs, but no one listens to them thinking things are great in my life.

"Dude, you are one miserable fuck," Devon says after we listen to a couple of my recordings. Normally, this kind of comment would make me want to hit him, but it's true. I wrote them over the summer when I was sitting in the cemetery. They're more real than anything else I've ever done.

The gig is about a month away, so we have time to learn a few new songs and tighten our older stuff. With Devon here, we need to get used to playing together all over again, and Neil's right when he says we should pick no more than three. There's a bit of pride that swells in me when I realize we'll be playing three songs that I wrote entirely alone. I refuse to show it, though, because I know what happens when you feel good about something you accomplish. There is always someone or something waiting to tear you down.

We practice a couple of our regular tracks and one of mine before we call it a night. It's just me and Neil and I'm about to head out when he stops me.

"They're dark," he says. "Your songs. They're really fucking dark."

"Too dark?"

"Hell no. Is there such a thing?"

I laugh, but I'm nervous because I know what he's about to ask. When he does, it doesn't come any easier despite preparing myself for it.

"So, are you, like, all right? I mean, you're not gonna snap and kill someone, are you?"

This is what I mean by the world waiting to tear you down. It's a normal comment. One that is probably said hundreds of times a day all over the world. It's not personal and Neil has no idea how deeply it cuts. But hearing it reminds me of what I am, of what I will become. If there is this kind of darkness in me, enough so that my writing worries even my co-songwriter, how long until it ruins me? How long before I'm sitting in my own prison cell, a product of nothing but hate and rage?

I can't answer Neil when he asks if I am all right, because I'm not. His question just proves it. *Fuck*, I think, and shrug. He says nothing when I turn around and walk out. There's nothing *to* say.

****

I call Alana that weekend; I need her. Again, I hate myself, because I know I'll sleep with her. That's how we both cope with anything that goes wrong. We call the other one and we fuck the problem away.

56

She's eager to visit, but she has to deal with some shit with her mom first, so I'm left sitting alone in my room for a few hours. I order a pizza and, after thirty minutes, I go to the lobby to wait for it.

The girl doesn't even notice me when she walks in. I don't know who her friends are, but they're caught in conversation. One is wearing all pink and is laughing about something a guy named Lyle said.

"I told him it was ridiculous. Seriously, there is no way that it would work, right?"

Strawberries looks at her pink friend and smiles. "He's trying. Give him credit for that. If Don had anything to do with it, it would be a disaster."

"If Don had anything to do with it, it wouldn't get done."

I watch them as they call the elevator. Their conversation is inane, but I feel guilty for criticizing. I also wish I was part of it.

I consider apologizing, consider approaching her and inviting her to have some pizza, but her friend catches my eye while I stare. It stops the crazy ideas, because I know what her friend would say. She'd tell her to watch out for guys like me and then they'd go off to some happy place where Don and Lyle and all their perfect friends do perfect things. Strawberries never even notices me and they're gone as soon as the elevator arrives.

My pizza sucks and I don't want to eat it anymore. I don't want to waste it, either, so I bring it to the lounge and leave it on the coffee table. Someone will come along, probably drunk, and finish it, no matter how crappy it is or how cold it's gotten.

Now, I have nothing to do but wait for Alana and, for some reason, this is the one time it takes her forever. I go back downstairs, keeping an eye out for Strawberries, but she's doing whatever girls like her do on Friday nights, and I head outside for a cigarette.

It's already dark when I see Alana walking up the hill. She's smoking and her hands are shaking. Something probably went down at home.

"Hey," I call out.

"Hey." She takes a deep drag off her cigarette and I watch her twitching.

"What's up?"

"It's my mom. She met some guy and she wants me to meet him."

"Again."

"Again," she says. Alana's mom is always meeting someone and introducing Alana to him. There have been several times when the guys have taken a liking to Alana. Sometimes too much of a liking.

"So say no. Jesus, Alana, you're twenty. Why are you even still there?"

"Some of us don't get to be swept away by a white knight scholarship." She throws her cigarette to the ground and lights another.

"You could've. You *chose* to stay home. You said you needed to be there."

"Yeah, well, I'm a fucking idiot. So sue me. Why the fuck are you lecturing me anyway?"

I don't say anything. I smoke my cigarette and let her finish hers. When she's done, she wraps her arms around my neck.

"I don't wanna fight. Help me forget," she says and she kisses me while she moves her hands down my back and around to the front of my pants. When she gets like this, she's unstoppable, and she'd probably have me naked on the sidewalk in front of my dorm if I didn't pull away.

"Let's get upstairs first, okay?"

She pouts, but takes my hand as I push the door open. Waiting for the elevator is frustrating, because I want to talk to her and fix whatever is happening for her, but I also want to give her exactly what she wants. As soon as we get into the elevator, she goes for my pants and plays with my cock while we ride up the four floors. Some kid is standing by the doors when they open and he sees Alana playing with my cock, which she's gotten out of my pants and is stroking like mad. His eyes get wide and I just laugh.

"Sometimes, why wait?" I say and I drag her to my room while she tries to get me naked in the hallway. Slamming the door, I strip and she follows, so we're both ready in a matter of seconds.

"Fuck me hard," she says. "I want it rough."

Alana is the one who introduced me to experimentation like this, but I've had my share of practice with other girls. Still, I always seem to come back to her.

I go into my drawer, where we keep a lot of the toys that we've found useful. I grab a small whip; I know how much she loves it. My cock is ready to burst and she sees the whip in my hand and grins.

"Perfect," she says. She spreads her legs for me and damn, I want in there. I can see how wet she is even from across the room. Alana moves her fingers to her pussy and starts to play, which makes me crazy. I know she knows what it does to me. I rush to the bed and flip her over, bringing the whip down on her ass. She continues to play with herself and cries out every time I hit her. I push her onto the bed and kneel behind her, still whipping her, and I adjust so my cock is right up against her cunt.

"I'm going to fuck you now," I tell her. "Unless you want me to wait." I know she doesn't want me to wait, but teasing her is fun, and she moans, spreading her legs even wider.

"Give me that cock, Jack."

I'm not sure who's going to argue with that. I toss the whip on the floor, entering her roughly and leaning over her so I can get my hands around her tits. I push into her as she tightens around me. Shit, I already feel like I'm going to come. Slowing my motions, I try to think of something else. Sadly, the first thing that comes to mind is Strawberries. I imagine having her bent over in this exact same position and, as much of an asshole move as it is, I fuck Alana even harder, thinking about the feel of another girl's pussy. I come imagining how good someone else would feel beneath me, and I almost forget where I am.

"Oh, Jack," Alana calls out, and I'm thrown back into the present. I've done a lot of shitty things, but I have never been out of the moment when I've been with her.

She didn't come and I can tell because she's looking hungrier than she did when she got here. She turns around and smiles, her head moving down to my cock. Alana's an expert at giving a blowjob. Her tongue runs along my shaft and I lean back. I feel a little guilty about where my thoughts went, but I want to satisfy her. I hate when she doesn't come. It just makes me feel worse.

She gets me hard again in no time and then she wraps her legs around my waist, sliding herself down over my cock. I take one of her tits in my mouth and lightly bite the nipple. Alana grabs my head and holds me close to her chest, her fingernails scratching the back of my neck. She smells familiar, like cigarettes and toothpaste, but I can't stop thinking about the smell of fucking strawberries. Alana's orgasm comes and I try to focus on her, but every sound she makes leads me to think about what I could do to that girl down the hall. The night on the quad, I thought she was going to let me. I remember her hands on my back, the taste of her skin along her breasts, the noises she made as I kissed her chest. I lose it and come with Alana on top of me, crying out, "Oh, fuck, princess. That's so fucking good."

Needless to say, it's awkward. Alana and I aren't dating, but she has those complicated feelings, and really, no girl wants to know you're thinking about someone else while you're buried inside of her.

She moves to the end of the bed and closes her legs. Never modest, she's still naked as she watches me. I don't feel right, so I grab my boxers and t-shirt and sit on the other end of the bed. I have nothing to say, although I should probably apologize. But I don't even know how to explain.

"Who is she?"

"She's no one," I insist.

"Really? She's no one? You just thought about her while you were fucking me, but she's no one?"

"I don't even know her name."

"Another anonymous fuck, Jack? Why do you do stupid shit like that?"

In case it wasn't clear just how fucked up my relationship with Alana is, she's the only person I tell about girls I fuck. There were a couple at gigs we played, although not as many as one would expect, and there were some random nights around town. It never happened at home because everyone knew who I was, but I've hooked up with girls who've flirted with me at work and one girl on campus when I was a freshman. That was a disaster, since she thought we were dating after we fucked one night. She was drunk after a party and I was there. That didn't seem like much of a relationship to me, but she expected a lot. I let it happen for a couple weeks, but she seemed to take issue with the fact that I let Alana spend the night, and it ended. I don't even know if she still goes here.

"I haven't touched her. Well, not like that. There was a brief 'accident,' as she called it, but clothes stayed on."

"So what's so special about her?"

She looks both sad and worried. I know she thinks this means something is going to break between us, but there is no future for me without Alana. I just don't want to be in a relationship with her.

"Nothing. She's an uptight, generic bitch and I have zero reason to be attracted to her."

"And yet..."

"Yeah. And yet."

"So what are you going to do about it?"

"Nothing."

"Nothing? Since when are you a pussy?"

"I'm not, but she has a boyfriend, which she has done nothing but remind me about, and I have zero desire to get involved with the kind of girl who loves having a boyfriend."

Alana laughs. "Maybe you could be her boyfriend."

"Maybe. Or maybe I could just fuck you again and stop thinking about some uptight little girl who means nothing to me."

"That works."

She lies back and spreads her legs and I undress so I can enter her again. This time, it's all about Alana. I love watching her come and she does three times, each time more intense than the last. Her nails dig into my ass and she loses herself as her entire body shakes around me. She closes her eyes, but I watch her enjoy what I do to her. After she comes the third time, I hold her legs up, and fuck her quickly until I finish. I let go on her stomach and try not to notice that she gets that dead look in her eyes again.

Ignoring the heaviness of what happens every time we finish fucking, I get up and grab some tissues. She doesn't move as I clean her off and I don't look at her face. I'm about to turn around when I hear her crying. It's a little nasty, but I stick the tissues on my desk and sit beside her, pulling her up so that she's leaning into me. She sobs into my bare chest as I hold her. There is nothing I can say, nothing I can do. I know what bothers her is bigger than me, but I also know I could make a small impact if I could just be what she needed. Sadly, I can't.

"You're gonna leave me. Just like everyone else," she cries.

I lift her chin and stare into her eyes. They aren't dead now, but are blazing with light. "I will never leave you. I don't care what happens. I'll fucking die before I leave you."

My words don't comfort her, only make her start to cry harder. "Don't say that."

"I didn't mean it literally. I just mean that I'm nothing without you in my life."

"Then why can't you be with me? We have everything. You're my best friend, you're the only one I talk to, and you fuck me like you love me. So what makes me not good enough, Jack? Why?"

"Nothing," I tell her and it's true. I do wish I could want to be with Alana in that way. It would solve so much, but I don't want to be anything to anyone. I like the system we have. It works well and I have no reason to change it. I'm loyal to her as a friend and somewhat faithful as her lover. I have my hook ups, but I always tell her. I know she sleeps around plenty. Sometimes, we've even been with other people at the same time. In the end, though, it's always her I want to see. That's the closest thing I know to love, even if it's not the right kind of love. Still, it's a big deal for me and I hate hurting her.

"Is it this girl?"

"She's nothing, Alana."

"But you were thinking about her."

"Because I'm an asshole. If there was ever going to be anyone, it would be you. But there won't be."

"Why? I know your shit. I can handle it."

"I just don't want anyone handling it. I don't want anyone to live it alongside me. I just want to forget that any of it happened."

She kisses me. I don't usually like kissing. It feels so … personal, but like I said, if there was ever going to be anyone, it would be her. Her lips taste like sugar. Although kissing is intimate and personal, I love doing it with her. She makes it both tender and hot. I try to control my body, but having her naked against me, her tongue slowly circling inside of my mouth, I feel my cock ready for more. She doesn't miss a beat and with the slightest movement, she slips her hand between my legs and strokes, while she keeps kissing me deeply.

"Pretend I'm her," she whispers. "Fuck me like you would fuck her."

"I don't even know her," I reply.

"But you want to. You want to fuck her, to break her, to prove that you're better than her by ruining her, don't you?"

"I don't want to ruin anyone." Although that's not entirely true. The idea of being in bed with Strawberries, of making her scream while I fuck her, is so tempting that I can't breathe. I wonder if her cunt tastes as sweet as the rest of her.

"What's her name?" Alana asks.

"I told you. I don't know. I've only called her princess and she's never corrected me."

"Well, then, pretend I'm your princess. Fuck me, Jack. Make me forget that I can't be her."

And because I'm an asshole, I do. I fuck her harder than I have in ages, bending her over and thrusting against her hips while I imagine how hot it would be to do the same to the sweet, innocent girl from the lounge. I even call Alana princess while we fuck. I feel a little shame, but not enough to stop.

Chapter 6

I hate long weekends. Columbus Day comes up quickly and my grandmother wants me home for a few days. I only go home when it's required or when I don't want to make her sad. I'm still a little annoyed about catching her at the prison, but she's my grandma. I'm not going to hold that shit against her only to have her die. That's the last thing I need on my already overloaded conscience.

Luckily, I get scheduled for Saturday and Sunday, so I just have to get through Friday night and Monday morning. Alana will visit, too, which will pass the time. She's been a little distant since she asked me to pretend she was someone else, but I ignore it and hope it will pass. What else am I supposed to do?

Grandma's late coming to get me, so I'm just sitting on the hill by the dorm, smoking, while I wait. I could take my bike home, but my grandmother enjoys our "sojourns" as she calls them, so here and there, I let her drive me around.

Besides, the weather is getting cold and it looks crappy enough to rain. Probably best.

I'm playing with blades of grass, tearing them from the ground and lighting them on fire, when I see Strawberries getting in a car with her boyfriend and some other guy. She looks exhausted and I wonder what could possibly tire her out so much. I wouldn't mind making her look like that, but I can guarantee she isn't tired for the same reason she would be with me.

She fits naturally alongside her boyfriend. He wraps his arm around her and there's a familiarity between them that says they've been together for a while. It pisses me off a little.

They're gone before I can think about it more and my grandmother arrives almost immediately after. I feel anxious for some reason, and I know why as soon as I get in the car. She's wearing a hat. She only wears a hat when we visit my father.

"I'm not going," I tell her as I put my seatbelt on.

"You know you need to make an effort. It's in his agreement."

"I don't give a fuck about his agreement," I snarl.

"Language."

"No. Fuck him."

"You're acting like a child," she warns.

"Right, because the *adult* thing would be to hang out with my dad who snapped my mom's neck while I screamed for help."

"You know there are-"

"No," I cut her off. "There are *nothing*. He killed her, she's dead, and I'm fucked because of it all. I don't want to see him."

She turns the ignition off and rests her head on her arms against the steering wheel. I want to feel guilty, but it's asking too much. I don't care what his reasons were. I don't care that the state feels he's a strong candidate for rehabilitation, provided he can show progress in patching things up with me. I hope he fucking rots in there for the rest of his life.

"No," I say through gritted teeth. "That's final."

My grandmother says nothing, just lifts her head, turns on the car, and starts driving. She stares straight ahead, not even trying to hide the tears that come, but I'm not backing down on this. Even when we get close to the prison and she takes the long way, probably hoping I'll change my mind, I say nothing.

I don't understand how she can forgive so easily and I'm not sure I ever will. It was her daughter after all. Addict or not, my mom could have been fixed. Maybe the state should've been thinking about rehabilitation then and not waiting to fix someone already too far gone.

We ride an hour in silence and I turn on the radio just to drown out the judgment in the quiet. If my father doesn't get put in this special program, it will all be on me. The only condition he hasn't met is establishing a dialogue with his son, but I'm not doing a thing to help the man.

My grandmother pulls into the parking lot of a liquor store and looks at me sadly. "Do you want something?"

I'm not 21, my family has a history of addiction, and my own anger is dangerous when mixed with alcohol. But the antidepressants they prescribed me in high school didn't help and I figure it's liquor or something harder eventually. I know Neil knows some people with all his club connections who could get me strong drugs, but I try to stay clean. I'm no saint and I've experimented, but my mother's story is too much of a reminder. So I stick to the numbing power of booze.

"Jack," I tell her.

She laughs a little. "Jack for my Jack."

In any other circumstances, maybe it's cute. In mine, it's just sad.

She goes into the store, a small, hunched woman who should have retired but can't afford to now that her entire savings went to paying legal fees. I think about the kids at school, especially Strawberries. I picture them all getting home for the first long weekend since school started, sitting around the dinner table and laughing over a home-cooked meal. Meanwhile, tonight I will be finishing off a bottle of Jack and hopefully fucking my equally screwed up friend if she isn't busy.

My grandmother comes back a bit later and hands me the paper bag. I shove it into my messenger bag and stare out the window for nearly the rest of the ride. We're almost home when she decides it's time to get serious.

"I know you refuse to take those meds, but are you seeing anyone? Are you safe?"

"I'm fine," I reply.

"Don't lie to me. You're not fine."

"Yeah, well, what should I say? That I hate him and I refuse to go? You keep telling me I have to move on, that it's not okay to hate him. What else do I say? That I'm sick of the way people look at me? That I know they see it in me? Because they do. I know I'm a loser and I know they can feel it coming off me in waves."

"You're not a loser. You're a victim of circumstance."

"I'd rather be a loser. I don't want to be a fucking victim of anything."

"I think you should go back to Dr. Nelson," she suggests and I push my face against the window, hoping the cold frosty glass will balance the heat inside me. Dr. Fucking Nelson. The fuckwad who somehow thought it was a good idea to give antidepressants to a 15-year-old before trying therapy. Like it was just a chemical imbalance that made my mom turn to drugs and my father become a lunatic. And as if the smartest move was to get the teenaged kid of a junkie hooked on prescription drugs. Fuck him, fuck his meds, and fuck his phony therapy.

"I know you're an adult now and technically, I can't force you. Unless there's another incident-"

"There won't be. I have been incident free for nearly two years," I remind her.

"I just worry that the people at that school can't treat you."

"I don't need to be treated. Fuck. Why am I such a case that everyone needs to fix?"

She shakes her head, but it shuts her up. Considering my life, I think I turned out fairly okay. I have a decent job that I've held down for years and I'm on a full scholarship to an awesome school. So I get drunk more than I should and I treat sex like a hobby. I'm not hurting anyone and I'm certainly not the only college guy who does those things. I know she doesn't see it, though. She's afraid I'll regress to the way I was in my senior year of high school, but it isn't going to happen. I'm too close to the end and too close to escape to give it all up now. At least most days. But no one needs to know about the exceptions.

When we get to the house, I excuse myself and call Alana. She doesn't answer, so I leave a voice mail, a little pissed off since she knew I was coming back tonight. I leave my phone on the nightstand and start working on a new song. I think about earlier tonight, sitting on the grass, seeing Strawberries and her happy relationship. It aches – and I hate the ache. She doesn't have the right to make me ache like that. I scribble fast, both thinking about her eyes and about how angry I am that I'm thinking about her eyes.

The lyrics are rough, but the song has potential. I'm about to start on the music when the phone rings. It's Alana.

"Yeah?"

"Sorry. Mom wanted me to go to dinner with the new boyfriend."

"And?"

"Well, he didn't hit on me when she went to the bathroom."

"Progress."

"Yup. So you're back?"

"I am."

"Whatcha doing?"

I put down my notepad and lean back on the bed. "Writing a song."

"Yeah? About what?"

"Strawberries," I say.

"Strawberries? Like the fruit?"

"Sort of." I don't want to talk about her. I don't want to face the fact that I'm obsessing over a girl who will never even notice that I exist. I'm the type of guy who lives in the periphery of girls like her and that's just how things go.

"The princess?" Alana isn't dumb. She knows me well.

"Sure. But I don't want to talk about her. Are you coming over?"

"Why?"

"Because I'm horny and my grandmother bought me a bottle of Jack," I tell her.

"Yeah, that's an amazing pick up line, but I don't know, Jack. I was thinking…"

"Don't do this. Please don't do this." I sit up and grip the phone tighter. I want to snap it, to break it into a hundred pieces, to go back to before I told Alana anything.

"It's just – if you're moving on, you're leaving me behind, right?"

"No. You're my best friend. You're the only person I love this much. You're the one who was so fucking worried about being abandoned and now you want to fucking walk away?"

"Cheap shot," she says.

"Well? It's true, isn't it?"

"I don't know. It hurts, though, you know."

"Stop making this something it isn't. You've dated. *I've* dated."

"You don't date. You fuck."

"Fine. But I've fucked other girls. I've fucked other girls with you in the room for fuck's sake."

"Yup. But you always wanted me. Now, you want someone else."

"Alana, please come over here. Please."

"Maybe tomorrow."

"Tonight. Please?" I'm begging, but the thought of her leaving, of losing her, of being alone – it makes me want to die. "You're killing me."

"Don't say things like that."

"Why the fuck not? You're making me want to die."

"Because I won't suck your dick? You're going to kill yourself because I won't suck your dick? Fuck you, Jack. I'm not listening to this shit. If you're serious, I'm there, but don't play that fucking card. Don't you *ever* play that card. You know what I went through last time."

"I wasn't playing any card. That's not what I meant. Please. Come over. I won't even touch you. I promise."

She's quiet for a minute. "Fine. But jerk off first or something."

"You're always so sweet."

"Fuck off." She hangs up, but I know she'll be here within the half hour. I don't jerk off, because I don't need to see Alana just for sex. In fact, I'm okay with simply being around her right now.

I decide to get something to eat while I wait. My grandmother is making cookies, which seems strange, since she never does things like this.

"Cookies?"

"I missed you."

"So you made cookies?" I laugh, caught off guard.

"Can you sit for a second?" She grows serious, and I worry. The cookies aren't just cookies. They're a warning, a bribe for something. I sit, but I choose the chair by the door so I can storm out if needed. As soon as she speaks, it appears to be needed.

"We have to visit your father this weekend. They won't even hear his case unless he tries with you."

"Good."

"I need you to do this, Jack. You can decide when. I didn't want to force it tonight, but you have to go. Please don't make this worse."

I know she's been fighting to help him get into this rehabilitation program. It's been her primary focus since he went in, but it was always an elusive concept, not a reality.

Do I think my father can be rehabilitated? No. I don't. I don't think people can be fixed after a certain point. Do I think he's a risk to the average person? No, I don't think that, either. But I don't want him to take the easy way out. He did what he did and he deserves the fallout. Why should I face it alone? Regardless of where he ends up, I don't get a chance at rehabilitation.

"Why? Why are you pushing this?" I ask.

"Because he's your father. You need your father."

"If he cared about that, he would be here, wouldn't he?"

I leave the room, without cookies, and I don't know what to do with my emotions. I open my paper bag and start drinking. It's half gone when Alana arrives and I'm nearly drunk.

"Stupid," she says and closes my bedroom door.

"Fuck you. Fuck her. Fuck all of it."

I collapse back on the bed and Alana takes the bottle. She starts cleaning my room, which is so degrading, but I don't want to do it, so whatever. I don't realize the lyrics are still on my nightstand until she picks them up and starts reading.

"'In the essence of a moment/in the flicker of a kiss/your eyes brought me to the edge/and there was only you to miss.' What's this sappy shit?"

I sit up and grab the notepad from her hand, ripping the lyrics up and tossing the shreds into my wastebasket. "It's nothing."

"Is that what you want?"

"Is *what* what I want?" I fall back onto the bed, but only after reaching for the booze. She takes the bottle away from me and sits.

"Do you want to be in love with someone?"

"No. I don't want to feel anything."

She lies down by my side and I wrap my arm around her; she rests her head in the crook of my arm. "Tell me what's going on. Are you okay?"

"Why does everyone keep asking me that?"

"Because you're not acting okay."

"I'm acting fine."

"No," she sighs. "You're acting like... well, like..." She doesn't want to say it and I realize what she thinks.

"I promised you last time it would never happen again."

"I can't go through that again, Jack. You know I would've followed you."

This makes me angry and I roll over on my side. "Never. Say. That. Again."

"Did you even think about what it would have been like for *me*?"

"No, I'm sorry. When I was wrapping a fucking rope around my neck, I did not think about your thoughts on the matter."

I move away from her and sit on the edge of the bed, my head in my hands. She doesn't move and her voice is a disembodied condemnation.

"They told me in math class. They came to get me and I thought you were dead."

"Well, I'm not. Hooray."

"You don't understand why I didn't go away to school?"

"No, I don't."

"Because I wanted to be able to drop it all if you needed me," she says. "Because I couldn't be in another state if you tried to kill yourself again."

I turn around and look at her lying on my bed. She's crying, but she looks so much more alive than I've ever seen her. The sobs shake her body and I consider hugging her, but then I remember that I'm still mad. Although I forget *why* I'm mad.

"I'm not worth that," I tell her.

"No, you've always been worth that. You've always been worth everything. You just don't care about my opinion. You always wanted everyone to like you, to please them all. For all your venom, for all your anger at them, you wanted their approval. You had me and you had Dave, but we were never enough. I could give up my entire future for you, but it didn't matter if some stranger in your dorm looked at you the wrong way. And now, I'm going to end up stuck here, because I planned my future around you and it's not good enough. Not if your 'princess' doesn't acknowledge you."

"That's not-"

"Just shut the fuck up," she interrupts. "I needed to say it and you needed to hear it. Now let's just forget about it and get drunk."

"I lost my buzz," I tell her.

"Good thing I brought more."

She takes out a bottle of vodka and a bottle of tequila. We drink until we both pass out in my bed. It's almost like sleeping, like disappearing. Except I can't stop seeing that girl.

Chapter 7

During work the next day, I find a quiet moment and ask Sandee for advice about my dad. We're out back during break, the door propped open with a box of hot sauce, and we lean against a stack of pallets, smoking. She passes me a bottle of something. I don't even look to see what it is. I take a swig and the burn feels so fucking good.

"Can I ask you something?" I ask.

She slips the alcohol back into her apron pocket and lights another cigarette. "Ask away."

"My grandmother insists I see my father before I go back Monday night. I can't stand seeing him. I hate him so much."

She nods.

I continue. "Like, fine, okay, maybe it would be better to have him in some program, but it seems really lame, you know? Like, oh, go ahead, fucking kill your wife, but now things will be a-okay because you said sorry. That's bullshit. No one stepped in to help her. No one tried to help me."

"You don't want anyone's help," she points out.

"Still."

I look up at the sky. It's a funny shade of pink, which inevitably makes me think of the same thing that's been on my mind for weeks now.

"Motherfucking strawberries."

"What?" Sandee asks. I didn't even realize I said it aloud.

"Nothing."

"What do you want, Jack? With your dad?"

"I want nothing. I want him to disappear. But I don't want to make my grandmother suffer."

"Can you handle him being out at some point?"

The rehabilitation program will speed up his parole, so rather than the thirty years he got, he'd be out in less than five more. Sure, it would still be a decade in prison and then endless "rehabilitation," but my mom was worth more than a decade. One condition of him even getting that far, of course, is an ongoing effort to repair his relationship with me. Maybe if I'm long gone, they won't be able to make me come back for him.

"I don't know," I admit.

"Can you handle just making your grandmother happy and doing the visit?"

I shrug. "I guess. It's just always someone else, you know? Always what makes someone else happy. I don't know why it bugs me, since I'm fucking miserable regardless, but just once, I would love to be the reason someone smiles. And not because I did something they wanted. Just because."

Sandee stabs out her cigarette and squeezes my arm. Most people don't touch me at all and no one but Alana and my grandmother hugs me, but it's a small act of comfort and I appreciate the gesture. I know she's only ten years older than me, and she is certainly not my mom, but I cling to her like she is.

"Maybe you're just desperate for the smile to come from the wrong people," she says. "If he isn't gonna change, it doesn't mean you can't be strong enough to go, if only to make it easier on your grandmother."

I finish my own cigarette. "Got more of whatever that was?"

I take another swig of the dark alcohol and sigh.

"You're the second person to say that in the last two days," I say. "That I seek the approval of the wrong people."

"I didn't say approval. I just think you feel like you need to prove yourself to people who doubt you, rather than loving the ones who already believe. You'll never make everyone happy, Jack. Even if you had the life you wish you had, someone would always be ready to tell you you're not good enough."

"People fucking suck, Sandee."

She nods and moves to the door. "That they do. I'm heading back in, but take your time. It's dead anyway."

I climb up the side of the pallets and sit on top, staring up at the sky. The pink has faded with the day, giving way to darkness. There's a weird cloud cover overhead, a strange greenish gray mass that blots out the moon and makes the entire back lot look eerie. I'm feeling guilty about Alana, about hurting her, about being such a letdown to her. It makes me feel worse about saying no to my grandma, even though what she's asking is the hardest thing for me to do.

I think back to when it all happened, about how she faced everything bravely. She sat through the trial and never shed a tear, never showed how much it tore her apart. I *have* to be able to do this.

I take out my phone and text Alana. I want to see her after work. She tells me she'll meet me in the lot when I get out and I decide I'll make things up to her. I don't know how, but I'll fix everything. I have to hope there's something in my life that isn't beyond repair.

****

When I get out of work, I find Alana passed out drunk in the backseat of my grandma's car. I take the bottle from her hand and sit her up, trying to stir her.

"Wake the fuck up," I say.

She mumbles and tries to slink back down along the seat. I push her against the door to keep her upright.

"Alana, wake the fuck up."

She doesn't, though, and I'm pissed. I know she wouldn't be stupid enough to drive here drunk, but she must have crawled into my car and finished the bottle fast. *This is what you get for the shit you do,* my mind tells me. Yeah? Fuck you, mind.

I buckle Alana into a seatbelt and crack the window a bit, hoping the air will stir her.

"You're pissing me off," I tell her.

I drive around for a while, waiting for her to wake up. I try everything – slamming on the brakes, opening the window more, blasting the a/c, blasting the radio. Finally, she wakes up when I make a sharp turn around a corner.

"Where am I?"

"You passed out in the back of my grandmother's car."

"I need to get laid," she whines.

"You need to get showered."

"Fine. Showered, then laid."

"I can't bring you home like this," I tell her.

"Here." She reaches forward and shoves a wad of money at me. It falls onto the passenger seat and a couple bills blow out the damn window before I shut it. I don't know what the money's for or where it's from, but its existence makes me angry.

"What the fuck am I supposed to do with that?" I ask.

"Get a motel room. I'll shower there and then you can fuck me."

"I don't want to fuck you. You're a fucking mess right now."

"Fuck you."

"Yeah, of course."

I keep driving, but she leans forward again and smacks the back of my head.

"Get a fucking room," she demands. "I can take a shower and we can go to the bar. Someone will want to fuck me."

She's right. Someone will *definitely* want to fuck her, but it's stupid. Still, I listen and find a cheap motel nearby so she can shower. I don't even go in. I'm so pissed at her right now. I don't know why I don't just bring her home. I guess I figure the shit she'll deal with from her mom if I do isn't worth avoiding what I have to deal with right now.

She doesn't take long to shower and she's more alert, although still pretty drunk, when she comes back outside.

"Bar. Now."

She's going to get a lot of attention tonight, dressed like she is. Her black pants are skintight and her silvery pink tank top shows off her bare belly and clings to her tits. She doesn't even have a jacket and her tattooed arms make her look both tough and sexy. She'll have no problem finding what she's after, especially at the shitty bar nearby.

They always serve us, even though they have to know we're underage. We started coming here when I was a freshman, because I'd heard they would serve anyone. I guess it was true and although the thrill apparently wore off for most of my peers, it never stops me from coming here. Some nights, it's busier than others. Tonight is one of those nights.

Alana walks in and strolls right up to the bar, putting herself between two guys who must be at least 35. They both check out her ass and I walk forward, annoyed that I'm the one who has to do something if they go further than she'd like. She orders shots for herself and the two guys and leans against the one on the left, a guy who looks like he's spent a lot of time here. He wraps an arm around her and I tense, but when she goes for his crotch, I guess there's no point in fighting. I sit at one of the tables by the wall and watch her get these two guys horny over her.

It's got to be less than thirty minutes before she takes the guy whose crotch she was massaging over to where I'm sitting.

She smiles. "This is Aaron. We want to go back to the motel."

"You're being an idiot," I say.

"Hey, buddy-" Aaron starts, but he's out for one thing, which Alana is happy to give. The problem is, he won't be the one dealing with the fallout in the morning.

"Alana, you don't want to do this."

She rubs herself against Aaron and grins, sliding a hand up under his shirt. "Yes, I do. Bring us to the motel, Jackie."

"You're not proving anything."

"I don't want to prove anything. I want to get laid and Aaron had kindly offered to fuck me."

"You know what? Fine. Whatever."

I drive them back to the motel, which is thankfully not far, because she's all over him in the backseat. If it was any farther away, she'd probably have already slept with him before we made it. When we get there, I wait for them to get out, but Alana runs her hand through my hair from the back.

"Don't you wanna watch?"

"No."

She's angry now and she turns the anger on me. "Fuck you, Jack. Fucking watch. If I can play your little princess, you can fucking watch."

I hate her when she's like this. I hate *myself* when she's like this, because I don't say no. I just follow her like a fucking idiot into the motel room and sit in the shitty rotting chair while she gets naked with some random dude she met at a dive bar.

Aaron doesn't seem to mind at all that I'm here, which is annoying. I could be her boyfriend; he doesn't know. Who just goes back to a motel with a girl to fuck her while another guy is in the picture? He doesn't even undress, just pulls down his pants and bends her over so she's facing me and he's behind her.

She gasps as he enters her. There was no foreplay and clearly Aaron has one goal here. She's enjoying herself, though, as evidenced by the way she closes her eyes and tilts her head back, pushing her ass toward him so he can thrust deeper into her. I don't want this to turn me on, but it does. Hell, it really does. I like keeping my eyes open with Alana, because I know the faces she makes when she comes and it makes me happy to be the one to make her come. However, this is incredibly hot. She's getting off on this and I get hard watching her get fucked. His cock slides in and out of her quickly and she moans.

"Oh, shit," I say, and I unzip my pants. It pisses me off so much, because I don't even want to be here and yet I'm about to jerk off watching this. Something is seriously wrong with me. Even as I take my cock in my hand and start stroking myself, watching some old guy from a bar fuck my best friend, I kind of want to cry.

Alana opens her eyes and smiles at me. "I love watching you watch me," she says. "It makes me so fucking hot."

"Great."

I'm horny and miserable and pissed off and I feel sick to my stomach. Aaron pulls out of Alana and comes all over her ass. He doesn't say anything, just gets up and goes to the bathroom to clean himself off. I'm still sitting in the chair with my dick in my hand while all this happens. I feel like an idiot.

"Fuck me, baby," Alana says. "Fuck me like no one else can."

"You're drunk."

"Not anymore."

"Well, too bad. This is stupid."

She stands up, still covered in Aaron's come, and walks over to me, kneeling between my legs. She starts sucking my cock and he comes out of the bathroom while she teases my balls with her tongue.

"Oh, fuck," I say, full of shame.

"She's pretty hot," Aaron says. "Think she'd be up for another go?"

Alana moves away from me and stands. She grabs my hand and I let her drag me to the bed. She pushes me down, kneeling in front of me on the bed. She goes back to sucking me off, while Aaron positions himself and starts fucking her. I am so fucking hot right now and her mouth is phenomenal. This is the worst way to treat my best friend, but I'm pissed at her and horny, so too fucking bad.

I come and Alana swallows, but there's nowhere for her to move with Aaron behind her, so she keeps me in her mouth. By the time Aaron is done fucking her, I'm ready again.

"You know you want to fuck me," she says and smiles. Damn her. I do, of course.

"You just fucked *him*. Twice."

"So I'll take a shower."

She gets up and Aaron looks at me awkwardly. I'm his ride back to the bar, which makes this whole situation uncomfortable. I shrug and follow Alana to the bathroom. She's so gorgeous and as soon as she steps into the shower, with the hot water streaming down her tits, I can't take it. I strip off my shirt and get in the shower with her, slamming her back against the wall.

"Be rough with me, Jack."

I lift her leg and she struggles to maintain her balance in the slippery shower. I'm not gentle as I slip inside of her cunt, but she's so wet that it wouldn't matter. I get my hands under her ass and lift her so I can thrust deeply, and she wraps her legs tightly around my waist. I bite on her nipples and she cries my name, but the water drowns out the sounds. I am so angry with her for making me feel like this and I push her harder and harder against the wall of the shower. She bounces up and down on my cock and I explode inside of her in no time. Fuck. Why do I have no self-control?

"I didn't come," she pouts. "Do it again."

"I fucking hate you right now."

"I don't care. Do it again."

She grabs my cock and tugs on it, but I'm not in the mood. I'm ready to walk away when she says, "Come on, Jack. Get hard. Think about the strawberry princess and that tight little pussy. Think she'd even be able to fit you inside of her?"

Fuck Alana. It works, because the simple thought of Strawberries naked under me, her pussy wet and hot while I slide in and out of it, makes me fucking wild. I yank Alana out of the shower, drag her back into the motel room, and push her down over the shitty table that probably no one has ever used.

"Beg for my cock," I command her. "You only get it if you fucking beg."

"Please, baby. Please give me that cock."

"No. Not good enough."

She looks at me over her shoulder. "Give it to me. Make me come. I want to come."

"No."

"Fuck you, Jack. You can't resist me. As soon as you think about that little innocent cunt again, you're going to lose it and fuck me hard over this table while you imagine doing it to her."

Oh, Christ. I grab a handful of Alana's hair, pull her head back, and slam my cock into her.

"You're a bitch," I tell her and it's awful. I hate myself for saying it and I hate that she laughs and clenches her pussy around me when I do. I hate that the rougher I am with her, the more she groans in pleasure, and I hate that it makes me love it even more. Finally, I really hate the things I want to do to that sweet girl who can't even imagine what I'm thinking when I look at her. I want inside that pussy so fucking bad it hurts. What the fuck is wrong with me?

Alana comes and it's intense. She screams so loud that I worry someone will call the cops, thinking I'm hurting her. It's a shitty motel after all, and who knows what kind of shit they see here? Alana is near tears as I slap her ass hard and fuck her until she almost falls over. I pull out, drag her over to the bed, and get back inside of her to finish. She's still shaking as I come and I let it squirt across her stomach.

"Thanks, Jackie. You always know just what to do."

From behind me, Aaron coughs. Shit. That asshole is still here. I don't say anything, but get dressed. I nod at Aaron and he follows me to the car. Alana looks at me, a little nervous, but I'm not going to leave her here for good.

"I'll be back in a bit."

I drive Aaron back to the bar so he can get his car. We don't say a word to each other. I fucking hate the bastard. After I drop him off, I drive around for a bit. I love Alana, but she knows how to bring out the worst in me. Or maybe, there is nothing but the worst to bring out.

Chapter 8

My grandmother is so happy that I agreed to visit with my father on my way back to school that I almost feel okay with the decision. Until we reach the prison and the familiar sickness returns. I can't turn around now and say I don't want to go in, but the sky is steel grey and I wonder why it's never sunny when I come here. Even the weather hates me.

She has a hat on, because it's a prison day, and I don't have the heart to tell her that she tries to look nice for a group of lowlifes. I feel like somewhere in her head she convinces herself that she looks like she's going to church or something and that people will think that's what she's doing. She seems to believe that if other people assume she's not the mother-in-law of a killer, then she's not the mother-in-law of a killer.

The security check is backed up today because some guy is arguing with the guard about his belt. They want him to leave it at the entrance, since it keeps setting off the metal detectors, but he's apparently really attached to the stupid thing and doesn't want to give it up. They argue back and forth and it's the dumbest conversation I've ever heard. And I go to college with frat boys.

"Buddy, you have to take off the belt and leave it, or you can't get in. Unless you can pass through here without setting off the machines, you aren't going to see anyone."

"You're just trying to rob me. You're all part of the system, man, and I ain't giving you shit."

"You'll get the thing back," the guard tries to reason.

"Fuck you. You're just trying to keep me down."

The guard sighs. "Look, just put the belt right here on this shelf. I will personally watch over it and make sure it's safe."

"Why should I trust you? You work for them."

"I do and I make less than twenty bucks an hour. I don't care about your damn belt."

"More than I make. Think you're so special, judging me, acting like you're too good for something that belongs to me-"

"Holy fuck, just give him the fucking belt," I yell. The guard, the random dude, and my grandmother all turn to look at me. "What? This is fucking stupid."

The guy seems so taken aback that he quietly removes his belt and hands it to the guard. He goes through the metal detector, this time without setting anything off, and turns back to look at me. He shakes his head and mumbles to himself, "Crazy ass motherfucker."

The guard just stares at me. I walk through the machine and the thing goes insane. It's my belt ironically. He raises an eyebrow and just holds out his hand.

"I need you to leave your belt here."

I don't care about the belt or this visit and the sooner we get in, the faster we leave. I hand him my belt and then my grandmother is through. The guard buzzes us into the next area, where a few more guards are sitting in a small office. I wait for them to lead us to the room where we'll meet my dad. The metal table shines in the fluorescent light. If I stare at it long enough, maybe I'll go blind.

"No outbursts," my grandmother warns.

"It wasn't an outburst. He was wasting time."

"I don't care. Your actions impact your father."

"Yeah, well, *his* kinda impacted me."

She shakes her head and turns to face the door through which my dad will enter. I hate it here. I hate the way the lights are covered in weird metal mesh grates that make it always feel like five o'clock on a winter evening. I hate the way the voices of other visitors and prisoners bounce off the walls, disembodied and incomprehensible, but invasive enough to remind you that you'll never be alone in here. I hate how the guards try to treat me like their own kid, as if by being sympathetic it will fix anything. And I especially hate the stupid look of hope that refuses to leave my grandmother's face no matter how many times we come here. Sometimes, I think maybe it's that look that makes me limit my visits as much as I do, more so than even hating my father. Because the fact that she believes someday things can be okay? Well, there is just nothing I can say about that.

My father is led in by the same two guards who showed us to the room. He doesn't make eye contact with me but smiles at my grandmother.

"Janine," he nods.

"Bobby."

He sits in the chair across from us, his hands cuffed and the guards standing close enough that if he decided to make a run for it, they could stop him. He has never tried to run for it, though. I feel like if the entire prison burned down around him, my father would be found sitting in the middle, unsure where to go, even with no walls left standing.

"Hi, son," he tries.

I grunt in his general direction and focus my attention on the flicker in one of the fluorescent bulbs. It's going to burn out any day now.

"Jack," my grandmother prods, but I don't reply.

"Leave it," my dad says.

They talk quietly about his case, the proposed plan to rehabilitate him, the halfway house program he'll have to go through if he's released. It all seems so pointless to me. If there are all these resources to ensure that he stays on the right path, to ensure that he stays sober and clean even though he never really drank or did drugs, then why were none of those things available to help my mom? Why didn't anyone try to stop this before we were sitting here, in this dingy fucking room, with everything grey and hopeless ahead of me?

I want to leave, to excuse myself, but I stay for my grandmother's sake. She and my father talk for nearly half an hour before the guards come and tell us time's almost up. He's not allowed to hug her, but she brushes his upper arm. Before he stands to go back to his cell, my father turns to face me.

"Jack, I hope we can-"

"No. I'll fake it, but that's it. I'll sit here so it looks like you're an all-American father and I'll say whatever bullshit I need to say the next time the lawyers come to see me, but don't even think of asking me to mean it. I'm only doing this for her."

He opens his mouth to respond, but then shuts it again and nods. The guards lead him away and we wait to be escorted from the room. My grandmother is sad, but I don't have more to give her. I came here after all. That's enough.

Outside, it's sunny now and it bugs me. Couldn't the world have stayed ashy and miserable?

Grandma brings me back to school and I'm barely out of the car before I run to the parking lot and hop on my bike. I put as much distance as I can between myself and the prison, wishing that the memories were like the miles, and as easily left behind.

****

For several weeks, school begins to become routine again. Classes, work, band practice - and repeat. I can't believe how fast the show comes up. I know we've been working on my songs, but suddenly it's the night before and I realize that my words, my music, will be shared with everyone. I know no one knows it's all mine, but it frightens me. People are so quick to criticize, and criticism of something so personal is intimidating. Still, after we practice for a while, I know the songs are damn good. I just hope it won't feel like walking onstage naked, with my entire history printed out for everyone to read.

Neil stops me again when it's just us left after practice. I can't believe the show is tomorrow and even my practiced calm can't hide the fact that I've bitten down my fingernails until they are bloody. *Stupid*, I think to myself. *You're going to suck because you can't even control your anxiety.* My self pisses me off, though, so I tune it out.

"You ready for this?" Neil asks.

"It's not the first show."

"No, but man, your songs are... well, they're more intense than usual. And I know you don't like to be that out there with everyone."

"They're just songs."

He shakes his head. "No, they're not."

"As far as *they* know? They're just songs."

"Okay, as long as you're sure. I think they're epic and I think they're gonna give us the boost we've been hoping for, but I'm not sure it's worth the cost of-"

"Neil. Enough. It's fine." I don't want to talk about the songs, outside of their musical parts.

Either the songs are good or they are not. No one needs to know how deep every word cuts.

"Okay. Well, I guess I'll see you at the show then."

I hesitate. Sometimes I think Neil and I could be friends, not just cowriters and comusicians. With Dave overseas and Alana and I, well, a mess, I could use a friend like Neil. But then I picture coming here, with my whole story hanging over practice, with the constant reminder of my parents, and the constant need to reassure everyone that I'm fine. I don't want to taint the only place I have that's a refuge from all the shit that surrounds me during every other minute of my pathetic life. As much as I want a friend, I want peace more, and so I blow it off, this feeling that I'm running away.

"Yeah, see ya," I mumble.

I take off into the night, wondering if I'll ever find it in me to make an effort.

****

Show night, the club is packed. We're only opening, but I know a decent amount of people are here for us. Neil knows everyone it seems and he's managed to develop quite the Facebook following, or so I'm told. I don't even use Facebook. Who would I possibly talk to?

He's told us that he's been getting a big fan base established, but I didn't expect there to be *this* many people. It's both thrilling and terrifying. I focus on the sound check and don't think about all these people and my own songs being introduced. I think I'm actually going to be okay, too, until suddenly I'm not. I don't know what happens. The room spins, the walls grow closer and closer, and I run from the stage, managing to hold in the puke until I reach the sidewalk from the loading door. Neil is right behind me, but he hovers in the doorway while I vomit in the street.

"We don't have to play those songs," he suggests.

I wipe a strand of sticky puke from my lips. "Fuck you. We're playing them."

"I don't think you-"

I stare him down. "We're fucking playing them. There is no way I'm backing down because I had a little case of the nerves."

114

I walk past him to the little area backstage and grab my messenger bag. I find the bottle of whiskey in the front flap and drink half of it. Neil's followed me, of course, but he says nothing. He just shakes his head.

"Don't fucking shake your head," I tell him. "I'll be fine in like five minutes."

I put the bottle back and grab my cigarettes. Outside, in the fresh air, even with the tastes of whiskey and vomit mixing in my mouth, I feel better already. I breathe in the smoke from my cigarette and try to forget the momentary anxiety. Neil stands next to me the entire time, but doesn't speak until I'm done smoking.

"Look, Jack. We aren't really friends, I guess, but you're a damn good musician and I don't know what's happening with you. But, you know, maybe you should see someone."

"Fuck you."

"Okay. Whatever you say."

He's not angry, because there is nothing to be angry about. He made his obligatory suggestion to help my mood and I denied it. The end. I wish more people were like Neil. If I wanted to stand out here and have a fucking moment, I would have it. I don't need someone forcing it or harassing the shit out of me when I clearly don't want to talk.

We go back in and get ready. The other guys are onstage still, finishing the sound check, and we don't have much time. I grab a mint from the table in the corner to get rid of the lingering vomit taste, and I splash my face with water. The lights in the club dim and someone announces us. Neil looks at me and I nod, following him out on stage. My bass is already set up and I put it on, feeling like a different person. It's like the sounds that the instrument produces are all the words I can never say and playing is cathartic.

We're barely a verse into the first song when I see her across the room. She looks so out of place; her jeans and t-shirt are too clean for this crowd. It's like she ironed them. Her gaze darts around the room and she's biting her lip. Damn, she is adorable. I almost call out to her when she starts chewing her fingernails nervously. She glances my way and we make eye contact for a moment. The lights are bright, but she's standing in just the right area that I can still see her. I can't explain it, but I think I love her in that instant. This silly, foolish girl whom I cannot get out of my head.

When we perform the new songs, the crowd erupts. They love them. I think of what Alana said recently, that I need their approval, and I wonder if she's right. As much as I hate most of these kids during the day, here, at night in this club, their opinions define me. I wish I understood why, because they haven't shown to be people with much taste. Yet their applause drowns out reason and I feel whole when they react to my songs this way.

I don't even like playing in front of people, but when they're like this... it's euphoric. They even demand an encore, which never happens for an opening band. We're offstage when we hear it and Neil claps me on the shoulder.

"Whatever is fucking you up man, hang onto it."

It's a weird comment, and it rests on me funny. Should I be offended? Is my life nothing but inspiration for art? As we play our encore, though, I realize it's the first time my past has not shamed me. In fact, I feel a slight bit of pride that the darkness settled on me the way that it did. Without it, I'd probably be no different than the empty people I see all day, every day.

After we perform, someone says we need to talk to a reporter from the school paper. What a joke. They probably sent some uptight asshole who won't even get the music. Then the reporter will write a stupid review that complains about the noise, because he or she listens to crappy pop hits that replicate the same shit the radio has played for years.

I get my bass into the van and we load up the rest of the equipment, except the drums.

"Hey, can you talk to that reporter?" Neil asks. "I'll be right out. I just want to make sure they don't fuck up the load in again. Last time, it was a bitch getting everything into my garage."

"Yeah, whatever." I don't want to talk to the empty-headed reporter, but I suppose I should.

"Feel free to brag about your songs."

"Right." Neil knows me so little. I wasn't even going to mention that I wrote them.

I push the felt curtain aside and nearly trip over Strawberries, who's sitting in a metal chair, looking lost. Huh. Did she come here to talk to me? I can't deny that my body hopes she did. My cock is already getting hard just thinking about bringing her back to my room tonight. The energy from the show is still making me twitch and now, near this girl, I want to put that energy to good use. I lean in closer to talk to her over the noise of the club.

"I thought that was you. Doesn't really seem like your scene, princess."

She rolls her eyes. "It's Lily. And what's my scene?"

"Tea parties and knitting circles?"

I try to lighten the mood, hoping she'll play along, hoping that it will be enough to loosen her up and maybe even get her to my room. I notice she's not here with anyone. Hopefully the boyfriend is no longer in the picture. Smiling at her, I do my best to flirt, but I feel weird about it. I don't flirt. I meet girls who are horny and I fuck them hard. This girl is not in my toolbox.

"You're an asshole," she says.

Well, that didn't work. Although asshole I can do. Far better than awkward flirting. And she seems to keep coming back, so maybe asshole it is.

"Yet you can't deny you want me," I tease.

I take my fingertips and run them along the lower side of her arm. The hairs on her arm stand up; she definitely wants me. I just don't know how to play this game, because girls I fuck don't play hard to get. Maybe that's why I want her so badly; I'm not used to chasing girls who say no.

She pulls her arm away from me, irritated.

"Did you like the show?" I ask. I'm dying here.

"It was good."

"How about a private performance? Just you and me?"

She opens her mouth, but then Neil and the others appear through the curtain. Damn it.

She turns to Neil and takes out a steno pad. "I need a quote from the band for the paper."

I try not to laugh. *She* is the airhead reporter. Perfect.

"Well, we're really excited that our outreach has worked and we've been able to establish a stronger fan base. I think that along with the amazing new songs Jack here has written, it will really boost our exposure. I know we'd all like to see our own show by the end of the semester. That's really the goal."

Strawberries writes down what Neil says and I watch her. She's biting her lip again and, holy hell, I want her right here, right now. I almost rip the steno pad from her hand and drag her to the bathroom or somewhere private. She doesn't strike me as the kind of girl who would be up for wild sex in a club bathroom. Oh, but how I wish she was.

She gets up to leave and the other guys look at me, waiting. I move close to her, whispering in her ear. "Remember. 401. When you're ready to admit you're interested."

It doesn't work. At all. She walks away and doesn't look back. I watch her ass in her tight jeans as she goes. Fuck. Now I definitely need to find the kind of girl who *is* up for wild sex in a club bathroom. Because I am desperate and horny and I don't even know how to make it happen with Strawberries.

Or Lily. She said her name was Lily.

"Are you sticking around?" Neil asks. I'm grateful for the interruption of my thoughts, because my cock is going to burst if I keep thinking about that ass, but I also kind of want to punch him for cutting my moment with her short.

"I don't know. Maybe."

"That girl's here."

"What girl?"

I turn toward the bar, where Neil is pointing. *Did she come back? Did it work?* But it's not Lily. Alana is sitting on a bar stool, not looking at us. We haven't talked lately and it's partially my fault. Well, that, and the fact that the last time we *did* talk, she made me watch her get fucked by some old dude she met in a bar.

I go to her and she turns to face me, her eyes sad.

"Hey," I say.

"Was that her?" She tilts her head toward the door where Lily just walked out.

"Was *who* her?"

"That girl you were just talking to? Is that the princess?"

"Yeah."

"She's cute," she says.

"Can we not talk about her?"

Alana looks at me. "Why?"

"I just-"

"She's not *that* cute, Jack. Control yourself." She reaches a hand down to my crotch and rubs my cock through my jeans.

"That's not helping, you know."

"So put it to use and fuck me."

"This is unhealthy," I say and lift her hand away.

She downs her glass of whatever she's drinking. "It wouldn't be the first time you've fucked me in a dirty club bathroom. It's okay. You need it and she's not giving it to you."

I actually *do* debate. I'm not as pathetic as I appear. There's a full on discussion in my head that involves me arguing against doing this, a loud voice that suggests that I go back to the dorm and try having a conversation with Lily, that reminds me that I continue to use my best friend because I can't seem to control myself. Of course, the full conversation in my head looks to a normal person like a grunt drowned out by Alana's lips on mine and her hand down my pants.

I drag her into the bathroom and lock the door. She pulls her pants down and sits on the nasty sink, spreading her legs for me. I enter her and stare at myself in the mirror behind her while I fuck her. It's dirty and grimy and I look dirty and grimy. Of course, my stupid, fucking cock doesn't care; it's having a grand old time in Alana's pussy.

She clutches at my back and screams my name. *I am a fucking idiot,* I think, but I keep right on fucking her. She comes, biting my neck, and I finish inside of her. It's dirty and wrong and I feel terrible about it, but it doesn't stop me from coming.

"That girl is never going to be enough for you, Jackie," Alana says and she sinks to her knees, taking me into her mouth. I've barely lost my erection before she gets it back and she blows me like a whore in the bathroom. I think about Lily's tight ass and I come in no time, shooting the load down Alana's throat. I really hate myself, but nothing seems to stop me.

"I wish you wouldn't do this," I tell her once she's back on her feet.

"What? Fuck you? Suck your dick?"

"You know I'm a fucking loser. You know I won't say no."

"Yup, and I love that about you," she says. "You think you want that sweet little girl, but you can't function without a girl you can treat like a whore."

She's right. She's trying to hurt me, but I'm not mad. Because she's right. I've never been a boyfriend, minus the little relationship I had with her, and I sucked at that. Although I never cheated on her, I was a mess the whole time and I treated her like shit. I still treat her like shit, but she seems to be okay with it most of the time. I no longer pretend that we're more than we are. It bugs me, though, because I know she's just waiting for me to change. But nothing has changed me yet. Even when I can rationalize that this is the wrong thing to do, it doesn't stop me from doing it. And now, because I'm a little stung by her words, I make it a million times worse.

"Turn around," I tell her.

"Why?"

"So I can fuck you like a whore."

Poor Alana. She does it, because she's as broken as I am, and it's the emptiest sex I have ever had. It doesn't stop either of us from coming, but it's all physical. The emotion is gone from us both and we are no longer even human. I feel like a cutout of a guy blowing away in the wind and it's all just darkness. There is never going to be anything but darkness.

Chapter 9

Alana ends up spending the night after the show. I wish I could figure out the endless conflict I have between what I know is right and how much fun it is to fuck my best friend. Although logically, we're not doing anything wrong, I do care for her far more than I ever show her.

Fortunately, I guess, she ended up getting drunk and hitting on Devon, so I lost track of them. By the time we were ready to leave, she'd probably fucked Devon's brains out, so she was too tired for me when we got back. Now, the morning after, she is lying strewn across my bed and I'm trying to decide what to do with her. I somehow managed to get the day off today, and now I have hung-over Alana in my bed and no idea what to do with myself.

I kick her a little to see if she'll respond, but she just grunts and rolls over. I move to my chair and turn on the Xbox. Maybe shooting something will help. I think I dreamed last night, although I don't remember it clearly. Still, my head is swimming with thoughts of lovely Lily and I need a distraction.

I feel a little proud that I choose Xbox over sex or alcohol, but virtual zombies don't dull the ache the same way. I've nearly maxed out the achievements on the game by the time Alana wakes up and joins the living.

"What time is it?"

She's still wearing her clothes from the night before. I ended up sleeping in a twisted position around her passed out body.

"Like four." Fuck. A zombie gets past me.

"In the afternoon?"

"Uh huh."

"Why didn't you wake me?"

"You clearly needed to sleep it off," I tell her.

She gets up and takes the controller from my hand. I don't even protest. I already beat the game; I'm just trying to get the last few achievements. It's a little irritating that she turns off the console without saying anything, but I'm not surprised anymore.

"Let's go somewhere," she says.

"Where? You're a mess. And you smell like shit."

"You're a sweetheart. I'll take a shower and you can take me for a ride."

I shrug and gather an old t-shirt she can wear, walking her to the girls' side for her shower. The lounge on this side of the hall is much nicer. They have flowers and some kind of dried smelly shit in a glass bowl on the coffee table. We have old pizza. I sit and wait for Alana, hoping that Lily will walk by, that I can see her, that we can talk.

She doesn't come into the lounge at any point and, when Alana is showered, we leave campus. I don't know where to go, but I drive with her hanging on to me until we're nearly back home. There is a weird part of me wired to this place, especially with Alana near me, and I wonder if that's part of why I can't fall for her.

I stop in the town next to ours by one of those old meetinghouse churches. There's a gazebo on the grounds, although it's rotting and falling apart.

"Here?" Alana looks around her, confused.

"I realized I was just heading home. Force of habit."

"So you stopped here?"

"I don't know."

I lean against my bike and take out a pack of cigarettes. Everything is so incomprehensible and I feel myself slipping. I can't tell Alana or she'll panic, but the heavy weight of misery that ebbs and flows in my life is starting to come back in full-blown waves.

I light a cigarette and walk to the rotting frame of the gazebo. It's probably condemned, but I go up the steps and sit in the middle, somewhat hoping the whole thing will crash down over me and end it all right here.

Alana follows and steals one of my cigarettes. We sit, smoking, until she puts a hand on my knee. "I know what you're doing."

"Yeah? What's that?"

"You're shutting down again. Don't shut down, Jack. You know I'm here. I can handle it. I've learned how to handle it."

"I don't even know what *it* is. How can anyone handle it?"

She sighs and looks out over the churchyard. "Do you think she'll make you happy?"

"It's not really a matter of debate. She hates me."

"You don't help yourself, you know. Make a fucking effort. I know how you are. You act like an asshole, like it will somehow insulate you against feeling a thing."

"It's worked so far."

"Has it?"

"Besides, you're the one who keeps reminding me that I'm a fucking idiot."

"I've always been what you need when you need it. It hurts like hell that you need something I can't be, but I'm not gonna stop being your friend just because you need more."

"You know we're a mess?" I ask her.

"I do. But the mess is the only thing I know and the only thing that keeps me going. I'll always be here, no matter what. I think you need to start opening up, though. You're falling apart and I saw it when you looked at her. You want to be something else. But you can't. Not if you fight it."

"That's not what you told me last night."

"Hell, I don't know what I am, either." She laughs, a sad and hopeless laugh, and wraps herself in my arms. Again, I wish I loved her, because I can't imagine a life without Alana. But I know she's right. Lily has made me want to be something I'm not, and it scares me even though I can't stop hoping it could happen.

"I don't have a shot," I whisper.

"Not if you don't try. Maybe start by being nice. She looks a little too sweet for what you are."

"That hurts."

She takes my hand and links her fingers with mine. "I'm sorry. But you need to face that part of it. You know how people judge. Just be prepared for it with her. I promise you she isn't perfect, even if you want her to be."

I don't say anything. I know Alana's right, but every time I look at Lily's beautiful eyes and smell her strawberry hair, I can't imagine a way she could be anything but.

****

The week flies by and it's Thursday night before I know it. I haven't had much time to do anything but work, study, and practice. With exams coming up, I'm also trying to focus more on school. Classes come easy to me, but I take my scholarship seriously and I value it.

When you're an antisocial person, you find studying comes a lot more naturally, of course. I've spent most nights in my room reviewing content and that's the plan tonight as well. I'm thwarted though as I walk into the dorm after getting off work, feeling nasty from the sticky heat of the kitchen. Because the weather is in that switch to fall mode, every building is obscenely hot to make up for the chill that's in the air. It's a pleasant chill, though, and I'm debating about taking a shower and studying outside on the quad when someone almost knocks me over.

It's Lily. Her eyes are wet and full of a burning rage. It's an emotion I recognize well. She's determined and it takes me a second to catch my breath after she walks into me. I reach out a hand; she's shaking and I want to comfort her, but she doesn't even notice.

"Hey, where are you running off to? Lose your glass slipper?"

As always, she misunderstands my caustic humor. "Fuck you."

"Ouch. What happened?"

"Get out of my way."

She starts to push past me, but I know this feeling. I live it almost daily. I take her arm and turn her to face me. The intensity mixed with the greenish blue of her eyes hits me deep in my belly. She's standing here, ready to fight, ready to run, and all I can think about is how unbelievably beautiful she is.

"Hey. Hold on," I say. "Let me take a quick shower and we can go for a ride. You look like you need to get a little wild."

"You have no idea," she replies.

I can't believe this is happening, but I'm not going to argue. I need to clean up because I smell terrible, but I don't want her to leave.

"I'll be down in like ten minutes," I tell her, and I hope she waits. I nearly trip on my way to the shower, so desperate to hurry up to get back to her. It feels like the longest shower ever. Once I'm dressed, I head back to the lobby, half expecting her to be gone. Thankfully, she isn't, but she is tapping her foot. I wonder how much longer she would've waited.

"Come on," I say and lead her to the lot where my bike is. She doesn't speak and I'm afraid to find out this is some kind of delusion. Anything I say could ruin the moment and I want to wait until I at least have her with me off campus before I test it. She doesn't ask for a plan and I debate. I consider taking her to a park somewhere, to the café, somewhere we could talk. However, she digs her fingers into me as we ride and I realize that whatever led her to this point is something she needs to forget.

Because it's the only way I know how to deal with that kind of pain, I bring her to a bar. It's a small townie bar, but I know Liam will serve us. He's a friend of Liz's and he's been serving me for years. It's one of the perks of knowing people in a small town where everyone is desperate to escape.

Strawberries doesn't strike me as a drinker, so I start slow. I grab two beers and bring them back to the table where she settles herself. She sips the shitty beer like it's fine champagne and I can't help but smile.

"What?" she snaps at me.

"You're looking like you need to disappear. It ain't gonna happen if you nurse that."

"What do you mean?"

God, this girl is too fucking precious. "Drink faster," I tell her.

"I don't really drink," she replies.

No kidding. "Well, I'd suggest you start. Whatever shit you're dealing with – it's still gonna be there in the morning. Maybe tonight – let it go."

It's probably bad advice, but I don't care. I've been through too much to think about the morality of drowning my pain in alcohol. It's kept me from suicide watch for several years, so I'll take it. If that's a problem, too fucking bad. This girl and whatever problems she has are no match for the shit that's been my life – and she can afford to take a step over the line once in a while. I get the impression she thinks the line is straddled by a fucking brick wall. It's my mission to break through that wall for her.

She stares at me and holds my gaze. It's a challenge again. I don't know how tonight will end, but I almost get down on my knees and pray that it ends with her in my bed. I need to be with this girl in the same way I need fucking oxygen and I don't know that I can deny it anymore. Her lip turns up in a quirky smile. She grabs the beer, downing it, and then she slams the glass on the table. Well, fuck. Maybe she really does have a wild side.

"Problems gone?" I tease.

"Nope. My life still sucks."

She says it in the cutest way possible. I wonder what she would think if she knew about mine. I don't know how to respond, so I suggest something a little harder. At this point, I need it as bad as she does. I'm fighting my entire body and mind by not reaching across the table and undressing her.

"Bring me whatever you think will make tonight have never happened."

Whiskey it is. I order two shots, but Lily downs both of them before I can even sit.

"Anything?" I ask.

"Two more. I don't want to feel anything."

I shrug. It's stupid. If she gets drunk, my one chance with her will be spent holding her hair while she pukes or helping her up the stairs at the dorm. However, I do what she asks because I'm so happy to have the chance to be here with her tonight, even if it is sad and meaningless. I haven't had anything except a little beer, but it's better this way. I want to remember her eyes and the way she looks.

I bring back the other shots and they're gone almost immediately. I sit, not sure more alcohol is a good idea. She looks at me, the hurt obvious in her face, and I want to make whatever is hurting her go away.

"Do you do this a lot?" she asks me.

"When I need to forget. Which I guess is a lot by most people's standards."

"What do you need to forget?"

Wow. Not the time to go there. "Nothing that is going to help you disappear."

"But this works?"

"Sometimes. Sometimes, I just wake up feeling like shit. And then I remember. And feel like shit some more."

Lily reaches across the table, looking for any last drops of whiskey in the shot glasses, but her hand brushes mine and my entire body tenses. Does she know what I'm thinking? Does she know what I want with her? Do *I* know what I want with her? Yes, it is physical and I can't stop thinking about bringing her back to my room and helping her forget in a whole different way. There's something else, though. I want to hold her, to shelter her from pain, to have her lift her face toward me with her eyes sparkling. I want to kiss her, to see if her lips taste like strawberries. I don't know how to feel all of this.

"Why are you even talking to me?" she asks. "I thought you hated me."

"I don't hate you. I just thought I hated your type."

"So you don't hate my type? Or I'm not the type you thought?"

"Good question," I answer.

"Why did you invite me out?"

"Seemed like the right thing to do. You can't seem to stop running into me, princess."

"I'm not a princess. I'm nothing." She looks at me again and I swear, I will say or do anything to make her keep looking at me this way. I can't remember a time when anyone has looked at me like this.

There is no way she's nothing. She matters to me, and although I may be an expert in worthlessness, I know she is not. "I really doubt that," I counter.

"It's true."

The hurt I feel at her sadness is palpable. I move the glasses aside and brush her hand with mine. "Princess, you're more than you think you are. And whatever made you come here tonight is not worth your time."

She looks down and makes a small choking sound. I think she's about to cry, but when I ask if she's okay, she looks at me again and it's all gone. *She's* gone, back to staring at me like I'm nothing to her and as if the pain she's in is my fault.

"I'm not gonna puke on you," she snaps. "Calm down. I just don't have anything to say. You're getting all serious on me."

And we're back.

Screw it. If she wants to play games, I can play. For a moment, I thought I could be open with someone. I thought there was a way my pain could be something less than pointless suffering, that it would make us closer in our misery. Now, I figure fuck it all.

"Wanna smoke?" I ask.

I stand up and gesture to the alley outside. She follows and I lean against the wall, watching her. She shivers and looks vulnerable in a place this dirty, but she doesn't back down.

"I can't feel my skin," she says.

"You're drunk."

"I thought it was supposed to be fun."

"It's fun when you have nothing in your head to worry you. Otherwise, it's just a means of covering the pain."

"You seem to be a real expert."

She has no idea. I hand her a cigarette, even though I can promise that she doesn't smoke. She takes it, though, and puts it between her kissable lips. My cock twitches at the move, as I picture her using those lips on me. Damn it. Why does this girl make me so horny?

I fumble with my cigarette pack, getting my own out and trying not to look as hungry for her as I feel. I light it and then go to her to light hers. It's tense being this close. The smoke obscures her face a little, but her eyes are still shining through the haze.

After she finishes her cigarette, she throws it on the ground and walks to me. She reaches down and runs her fingers across my waist, her lovely fingertips resting inside the loops of my jeans. I drop my own cigarette and breathe deep. This is dangerous and my skin feels every flicker of hers.

"I'm feeling down," she says. "Wanna cheer me up?"

Breathe, I tell myself. "What'd ya have in mind?"

I think I'm going to die when she reaches down into my pants and begins to move her hand up and down along my cock. Her skin is so soft and I feel like I'm going to come just being here next to her like this. Her touch is everything I pictured it being and I need to be inside of her. I groan and she whispers close to my ear, "Do you like that?"

"I do."

"Would you like me to do something else?" Her hand moves faster and I'm trying to stand still. I want to throw her against the wall and fuck her so hard her screams echo through the night. Instead, I just close my eyes and try to focus on not coming yet.

"Are you teasing me or are you for real?" The words are nearly impossible to speak.

"Do you like to be teased?"

She pushes her body against mine and grips me tighter. It's too much. I can't take it anymore. I push her across the alley, slamming her against the wall. I get her pants down and feel my way to where I want to be. I slip my fingers between her legs, just to see if this will be okay, and she's so hot and dripping wet that I know I'm going to lose it. I don't even ask if we can go further before I shove myself into her.

Her pussy is so tight and as perfect as I imagined it would be. I breathe in the strawberry scent of her as I thrust, rough and desperate. It's not sweet and it's not the way I would have wanted it to be with Lily, but I need her so bad.

I look up from burying my face in her neck and her eyes meet mine. She smiles.

"Who's the princess now?"

Oh, Lord. I can't stop myself and I know I'm being rough with her. It's probably terrifying to her, but I can't get deep enough, can't get close enough to her. Every thrust is better than the last and I'm losing my mind. I've fucked other girls, but I have never felt so overwhelmed by being with someone. She makes the softest noises, like small purrs and sighs, and every sound sends a pulsing shock through me. The orgasm is fucking insane when it comes and I pull out, letting go all over the nasty alleyway pavement. I feel both ecstatic and ashamed. She didn't even come. For all my big talk and teasing, I came before I could please her.

I want her again immediately, but I don't know if she'll ever look at me again. Just having touched her has given me an entirely new hunger. I try to catch my breath. I don't want to go back. I don't want this to be it.

There's no right way to approach this. If I invite her back to my room, she might panic when she realizes what we just did. If we stay here, the moment might be lost. I hope she can't see how much I'm shaking right now.

"Do you want another drink or do you wanna head back?" I ask her.

She smiles as I button my pants and she rests her hand on my hip. "Can I stay with you tonight?"

I sigh, the shaking getting worse. She deserves to be warned. "I'm going to fuck you hard all night if you do."

"That was the plan," she replies, and they are the most beautiful words I have ever heard. I can't get to my bike fast enough and the entire ride is full of anxiety. I won't be happy until we're in my room and she is naked underneath me. There are still so many things that could go wrong, but I try not to think about them.

I lose myself in the smell of strawberries, now more intoxicating than ever.

Chapter 10

The walk back from the parking lot is agonizing. I am so fucking hard and Lily walks a foot in front of me, her ass gorgeous as she moves. I cannot wait to have her pants off, to bury myself deep inside her, to lose myself against her strawberry hair. I want to make her come, since she didn't in the alley. It's unacceptable and I won't be satisfied until she screams my name tonight.

When we make it to the lobby, we have to wait for the elevator and she won't even look at me. She's breathing fast and her breasts rise and fall in a way that makes me even more impatient. I take her hand when we make if off the elevator and lead her to my room. Shutting the door behind me, I rush her, dropping her shirt and pants to the floor within seconds.

She is simply stunning. She looks at me, nervous and yet ready. I undress, my hands shaking because I can't get to her fast enough. She falls to her knees to suck my dick, but I lift her back to her feet. I'm going to make this sweet little princess cry my name as I give her the best orgasm she's ever had.

"I don't want your mouth. I want your cunt," I tell her and I push her face first onto the bed. I reach between her legs and play with her pussy. Her legs tighten and she tries to pull me in deeper. I don't want to wait, but I also want her to come back for more. I move against her, still finger fucking her, and I rest my cock against her ass. The tip of it brushes her wetness as I slide my fingers out and she moans.

"Beg me for it, princess. Beg for my cock," I say in her ear, pulling her hair to the side.

I back away and she gasps.

"Please."

"Scream it," I instruct her as I turn on some music.

She slips her own fingers in and out of her pussy. I can see the wetness on them as she pulls them out and I need it. I need to feel her warmth around me. I need to kiss those beautiful, soft tits. I need to have this girl do everything I've dreamed of her doing, but I love that she keeps saying my name and begging. She moves her other hand to her breasts and flicks the nipples, her eyes rolling back in her head as she continues to call out, "Jack."

"I can't hear you," I tease, my cock ready to pop.

"Jack, fuck me. Fuck me so hard I forget what I'm doing." The request echoes through the room and probably down the hall.

"Oh, fuck, princess. Yes."

I flip her over and push her face down against the bed again, while she still stands against it. It's only a moment before my cock is enveloped by the heat of her pussy. I can feel her starting to come. Maybe she isn't the good girl I thought she was, but oh fuck, she is *good*. I pull on her hair and it's rough and dirty and so fucking amazing. I definitely love this girl. I push harder into her until she can barely stand up.

After she comes, I turn her around and stare into her eyes.

"You're not such a sweet, innocent princess, are you? No. You're my dirty little whore."

"I am. Fuck me again," she asks, just as I'd hoped.

I move her to my desk, clearing the top, and I run my fingers over her clit. Her hand goes for my cock and she strokes me, slowly at first, but picking up the pace as I slide my fingers into her. There is no way I can just do this, so I spread her legs to get inside of her. I want her to love every second of it.

I slide the head of my cock in, just to see if she'll say no, and I tease her with it. She says nothing, but her eyes move down to where I'm slipping into her. She smiles and I play with her clit again, until she digs her fingernails into my back and screams my name louder than before.

"Fuck me, Jack. Fuck me! Please, oh, please, fuck me so hard!"

Perfect.

I shove all the way inside and her orgasm is instantaneous. She clutches at my ass and I bite down on her shoulder, smelling strawberries and feeling her tight, hot cunt wrapped around me. She just keeps crying my name and I can't hold back anymore. I come inside of her and rock her on my desk as the feelings slow. Suddenly, it's over and I step away, scared to say anything.

She looks down at the floor, where I've left quite the mess, but she doesn't speak. What's the next step with a girl like this? Do I cuddle her? Send her away? Beg her to come back tomorrow? What if she's still drunk? Why am I so terrified that I'll never get to touch her like that again?

I clean up and suggest we get some sleep. I don't know the etiquette for these kinds of things. Normally, it's Alana or some girl I have no intention of seeing again. I don't know how to get Lily to come back.

"Are you busy tomorrow?" I figure it will help me feel it out, to see if she's interested in more. I know I can't be her boyfriend, but tonight was fucking phenomenal and I believe she loved it. That's got to be enough, right?

"It's my birthday," she says about seeing me again. It's a strange comment and I don't know what to say. Am I supposed to take her out on a date?

I offer to help her enjoy it after classes and work. She smiles. "I'm sure you have something in mind?"

I touch her breasts, her naked body amazing. "It'll be a happy birthday indeed," I promise her. If there is one thing I can guarantee her, it's that I can make her come. I know I've had a lot of practice and tonight was just the start. With preparation, I'll have more control with her.

She dresses, but we don't talk again. After she's gone, I sit on my bed and finally breathe out. The whole room smells like her and I can almost still feel her cunt wrapped around me.

****

Work is unbearable. I just want to get to Lily, to celebrate her birthday, to feel her against me. Instead, I have to deal with a mob of dickheads who decided today was the day they wanted to check out the local restaurant scene. Although I don't recognize them from school, I can almost guarantee they're in my classes. Or some assholes just like them are. Poor Sandee is stuck working another double and she's been on her feet since five this morning. Of course, that's just opportunity for these fuckers.

"Move your ass. I'm not paying for you to take your time," one says to her after she takes their order. It's unnecessary as the size of the café is approximately that of two dorm rooms and they're the only customers other than an old dude reading the paper. If it wouldn't fuck over Sandee, I would take a two-hour break before making their stupid food. As it is, I debate how best to fuck with their meals.

She comes into the kitchen and she's near tears. I know it's not just the assholes, but we don't have much time to talk about it. Still, it drives me to near blinding fury and I throw their burger buns against the wall.

"All you're doing is squishing the bread," she laughs. "And the bread did nothing to you."

"I fucking hate people like that."

"I know, sweetie, but they're just hateful. Nothing to be done."

I flip the burgers and spit on two of them. She just shakes her head.

"What's wrong, anyway?" I ask.

"It's nothing. The school is just giving me a hard time again."

"Your son?"

She nods. "Isn't it their job to figure out a way to make sure he's not getting picked on? What am I supposed to do?"

I sigh. By the time I really had to deal with this shit, I was in high school. But it still hurt and I still remember coming home several times and wanting to die. I worry about Sandee and her kid. If it's starting now, what does that mean for later?

"Like you said, they're hateful. The way they are now? They'll be those assholes out there in a few years."

"I know," she says. "It's just tough, you know? He doesn't understand. I can't explain to him why people are so mean."

"Hell, Sandee, neither can I. And I'm supposed to be all grown up."

The order is up and she doesn't need more harassment from the table, so I drop the buns on the floor first and then finish putting the burgers together. Fuck those guys. They eat fast and, of course, leave her a two-dollar tip on a seventy-dollar tab. Because some people are just not human.

I don't get a chance to talk to Sandee again before my shift is over and I debate. Should I stay and talk to her, or should I head back for Lily? I'm torn, but I realize Sandee would tell me to go for the girl. She'd probably be thrilled for me. However, I still feel bad and I promise myself I'll make it up to her somehow soon.

When I get back to the dorm, I shower quickly. I've been antsy all day. There's been a strange vibrating nervousness forming and it gets worse every second I get closer to seeing Strawberries. It's such a delusional hope, this feeling that by next week she'll even be talking to me, but I ignore the constant warnings. I just want to lose myself in her taste.

I go to her room and try not to laugh at how pink it is. Then I see her roommate sitting on the pinkest bed I've ever seen and I see Lily's black and white one. My little strawberry princess has no more decorating style than I do. Nice. Another assumption broken. She doesn't say a word, just pushes me back out into the hall, closing the door behind her.

I run my eyes along her body. She looks gorgeous. Her hair is down and she's wearing an incredibly tight sweater and the smallest skirt I think she could get away with owning. I still don't know what kind of date I'm supposed to have planned, but seeing her like this makes me forget everything except what it felt like to be inside her. I don't think I can go anywhere. I don't even think I can walk.

"Did you want to go out or do you have something else in mind?" I ask her. It's her birthday; she should get to do what she wants to do.

"We could stay in," she replies. "Unless you don't-"

I stop her there. "Oh, I do. I certainly do." That is all I want right now and I bring her back to my room.

Lily sits on my bed, crossing and uncrossing her legs. I can feel the anxiety emanating from her. She opens her mouth a few times to say something, but reconsiders and shuts it again each time. Her eyes move over my crotch and I realize she wants to request something, but is afraid to ask me.

"Princess, there is nothing you can say that will shock me – and there is nothing I would not do with that sweet cunt."

She sighs and admits that she's not sure what she wants. Hell, it's her birthday; I have several ideas. "How about you let me surprise you?"

Since she's up for it, I open my drawer and debate. I know I want her. I want to own her. Not in a patriarchal controlling way, but I want her at my mercy. I want to make her mine and make every nerve ending succumb to my desire. It's not always my way sexually, but the idea of having her give in to me entirely, of letting me dictate her pleasure, gets me so hot that I almost come before I even move.

I take out handcuffs and a scarf, along with my favorite – a ball gag I've never used with anyone. I love the idea of having the sounds of her pleasure stifled so that only I know how much she enjoys it. Like it's our dirty little secret.

I turn around, the toys in hand, and Lily's eyes grow wide. She lets out a deep sigh and uncrosses her legs again, showing her agreement. I run my hands along her arms before flipping her over and cuffing her to the bed. Once the gag is in place, I tease her by dancing my fingertips down her back and ass.

"I'm going to enjoy making you scream and being the only one who knows how much you like it," I whisper in her ear. I slide the teeny tiny skirt up to her waist and I'm greeted by her soft naked ass and cunt. "No panties. Oh Christ, you are amazing." This girl is surprising; I would never have guessed she was the type to be this willing.

After she's blindfolded, I slip my fingers into her. She bucks wildly under my touch and the soaking pleasure spills down my wrist, onto the bed. She comes with just my fingers inside her and I'm not even trying. Holy hell, she blows my mind. I both love her and want to do things to her that are so dirty that I feel slightly guilty for even picturing them. I rest my body against hers and touch her cunt just slightly with my cock. Nibbling her earlobe, I pause, and then force myself all the way into her while she jerks upward against me.

"Scream for me, baby," I tell her and it's awesome, because she can't. I can tell she wants to and she's fighting the handcuffs and gag. "You have the wettest, hottest pussy I have ever had. You're all mine, you little slut."

Maybe I shouldn't talk to her like this, but she tightens around my cock even more when I do. Although she's jerking all around, it's not out of pain or agony. I can't believe how much she's getting into this. I had this idea of her being so innocent, so pure, yet she is wilder than any girl I've ever met.

"Come for me," I beg and slap her hard on the ass. She meets my thrusts and I don't know how long I can hold on. I try to think about anything else, anything to keep this from ending. I hold her down against the mattress, pushing on her shoulder with my palm. I feel her orgasm several times, her body making the tiniest shudders underneath me. She's almost in tears, but her hips are not stopping. Eventually, it's just impossible to ignore how good she feels. I close my eyes and forget everything but the feeling of sliding in and out of her. I don't think I will ever feel this good again.

I pull out and come across her ass, collapsing against her and reaching up to uncuff her. When she's free, she rolls over and I run my hands along her body before taking off the blindfold. As soon as I see her eyes, I'm ready to go. She looks so sweet with her wet eyes, both nervous and yet desperate for more.

I stroke myself until I'm hard enough and then I take out the gag. I want to feel those lips on me. She takes so much of me down her throat and I could easily come like this. Holding her down, I fuck her mouth. She moans as her tongue swirls around my cock and I love it, but I want to hear her scream my name so I break free of the insane pleasure of her lips.

Lifting her legs up, I watch her face as I enter her. She gasps as I slide all the way in, and her eyes are on fire. I kiss her neck and chest and feel her body twitching. I love how easily I can make her come; it feels like I finally do something right.

"Say my name," I plead.

She screams it, a loud, guttural scream, and we fuck like there's nothing but each other. She's not even moving anymore. Her body is shaking under me and her mouth is quivering. I want to bite down on her lip, to be fully in control of her, and to be able to fuck her endlessly. Sooner or later, though, I have to come, and I do. I clean myself off and turn back to her on the bed.

Something changes in her expression. We just had the best sex of my life, and obviously of hers, but she closes herself off to me as I look at her. I don't know what's going through her head, but it reminds me of what this is. I'm the kind of guy girls like her fuck when they want to be "bad," but I'm not a person to her. She will never care about me. Her eyes are wary and I try to pretend it doesn't bother me.

"Princess, I'm exhausted. Are you planning to stay the night?" I ask, trying to hold back any emotion.

Although there is nothing I want more than to hold her right now, she looks like she wants to run away. She's probably regretting what just happened, which makes me regret it. I thought we were having fun. I thought she liked it. I mean, she *definitely* liked it, but I hate seeing the guilt in her eyes now that it's done. She'll despise me in the morning.

She says nothing, so I try again. "You can stay if you want, although I do have to work early in the morning."

"Yeah, I'm going out for dinner with my parents," she replies, as if that is relevant or even an answer. I don't know how to respond and she adds, "I should probably not be... distracted tomorrow."

I move back to her, tentatively, and run my hands across her thighs. I don't want this to end yet. I press down on her clit with my thumb, just to remind her that her body is completely okay with what we've done these past two nights, and to convince her that she wants more. She lets out a soft moan and bites her lip.

"When you get back tomorrow night, come over. I have a distraction in mind that I think you will love," I say.

I'm not sure I'm going to be able to pull off what I'm thinking and I have no idea if she'll go for it, but

I need to give her something to look forward to, some reason to come back.

"Really? Something like tonight?"

"Better. Just for your birthday. Real princess treatment."

I feel her grow wet again under my thumb, but she doesn't try to do anything about it. I tease her some more and I love how her face betrays her attempt at being cool.

"I don't want to go," she complains and I move quicker over her clit. Perfect. I have her just where I want her.

"Good. I want you desperate tomorrow."

I leave her like that and toss her clothes toward her. She'll definitely be back and I watch her leave, questioning. She wants more, I know it, but I want to leave her wanting. This way, she won't disappear.

As soon as she's gone, I text Alana and tell her I need her to come up the next day after I get out of work. She promises she will and I consider telling her why, but figure it'll be easier to convince her in person. Once that's done, I put the phone down and lie back on my bed, still smelling Lily's scent on my pillows and sheets.

Chapter 11

Alana meets me at work, so we go out to her car to talk after my shift's over. I don't how to express what I want from her, what I need her to do, or why I need it. I spent all day agonizing about it, but now, sitting in her car with the heat on way too fucking high and her smoking nonstop and flicking ash against the vent so I keep breathing it in, I realize there is no way to do this tactfully.

"I've had a crazy couple days," I tell her.

"Yeah?" She doesn't look at me, staring out over the empty parking lot. I don't get it. Last time we talked, things were okay. Her moods drive me insane.

"I talked to her," I say

She flicks the cigarette again, but I'm prepared this time and I don't breathe in for a second.

"Actually, well…" I don't know what to say. It feels wrong somehow to announce that I fucked Lily, although let's be honest. That's what it was. We didn't have a romantic outing. There was no date that ended in an innocent kiss with the promise of more. I fucked her like I wanted and it was amazing, but there has been nothing discussed. I'm here to ask my best friend and the girl I've been fucking for years to join us, and yet I'm acting like a nervous prepubescent boy before a junior high dance.

"Did you fuck her?" Alana gets right to the point.

I nod.

"Was she any good?"

I don't want to discuss this. I don't want to tell Alana that, in two nights, I experienced more than in all the years I have known her. I don't want to minimize the something else that gnaws at me when I look at Lily. So I just nod again, like a fucking idiot.

"And?"

"Well, it's her birthday. And she's interested in experimenting. So I thought…"

Alana laughs and stabs out her cigarette. "You want me to have a threesome with you and your little princess?"

"Are you mad?" I ask.

"Hell no. Sounds fun. But I promise you, she is never going to go for it. I'm sure she's had fun sleeping with the bad boy, knowing she's being rebellious, but that isn't the same. Girls like that? They don't do kinky."

I keep my mouth shut, not wanting to tell her about the gag and the handcuffs, about how wet Lily got just by looking at them in my hand. There's a weird jealousy in Alana, but it's not about me. I don't know if that comforts me or bothers me more. Something in her wants to hate Lily, but it's for a reason I just can't pinpoint. I thought she'd be heartbroken that I'm moving on, but she doesn't even seem to care.

"Are you sure you're not mad?" I ask again.

"I've been thinking a lot about Dave. I love you, Jack. I always will. But sometimes, I wonder if that will ever be enough for either of us. Maybe I should have tried harder with him."

"He didn't try, either, you know."

"It wasn't worth trying. I was all about you. He knew it and I knew it. Only you didn't know it," she says.

"I'm sorry."

"I'm starting to deal. At the end of it all, I just want you to be okay. But I won't pretend that I don't have serious doubts this little rich girl will be anything but another trigger."

"Maybe she'll surprise you," I suggest.

"Yeah, maybe."

****

I probably should have asked Lily how she'd feel about this, but I want to give her what she wants. I know she looks at me as some kind of sexual experiment, so I figure the least I can do is test the limits of that. There's nothing else I can offer her, and nothing else that she would want, but if I can keep her sexually drawn to me, at least I'll have something.

She shows up wearing the tightest pants she could probably fit in and a shirt that showcases her gorgeous tits. I'm immediately hard just looking at her. Alana is sitting on my bed and she raises an eyebrow when Lily comes in the room. I smile at Lily, but her face falls when she sees Alana.

"It looks like you already have company," she says.

"This is Alana. Alana, this is the princess."

Alana laughs, doubtful, and challenges Lily immediately. She pushes a strand of hair behind her ear and I feel protective of Lily, who's staring at Alana and clutching her purse to her chest; the poor girl looks terrified. I know Alana is gorgeous, but I get the impression that Lily has no idea how beautiful she is herself. I move closer to Lily and smile, trying to put her at ease.

"Our little princess is not so innocent when you get her going," I tell Alana. "Are you?"

Lily stiffens at the question, but her face grows determined. She's not going to let Alana intimidate her.

"Lily," she introduces herself. "I have a name."

When she turns back to me and glares, it's both adorable and sexy as hell. I wish I could understand what goes on in my head when I look at this girl, but I don't even care. All I know is I will never have enough of her.

Alana runs her eyes over Lily's body. "Listen, sweetie, you're cute, but I think Jack misunderstands you. All apologies."

Lily turns around and locks my door, dropping her purse onto the floor. She flashes me a smile and runs a hand through her hair. "Misunderstands what? Why does everyone think I'm such a good girl?"

"I don't think you are anymore," I tell her. "I think you are one very, very naughty girl in fact."

Alana's still doubtful, but Lily's not going anywhere. I move to Lily's side and spank her hard on the ass. She cries out and then follows the cry with a soft whimper. The sound puts me on edge and I feel like I am going to die if something doesn't happen soon.

"Go ahead, Alana," I tell her.

This is every guy's fantasy, although it isn't really new for me. I've seen her with other girls and other guys, but when she kisses Lily, it's like nothing else I have known. I'm both turned on and jealous as hell. I want to be the one Lily's lips touch, but I can't deny that my cock doesn't mind me watching. Lily takes Alana's breasts in her hands, cupping them and brushing her fingers against the nipples tentatively. Her eyes are wide and she seems almost oblivious to the fact that Alana is undressing her.

"Does that turn you on?" I ask. "Touching her like that?"

It turns *me* on and as Lily and Alana's breasts touch, I collapse into the chair behind me. Lily looks at me, pride and pleasure and a little longing in her eyes, and I can't get my cock out fast enough. I almost come when Lily says, "Someone needs to fuck me."

They're both naked and I direct them to the bed. I can barely speak, but this is about Lily, not me. I slow my hand, although it's futile to think that I'm not going to come hard very soon. Alana warns me to stop, which is impossible. I watch her slip her fingers into Lily's pussy, and the sudden sound of shock and ecstasy that bursts from Lily's lips makes me bite down on my own lip, hoping to hang on.

Alana slides down along Lily's body, until her mouth comes to rest on her clit and I have to stop touching myself. Lily moans in pleasure and looks at me. I need to fuck her, to touch her, to kiss her, but she's enjoying Alana's mouth way too much for me to interfere. I feel the insistent throbbing in my cock grow faster while Lily comes and keeps her eyes on me. Alana smiles and suggests they switch places. When she takes Lily's hand and shows her how to stroke her pussy, I can't wait any longer.

I get up and position myself behind Lily. My fingers move into her wet cunt almost on their own and she sighs, while fingering Alana beneath her.

"I want to fuck you while you eat her pussy," I tell Lily. "Do you want that, Alana?"

"God, yes. Lily, please."

"C'mon, princess. Spread your legs for me. Let me come inside," I plead.

Lily moves her head between Alana's legs, while lifting her hips and spreading her own legs for me. I can't even tease her since I need her so badly and I clutch her hips as I shove myself deep. I grab her hair and fuck her from behind while Alana holds Lily's face tight between her thighs. Alana's nails leave red lines down Lily's back. All the times I've done this before disappear. Lily is not another girl. She's not an anonymous fuck or a plaything. She is beautiful and sexy and willing and perfect.

Her orgasm is intense, but her cries are lost against Alana's body. She collapses under me and I can't hold on to her. The twitching spasms run through her and Alana smiles when she sees what Lily has been reduced to. I haven't come yet, and I need to come. I don't even know how I've held back.

"Watch me fuck her," I tell Lily and I drag Alana over to the desk chair. I bend her over in front of me and watch Lily as I slip into Alana. I wish that it didn't feel as good as it does, because I feel a hint of guilt as my cock reacts to the clenching of Alana's pussy. However, Lily never ceases to surprise me. Instead of being upset or shocked or even a little angry, she sits up and slides her fingers into herself. Alana is screaming my name and I close my eyes, trying to hang on. I want to come in Lily, but it's growing impossible when I look at her. I slow my motions, but Alana comes around me still. I open my eyes to see if Lily is still playing along. She has three fingers shoved all the way in her cunt and then she starts to orgasm. I think I may be able to hold on a little longer until Lily cries, "Fuck me again. I want to be the one to make you come."

I want that too – so much – and it's too late. I come across Alana's back and Lily finger fucks herself to orgasm. We all end up lying in bed together, touching and letting our mouths explore even though we're all worn out.

"Happy birthday, princess," I tell Lily, while my lips run along her collarbone.

She starts playing with Alana again and I respond by mimicking her movements on her own clit. I think we're all done, however, until she grins and takes my cock into her mouth. I don't want to come like this. I want her – all of her.

"Ride me, honey," I beg. "It's your birthday. It's all about you."

Alana masturbates while Lily climbs on top of me and moves slowly. It's sensual and wonderful and I fall so desperately in love with her it hurts. She continually surprises me and does so again when she fingers Alana, ensuring that everyone orgasms before the night is over.

"Lily, you are absolutely perfect," I tell her and reach up to brush my fingertips along her back.

"You only think that because I'm fucking you," she teases.

Although that might have been true a month ago, there is so much more happening, but I don't want to ruin tonight by thinking about it. Guys like me don't get to talk to girls like Lily, never mind fuck them. At the very least, I know she'll never forget me and tonight. I need to stop hoping for more. Sometimes you have to take what you can get and not demand anything else from the universe.

Chapter 12

Waking up next to Lily, with her arm across my chest, makes me feel like everything is perfect. My entire life disappears for the second in between sleep and wakefulness and it's all about her.

Alana's sitting at my desk, dressed, and she's reading one of my books. Lily's still asleep, so I turn my head to the side.

"Hey."

"Hey," she says. "I need to get going soon."

"Okay, do you want me to wake her?"

"No, give her a little more time. She needs it." She smiles, but it's genuine. There's no longer the unspoken criticism in her eyes that existed in her car the night before. "She's wonderful, Jack."

I grin like a little kid. "Isn't she?"

Alana's eyes grow dark. "She is. But you are, too. If things don't work... If she changes her mind... Please swear to me..."

"I won't. I promise."

She nods, but she doesn't believe me. The scary thing is that I don't really believe me, either. I've forced myself to make this what it is, to resist how I've been feeling, but I can't deny that I'm scared. When Lily finds out who I am, when she realizes what I come from, she will run away. I know I'm not boyfriend material and I don't want her to fall in love with me, because I'll never be the sort of guy she needs. She's the type of girl who has boyfriends, who goes on dates, who brings guys home to meet her parents. I'm none of those things and I'll never be able to be those things. And yet, I'm already dreading how and when this will end.

I have to turn it off, because Alana's right. When I give in to emotions like this, it ends badly. Last time, it ended with a noose in my bedroom closet.

"You have to let it go, Jack."

"I'm trying," I say. "But I know what's coming."

"Look, even if things fall apart, she cares for you *now*," Alana says. "She thinks you're worth it, because you're better than you think you are. You deserve more than you think you do."

I don't respond to that, because it doesn't resonate with me. Still, I appreciate the attempt.

Lily stirs next to me and I almost bend down to kiss her good morning, before I think again of how painful this will be when it ends. Instead, I get up and get dressed.

"I have to leave, Lily," Alana says. "Walk out with me?"

Lily looks at me, but I turn away, trying not to feel anything.

"Sure. Just let me get dressed."

Alana hugs me goodbye, but I keep my eyes down. After they leave, I go to my desk and I'm about to pick up the book Alana was reading when my phone buzzes. It's my grandmother.

"Yeah?" I answer. I pick up the book and shove it into the bookshelf.

"Jack, I've been calling you all morning." She sounds agitated and I glance at the clock. It's nearly noon. Oops.

"What's up?"

"They had an emergency meeting with the lawyers last night. Your father's case is being fast tracked, but you have to go see him today."

"Why?"

177

And just like that, the real world comes crashing down over me. All my happiness, all my escape, all my hope of something else was for nothing, because this shit will fucking haunt me forever.

"They want you to see him today, so they can assess his relationship with you. To see that he's trying to reconcile."

"We don't *have* a relationship. As I have told you over and over."

"Please, Jack. It's important. He needs you."

"What about me? What about what I need? Does anyone ever think about that? Maybe I was going to have one good day in my sad, pathetic fucking life. But no, drop that. Drop everything because your murderer dad needs you."

"You're being unreasonable. It's an hour at most."

"Fine. Whatever."

"It has to be today, though," she reminds me.

"Of course. Perfect. I'll head over in a bit."

"Thanks, Jack."

"Yeah, sure," I say and hang up.

I could have said no. I could've pretended for just one more day that I lived in a world where a girl like Lily would come back to my room and we'd snuggle and then go out for brunch and maybe sit in the park and talk about our futures. But why bother? Because I don't have a future and doing those things with her would only make the inevitable hurt that much more.

I clutch my phone in my hand and try not to feel broken, try not to hate her for being beautiful enough – both inside and out – to provide a reprieve of a few days.

She comes back in the room and her eyes are sad. I wonder if Alana said something, but whatever it was, it was probably the right thing to say. The phone call from my grandmother just solidified the fact that this has been nothing but a stolen moment in time.

"What happened?" She looks concerned, but she doesn't walk forward.

I shove my phone in my pocket. This isn't her fault and it isn't her problem. It's her birthday weekend and I'll make today count. I can always back away tomorrow. She'll need to go back to her room eventually and my dad isn't going anywhere.

"Nothing. So, what should we do today? Wanna go for a ride? It's nice out and-"

"Just tell me what happened," she says.

"There are some things you don't need to know about me, princess. Nor do you want to."

"You could give me a chance."

"Yeah? You want to hear about my fucked up life? Are you gonna rescue me?" She doesn't deserve it, I know, but my anger at the fact that she doesn't belong in my world is hard to keep hidden.

"I can't even rescue myself," she says sadly. I can't imagine what she needs rescuing from, but we don't move in the same circles and I don't want to shatter her illusions.

"Look, just let me deal with my own shit. It's your birthday. What do you want to do?"

"I want to get to know you."

"No, you don't."

I go to where she's standing and pull her body tight against mine. Rage is tightening all my muscles, but Lily tries to soften it. She kisses down my neck and takes my cock out, teasing me and trying to make things okay. Of course, I get hard and I hate that she already knows how to make me need her.

Pissed, I throw her onto the bed and enter her. This is what I know. This is how I deal with things. This is why, no matter how much she makes me imagine and dream of something else, I will never belong in her life. For every thrust, for every ounce of pleasure, there is an equal measure of pain, of knowing that it won't be long before Lily recognizes that this is *all* that I am. I don't want to stop because I love being with her like this, but also because this is the only way I *can* be with her.

I feel the orgasm coming and I give into it, trying to forget that it will be one moment closer to ending this. As my body rocks in total bliss, my heart shatters.

"Oh, Lily," I cry, half in ecstasy and half in agony, and then I fall on top of her. I feel the tears before they actually emerge, and they're unfamiliar. I don't cry. I don't feel. I don't let it stop me. It's dangerous to feel this much.

Lily doesn't speak, but she wraps her arms around me and cradles me, as if she could love me, as if I could be worthy of her touch. "Talk to me," she begs, but there is nothing I can say to her. I am nothing. I give nothing and I take so much.

Her eyes are gentle as they meet mine, but it stings to know that she's oblivious to what I am. I want her to be happy, to have memories of me that bring a smile to her face, but all I have to offer is physical. I stop my sobbing and smile. My hand moves between her legs, because I *know* I can do this well and I know she'll remember me well for it. Let her think I'm an asshole when I stop talking to her tomorrow. At least she will have had fun.

She doesn't argue and, in fact, she's far more receptive than I would have expected. A low growl comes from her and I realize that my touch does to her what hers does to me. It's an amazing feeling and I let it drown out all the doubts and fears that plague me.

We have sex again, but it's simple. Nothing kinky, nothing rough, and nothing more than the base physical act, but we both come and that satisfies me. I wish it wasn't going to be the last time, but I have to see my dad and I don't know how to send her away.

I roll off of her and take in her body. I've basically spent three days just like this and yet I cannot imagine ever having enough of her. She leans across my body and her lips meet mine. They're soft and, no surprise, taste of strawberries. I almost meet her in the kiss, almost let my tongue slip into her mouth to explore her deeper, but the way she kisses me is too kind.

I break away, the dark cloud returning.

"What are you doing?" I ask. I'm shaking and I can't stop it. Why would she do that? Doesn't she realize she's given me a taste of something I can never have?

"I just wanted to kiss you."

She looks confused, but I remember that she lives in a reality where people fall in love and things end happily. She lives in a reality where kisses lead to love and love leads to family. She could never comprehend a world in which people fall in love with something else and then hurt each other endlessly until the entire ground swallows them.

"That's too intimate," I explain. "Don't do that." I'm saying no, but Christ, all I want is to kiss her again. I grip the sheet, forcing myself to keep her world pure and untainted by mine.

"We just spent the last few days fucking and you think a kiss is too intimate?"

"It's just sex, princess," I say, as if it means nothing to me.

She's pissed and I don't get it. Why won't she leave? Why won't she walk away?

"I never asked for a relationship, but you could use my name. You just freaked out in front of me. Don't act like *that* is not an act of intimacy."

"Lily, you don't belong with someone like me."

"Maybe you should let me decide," she says and it's adorable. But there is no room for adorable in a life like mine.

"Decide what? If I'm only reasonably fucked up? If my problems are fixable?"

"I'm not looking for a boyfriend I need to fix."

And that's it. She's looking for a boyfriend. I can give her everything else, but I cannot give her that. Boyfriends go to holiday dinners. Boyfriends have the emotional stability to share their own pain and suffering. Boyfriends become husbands – and husbands do not kill their wives. However, I know nothing else and I won't be with someone like Lily, only to watch her learn how to hate me.

"You need to stop taking your shit out on me," she says.

I smile. "I think that's the first time you've shown a spine, princess."

She says nothing and the world opens up. There are two roads ahead of me, two paths that lead into a dark haze that I imagine must be the future. Having never believed in the future as anything more than an illusory concept that other people, *normal* people, cling to, I don't recognize it at first.

One of the paths involves me freaking out, forcing her out of my room and out of my life forever. I need to see my dad and she doesn't belong there with me. However, the second path says something different. It suggests that maybe, just maybe, I give her what she wants. I show her my life – and let her choose what she does with it. I have only a moment to decide and I don't know why I say what I do.

"Look, come for a ride with me. We'll talk. I can tell you all about how fucked up I really am."

It's a strange feeling, this decision to try. I wonder if I would have chosen it had I had the time to consider it, but now that the words are out, Lily dresses and waits for me to bring her into my world. It's frightening, but it's time to let someone in.

Chapter 13

It's fucking sunny. How is that even possible? I've had the best three days of my life and here is this girl, this foolish girl who thinks she wants to know me, riding with me to the prison where she can face the darkest demons of who I am – and it's fucking sunny. Sometimes, I think the universe just hates me.

Lily doesn't say a word as we pull into the prison, walk in, go through security, or walk to the room where she'll meet my father. She doesn't speak when I take her hand, which is probably a dumb move, a move of hope and silliness, but I need to hold onto her. We sit at one of the tables and I'm restless. *This was a terrible idea*, I think, but it takes me too long to change my mind. I get up, but before we can leave, there he is.

He looks like hell, which is a little satisfying. I know it's mean, but he used to be a good looking guy. When I was a kid and he'd take me places, usually school things, all the women would ogle him. It was kind of annoying. I think they assumed he was a single dad, since after a certain point, my mother couldn't get herself clean enough to care about meeting my teachers, and he used to work that angle as much as he could. Even at eleven, I knew it was fucked up to act that way. Now he's got dark circles under his eyes and a scraggly ass beard. Serves him right.

"It's been a while," he says. Which is bullshit, because I was just here. His guilt trip shit pisses me off.

"I changed my mind. We're going."

My grandmother said I had to come. I came. Nowhere was there a mention of socializing.

"You can't hate me forever," he says.

You'd be surprised, I think. "I don't know. I think maybe I can."

He pleads with me, but I am done with this. Poor Lily looks like she is going to pass out.

I bring her outside and, once we're out, I lean against the wall of the building. The fucking sun and its stupid glare make it impossible to see her eyes, but I'm sure they're judging me. *No*, I fight with myself. *You can't lose her. Not now*. I don't know why, but I'm unwilling to let this go. I won't give in to this today and I grab her, pushing her against the wall, and I kiss her hard. It isn't the intimacy she was craving, but it's a huge step for me.

She does taste like strawberries, and my hands start working without direction from my brain, touching her, needing to feel her, desperate for confirmation that she is real. She moans softly, but pulls away.

"Not here," she says.

"I need you, princess." It's the first time I've said it and meant it so much.

"I know, and it's fine. Just not here."

It's overwhelming. She doesn't hate me. She isn't running. She's happy to let me hold her, just not here in this shitty prison parking lot.

I don't know what makes me do it, but I drive home. She's seen a huge part of what scares me, and she might as well see more of it. I know where I live will disturb her. I'm sure her house has multiple bathrooms, probably more bathrooms than people, and I bet the lawn is landscaped by some guy they pay. We don't even have a real lawn. It's mostly dirt, which is good, because my grandmother could neither pay someone nor afford to keep it up. There's a rusted tricycle in the yard when we pull up. It wasn't here when I was just home, but who knows how long it's been here since?

My grandmother is reading when we go in. I don't want to chat, don't want to explain. I just take Lily to my room and undress her. I should try a different move, but hell. There is absolutely nothing about me, other than what I've shown her this past weekend, that even gives her reason to talk to me. She doesn't resist; she just lies back on my bed. I can't look at her. I want to look at her so bad, but I am so scared of what I'll see in her eyes. What if she's already starting to put it all together? What if I see that she's already changed her mind?

I don't say anything before I slip inside of her. It's animalistic sex, the kind you have when you have nothing else to hold onto, and right now, that's what I have. After I come, I move away from her. Her hand brushes against my back, but I cringe. It feels like it burns me.

"Do you want to talk about it?" she asks.

We're both still naked and she leans closer, but I can't look at her. "You couldn't possibly understand."

She rests her hand on my shoulder. "Let me try."

I turn to face her and my heart snaps in half. Her eyes are so kind, so sweet, as if I am worthy of her. There are so many emotions running through me right now. I want to hold her, but I also want to tell her to get the fuck out and never look back. I want to hide inside of her and breathe in strawberries for eternity, while another part of me wonders if a rope would still hold me.

In Lily's eyes, there is also a little bit of fear, and it's what hurts the most. I would never, ever hurt her.

"You're going to hate me," I tell her.

"I don't think so," she says and reaches out her hand to caress my cheek. It's weird being this close to her, both of us naked, and yet it's not sexual. It's vulnerable and beautiful and more intimate than I ever knew I could be with another person. I certainly don't want to answer her questions, to watch her eyes burn out as I speak.

"Look, this is my shit life. I'm sure it's nothing like Daddy buying you a BMW for your sweet sixteen." *What the fuck are you doing?* I yell at myself, but my mouth just keeps spewing hate. I should tell her I love her, should beg her to love me back despite it all, but instead I'm being an asshole. I really am the world's biggest fuck up.

"You really need to stop blaming me for whatever made your life suck or whatever. I'm trying my best, Jack."

"Maybe you shouldn't," I say.

"You know what? Fine. Let's just fuck and the next time you get a phone call that pisses you off, I'll leave. Easier than this."

My brain thinks a lot of things, but they're all lost when I slam my hand through the wall next to me. The drywall shatters into a fine dusty haze. My grandmother is going to be pissed. I reach into my dresser and take out my plaster and putty knife. She bought them for just such an occasion. The tub is almost empty.

Lily waits until I'm done patching the wall and then she takes my hand in hers, reaching up with her other hand to brush my hair back. "Tell me what's wrong. Please."

Oh, this beautiful, beautiful girl. Why doesn't she know how to save herself? "I'm not ready for you to hate me yet. For a few days, I almost thought there was a chance…"

She's frustrated with me and I try to fight it. I try not to give in to wanting her, to needing her to care. But she refuses to leave, no matter how vile I am, no matter how much I push her away. Finally, I let go, and I meet her eyes. "You saw what I will become," I tell her.

"I saw a man in a prison and I saw you lose it. I don't know who he is, why he was there, or what you think it means for you. But I don't think you automatically become anything."

"That's my dad."

The confession rolls off my tongue surprisingly well, given how long it's taken me to face it, and how few people I've told. I expect many possibilities, but what I don't expect is for her to clutch my hand and say, "That still doesn't mean anything."

Everyone has always told me it means something. All I've heard is that he is my future. How can she still look at me like I'm not him, like it has nothing to do with me?

"Maybe it wouldn't if he'd robbed a convenience store or sold drugs. However, what he did... It doesn't go away," I warn her.

"What did he do?"

I get dressed, since I know as soon as I tell her my story that she'll want to leave, and then I sit back down next to her and tell her everything. The fighting, my dad's being on the road, my mother and her addictions. I even tell her about how lonely I was, about the time my mom disappeared for an entire summer, about how much I loved her in spite of it all. Lily moves closer to me as I talk, and she runs her hand along my leg, not speaking, but not backing away. Finally, I get to the thing that changes it all, the one thing that's held me back from almost everyone I've ever met, the thing that makes me unlovable. Seeing my father snap my mom's neck, watching her die on the living room floor. Knowing it was somehow the end of everything. I was fourteen.

Lily looks at me and says, "I'm sorry." That's it. *I'm sorry.*

"Yeah, I hear that a lot." Although that's not entirely true. Usually it's followed by a qualifier. *I'm sorry, but based on your background, we're not sure this would be a suitable school for you. I'm sorry, but you are too fucked up for me. I'm sorry, but you're simply not welcome. I'm sorry, but you'll probably never get better, and these meds are really your best bet.*

She nods and reaches for her clothes. So that's it.

"Don't leave, Lily. Please." It's begging, I know, but if only...

"I don't think I can handle this," she says.

And it's over. My heart doesn't even break; it just stops beating. I swear, I am no longer even alive. The numbness settles over me, consumes me in a way that all the alcohol and meds never could. Those seven words and my world ended.

I look at her, hoping to see doubt in her eyes, but there's none there.

I shrug. "I'm not asking you to handle it. I told you I can't be your boyfriend. This is why. I can't be a boyfriend. I won't end up like him. I refuse to put anyone through that. You don't have to feel guilty." It's weak, but it isn't her fault. I knew this would come. I just didn't think it would hurt this bad. Why does it hurt so bad?

She tries to console me, to tell me she still wants to know me, but how is that possible? She's running away, like she should, and like I expected. The conversation is hopeful, but the end result is the same. She wants to leave and she can't handle what I've told her. Finally, I give up. It's pointless to delay this. The pain is not going to be any less because we talk it out.

I bring her upstairs and my grandmother makes us sandwiches. She doesn't talk to us. I know she can see it in my face. She probably saw it the second Lily walked in the house. This girl doesn't belong here, in my house, in my life. I was the one who was too stupid to face it.

I love my grandmother, but sometimes, I wish she would yell at me, would tell me how fucking dumb I am. She's a perfect enabler, having lost her husband to alcohol and her daughter to drugs. She buys me booze and lets me be miserable, because it's that or lose me to suicide. But how can she see someone like Lily and not warn me that this beautiful girl who smells like strawberries is far more dangerous than even the most deadly drug? Because I see it, and I know that this is pain that I can't bear.

I bring Lily back to school. We don't talk on the walk back to the dorm. We ride in the elevator together in silence and I contemplate touching her, kissing her, begging her not to hate me, but when we reach our floor, I walk away. Inside my room, I cry, and it's pathetic and embarrassing, and I feel weak. I don't have any alcohol left and, even if I did, it would never, ever dull the agony that is growing by the second.

I lie on my bed and wouldn't you know it? The whole fucking thing smells like her. I can't even sleep now without the faint hint of strawberries taunting me, reminding me how utterly alone and empty I am.

Chapter 14

I wake up in the morning and go to classes, but it all feels pointless. It was four days. I keep reminding myself that it was only four days, but somehow, I feel like the entire ground beneath my feet is missing. I swore I would feel nothing. It was supposed to be fun. She was a temptation, a challenge; she was never supposed to matter. Yet here I am. I'm mourning the loss of something I could never hold onto in the first place.

I decide I'll call Alana after classes end and we'll go to the bar. We can get really drunk and maybe we can have another threesome. Why the fuck not? It's all I'm good for anyhow.

I have a stupid paper to write and although my heart isn't in it, I work on it in between my classes. There's a soft giggle from the girls at one of the other tables and I look up, thinking it's her. It isn't, though. Just another generic girl. At one point, I see her roommate on the other side of the library. I even debate about chasing her, of asking her to tell Lily to come by my room and see me, but then I realize that if she *did* pass the message along and Lily never showed... well, I couldn't deal with it. So I just keep typing.

I finish the paper and print it, since I don't have my own laptop. It really sucks trying to get my work done like this, especially as a game design major, but working part time at a café is not exactly computer buying money. The school offered to give me a loaner, but I took one look at the thing and decided the library was best. It was not only huge, but also bore a giant university logo on it and the words, "Property of IT," because it's not embarrassing enough to be poor. Neil has been nice enough to lend me his when I get really stuck, but I do try to get as much done as I can here. I hate charity.

After my last class, I head back to the dorm and I'm about to call Alana when I change my mind. It's weakness, but I shower instead and steel myself as I walk down the hall. I'm not even sure she'll be home, but I knock anyway. She answers almost immediately.

"Hey," I say. I will myself to look into her eyes and they're positively radiant. It gives me the confidence to ask what I came here to ask. "Do you want to come to dinner with me?"

It isn't a big deal, I know, but it's something, and I am so happy when she says yes. Outside, on the quad, I take her hand and it feels almost like something real. These are the kinds of things people do. People who don't feel like their lives are always in turmoil. I pause for a second and face her. "I thought you'd run away and never come back."

"Well, I didn't," she says.

"Even after you saw what I am."

"I told you. You're not your father."

"Tell that to everyone else."

"Everyone else is stupid," she replies and smiles.

This fucking girl. I laugh and it feels fantastic. Her grin gets even wider and she gives me a quick kiss on the cheek. I feel like I'm fucking twelve and I love it. Damn her. "That they are," I agree.

As we walk, we talk about my past, about my friendship with Alana, about Dave, and about how we all found each other. I realize just how much I miss Dave, but he made the choice to leave us behind when he joined the military. Still, I wish he would write or something. I don't have a lot of friends, and I love the dude, even if he is a mess.

Lily's mostly curious about Alana, and I try to put her mind at ease. I know she can't help thinking about us together, but it was for her. I would swear off everything in the world for one moment with Lily. We get to dinner before I can make any unreasonable professions of love, which is good, because that would be humiliating. Especially if she told me she just wanted to fuck Alana again.

She waves to her friends as we pass them, and I don't know if she wants to sit with them or not. I have no idea what to do in this situation, because our "date" is shitty cafeteria food, surrounded by people I never even talk to. It's awkward and uncomfortable, even though she sits with me in the back. I pick at the crappy food and try to figure out how to blend in, how to be someone like Lily, someone she would want.

"Do you wanna get out of here? Let's go somewhere else to eat," she says suddenly.

I could kiss her. I bring her to the café, of course, but it's nice, because she's seen the worst of me, and now maybe she can see something good. I forgot that I saw her here with that guy, but the memory stirs when we sit in one of the booths, right by where they were sitting. What if she remembers that morning? What if she decides she's an idiot and she wants to be with him?

Liz gives me a knowing smile, but I shrug it off. I don't know how to be this guy – the guy I make dinner for several nights a week. How do I sit here, on a date? I can't remember ever having been on a date. *Is* this a date? Do people go to cafés because they are so fucking socially inept they can't eat in the college cafeteria and then call it dating? Why am I incapable of even sitting here, having dinner with this girl, without making everything so complicated?

"Thanks for taking me here," Lily says while we wait.

"You're welcome."

I take a sip of my soda and watch her. She doesn't say much, but her lips stay partially open, as if the words are resting there, waiting to fall into the silence between us. I want to talk to her, but there is comfort in the quiet and I'm afraid to remind her of the multitude of reasons she should not even be here. So, while we wait for the food, I stare. She doesn't seem to notice, her eyes scanning the café like she's memorizing every detail. She blows a loose strand of hair away from her face and it's incredibly sensual somehow.

When the food comes, the silence turns to something else – a satisfied stillness because the sandwiches are that fucking good. I realize after we finish eating and I pay that we've said nothing on our date. By the time we get outside, I feel the anger and the worthlessness tearing the night apart. I go for my cigarettes and light one, letting the burn singe away those last little tendrils of peace. What in the fuck was I thinking?

"I'm glad you came out with me tonight," I concede, the parting words kind rather than bitter.

"Me too."

"So what now?" The three words carry so much weight. Does she want to carry on the insanely amazing sex we had, now that she knows what makes me so carnal? Does she want to pretend there's anything else? She doesn't answer me, just looks out over the parking lot and sighs.

"Why'd you choose to live on campus? I mean, your house isn't that far from school."

It's an odd change of subject, but I embrace it. "Like I said, all I wanted was to get away." I confide my hatred, my exhaustion with the petty gossip, and she nods. I don't get the impression she's ever been on the receiving end of rumors that crack you apart slowly, from the inside out, but at least she doesn't dismiss it.

"Has it helped?"

"Helped with what?" I ask.

"With escape."

It hasn't. Especially not now, not tonight, not with her. Because standing here, with the dwindling ash of my cigarette fluttering across the back of my palm, and watching her trying to connect with me, I think I will never get away from this. From this desire to feel what she makes me wish I had. A girl like her could change everything. She's the kind of girl you run to, instead of leaving behind, and that means facing a lot more than I know how to face.

I shake my head.

"There will always be people like Dave and Alana," she tells me.

"And you?" Is she suggesting that she could let it all go? That she could see me beyond what everyone else sees? There is still so much she doesn't know, doesn't understand, but if she thinks she could try...

There it is again. That faint elusive ghost known as hope.

She doesn't answer. She changes the subject and asks about school. Talk of classes, of homework, brings us closer together, though, and suddenly my body is tight against hers, the cigarette long forgotten on the pavement, and I'm desperate for her. She doesn't speak for a moment, but as she exhales, the smell of strawberries brushes against my lips and cheek. I want to grab her right here, to destroy her, to have every inch of her against me and to touch her everywhere. I don't know how I resist her, but I suggest going back to my room.

She steps back and yet again changes the subject. Now she wants to talk about the rooming logistics on campus. I try to repress the vehemence that explodes within me, but I can't and I almost growl as I light another cigarette.

"I don't play well with others, Lily. I thought you got that," I say in answer to her questions about my roommate situation.

"You certainly play well with me," she says. Holy fuck, this girl. As soon as I start to tame myself, start to control what is causing the frenzy inside of me, she's back and her fingers play with mine, following a path up to my wrists. The faint touch of her fingertips is enough to make me throw the cigarette to the ground and hold her body against mine. I breathe in her hair and kiss along her earlobe, down her neck, my hands holding her hips hard in position.

"You're gonna spend the night, right?" I ask, but my voice is not that of a sane man.

She doesn't move, answering with her lips just brushing against my own.

"I don't know," she whispers. "What are we, Jack?"

"I don't know. Do we have to decide now?"

Now is not a good time. Now I would promise her anything she asked for, because I need to bury myself in her, to touch her where she's wet, to feel her buck against me and beg me for more. I need to lose myself with this girl who's already making me question everything I believe and know.

"What do you want this to be?" I ask her.

"I'm not sure."

"So why isn't that enough? Let's just see. This isn't the kind of thing I do, you know."

I slide my hand up the back of her shirt, feeling the heat of her bare skin. *Ask me for anything*, I dare her silently. *I will give you everything I have for one kiss.* I fight this desire, this incredible need to be with her. I want to lean down and taste her, but kissing her is deadly. And yet I'm about to do it when she backs away again. I clench my fists, trying to fight both the sexual frustration and the hate that threatens to take over this moment still full of potential.

"That worries me," Lily says. "You said Alana was your best friend, but you couldn't date her. Are you going to give up on me, too? I'm not the kind of girl-"

"Oh, right. Now we're back to being innocent."

I kick a Styrofoam cup that was left in the middle of the parking lot. The tension in my forearms is intense, and my clenched fists shake by my side. Lily's eyes grow wide and I look up to meet her gaze, knowing she sees what I really am in that second.

"I'm gonna call a cab," she says and walks away.

Say something. Salvage this, my mind screams, but I can't speak. The violence and the rage and the hopelessness rush through me, pulling the air from my lungs and crushing my hope. I watch her walk across the lot and it's like seeing every good possibility torn from my life. She's nearly to the door when I call her name, the sound and my breath returning to me in a gasp. I'm shaking throughout my body and I hang onto my bike, hoping I can form a coherent sentence, maybe even something resembling an apology.

She turns around and looks at me. Neither of us moves for a moment and I want to say something, but I don't know *what* to say. She walks back toward me, determination in her face, but doubt in her eyes.

"Start talking," she demands.

"Look, princess, I'm sorry. But I thought we were clear. I'm trying to be better with you, but I'm not boyfriend material." She shakes her head and I go on. "Why does it matter? You certainly didn't care that we weren't in a relationship for the last four days when you let me fuck you nonstop." It's a classless statement, but this is a power struggle and neither of us knows how to back down. Being matched in fortitude is new to me and I fall for her just a little bit more.

"No, but the last four days were something else. They were temporary," she says.

"I don't do permanent, Lily."

"Maybe I'm not even ready for permanent."

"So what's the problem?"

She looks up at me and her eyes are sad. "I'd just like to know I was worth it to you."

I laugh. It's not a cruel laugh, but the comment is so ironic, so out of place. She cannot even imagine how willing I am to sacrifice everything just to have her look at me with those fucking perfect eyes and she thinks *she* might not be worth it to *me*. Me? The epitome of worthlessness? "I have no idea what it means to be worth it," I tell her.

"You're not worthless," she says and she cups my face, bringing her lips in closer, but the moment is gone. I don't want to have sex with her. I want to love her and it terrifies me. Watching my mother die is the only other thing that made me feel this out of control. I have spent years planning, arranging, knowing my limits. There were episodes of depression, of darkness, but with Lily, there is no answer, no clear path. And I want to scream because I cannot stop myself.

"If I could be the kind of guy that gets to be with a girl like you, I would be. I would give everything to be that kind of guy. However, it isn't reality, princess. *This* is reality. I'm a piece of shit screw up who can fuck you like no one else can – and I have to be happy that you'll even let me do that. That's the best I can hope for; sooner or later, you'll realize it."

She looks at me and smiles faintly, before lifting up on her tiptoes and kissing me. It's over before it even starts, in oh so many ways.

"I can be your friend," she says. "But you have to let me."

I grab her and kiss her this time, my tongue moving into her mouth. She mews against me as I do and it's soft and perfect and I am so completely fucked. Her hands reach into my hair and pull me deeper into the kiss and I lose track of my own hands. We are no longer two bodies, but some sort of force, standing here in the empty parking lot, a force that annihilates everything that has come before us like a fucking atom bomb. All that stands ahead of us is a blank canvas, a wasteland, but somewhere on the horizon, there is light and an oasis. And Lily is the one who will guide me there. I love her – entirely. It's something I don't understand and I don't want to understand.

She steps out of the kiss and smiles at me, her eyes dancing, and I want to cry. She may be my guide, but I am her apocalypse. An oasis in a barren world may be hope to someone like me, but for her, it's a sad remnant of a world that used to be thriving. And I am the cause of that desolation.

Walk away, I plead with myself. *Let her live her life without you ruining it.* But I can't walk away and I hate myself for holding her in an embrace. Still, I try and I beg, "Don't fall for me, princess."

The words fade into the night, though, unheeded, and she kisses me again, before gesturing to my bike and telling me to take her home.

Chapter 15

Back in my room, I undress her and I need to take in every detail. For all her willingness to play my games, for all her kinkiness, I'm still afraid to touch her. It was one thing to fuck her when I thought it was some sort of escape for her, but now that it's *her* and not some idea of the good girl gone bad, I don't know how. I run my hands along her skin and every inch of her makes me feel so unworthy, yet she gives so willingly.

"Please, Jack," she says, but it's not a teasing, sexy plea. It's the plea of someone who wants to cross a line that I have never crossed, the plea of a girl willing to put her entire life in my hands and willing to trust me entirely. I don't know what to do with that kind of trust, and I'm terrified she will shatter into pieces.

I stare at her body and she's just so *good*. How did she get here? She smiles sweetly and lies back on my bed, beckoning me to her, and I rest myself over her, still scared that this is a dream. She bites down on her lip and slips a hand down my body, stroking me slowly. I love that she can be so sweet and so kind – and yet also so wild when she's with me like this. I feel like Lily has shared a secret with me, some part of her that she's reserved for only us, and it's such an honor to be that guy.

I smile back at her; I want to give her what she seems to be craving. As I enter her, I can feel her take me in. I move on top of her and cup her face before losing control and pushing harder. She feels so unbelievably amazing, and I just can't get enough of her. I flip my hand over and run the back of it across her cheek, whispering her name.

She looks at me with so much love in her eyes that I feel like I'm falling apart and I lean down to kiss her. It's the kind of kiss I never imagined I would have, the kind you see in movies and read about in books, but that doesn't seem to exist in real life. The entire world stops moving as I kiss her. She is all I can feel and I want her and need her more than breath.

She reaches for my hips and guides my thrusts. I'm losing air and I can't stop looking at her. She must think I'm crazy, because all I can do is say her name. Over and over again, as if it's an incantation to keep her here.

She comes underneath me, her body tightening and then letting go as she digs her nails into my back and holds me inside of her. I feel her arch upwards and her eyes grow wet, tears of ecstasy slipping down her cheeks. I move faster and, once she falls back onto the bed satisfied, I seek my own satisfaction. Part of me wants to drag it out forever, but the realist part of me knows that will never happen. It just feels too right to do this with her, and I'm close to orgasm when she pulls me down to her, kisses me, and whispers in my ear.

"I love you, Jack."

The words are the trigger for the explosion that rocks my body. Four syllables and the entire world as I know it is annihilated. No one has ever said those words to me like that. And the fact that it's Lily, this perfect, wonderful girl, saying them? I don't know if I should hold her close to me and never let go – or if I should run away before this goes too far.

I come inside of her, but after, I'm anxious. I'm not ready for love. I'm not ready to mean that much to anyone. And I am definitely not ready to know that I feel it back. Because if she changes her mind, I'll be devastated.

"It's only been a few days," I argue. I can hear all the logical voices telling me this won't work, all the rational reasons that we are so wrong for each other, but her eyes speak louder and I give in to them. I would so much rather listen to her eyes.

"So what? Something in you makes me want to believe in you. Believe in us."

"We aren't ready to be an us."

"Maybe not, but I do love you," she says. And with that, it's been said, and there's no taking it back. I'm not ready to say it to her, although I feel it through my entire body, and my heart breaks knowing the words exist within me. I hope she realizes how I feel, but saying it? That's just too real – and I can still picture a bleak world in which she is missing, and knowing those words are out in that place? It's too much.

Lily sighs contentedly and wraps my arms around her as she falls asleep. I spend the night cradling her in my arms. I have an exam in the morning, as does she, but I can't sleep. I don't want to wake and find out none of this happened, so I stay on guard all night, holding her and listening to her soft breathing as she dreams. I hope it's of a place where she and I are happy.

In the morning, I realize we have to get ready for our exams. I wake her by kissing along her face and she smiles up at me. I'm hard, even though I wasn't asleep, but it's not really new being around her. I press my erection into her thigh and play with her clit, bringing her to full wakefulness.

"We don't have time," she laughs.

"I can be quick," I argue.

I kiss her and she moans under me, but pulls away and then slides down my body until she has me in her mouth. She takes in my entire length and her tongue moves along my cock as she clutches me from the base and strokes in tempo with her mouth. I roll onto my back and she moves with me, going faster and deeper now that she has a better angle. I push her head all the way down, wrapping my fingers in her hair.

"Oh, fuck, Lily, yes. You are fucking beautiful," I cry and I burst into her.

"More later," she teases.

Hell, I want more now, but we need to study and she's right to suggest breakfast. Otherwise, breakfast would be something very similar to what just happened. I follow her to the cafeteria and, this morning, I don't even care that I don't belong here. Lily looks at me like I do and it blurs the edges of the world. She has an incredible ability to make me feel like someone special, and I want to hold her and kiss her and tell her that I love her, but instead, I focus on my geometry textbook and eat pancakes.

There is an odd normalcy of being in this moment, eating in the cafeteria, studying for a test, and sitting with my – girlfriend? – and I wonder what it must be like for people whose lives are always this normal. Do they even appreciate the wonderfulness of such mundane moments? Do they know how lucky they are? If I died right here and now, this one morning would be the memory I'd most treasure.

I go to my exam, leaving Lily by her classroom, and despite my lack of sleep, I feel like I can take on the world. I think I do well and when I get outside after the exam and the sun is shining, I start a list in my head of all the things I want to do. Somewhere in the back of all my racing thoughts is this nagging voice reminding me not to get too comfortable, that this is a borrowed moment from someone else's life, but I drown it out with more ideas and plans. While I wait for her to finish her exam, I write a few songs and I text Neil about tomorrow's practice.

Lily comes down the steps toward where I'm sitting on the grass and she glows. It's ridiculous. A giant grin breaks across her face as she waves. I turn around as a reflex, looking for the person who's made her smile like that, and then it hits me - *I* am that person. Holy shit.

She looks like she's waited years to see me. She runs down the last few steps and tackles me on the quad, kissing me across my face and neck.

"Bring me back to your room and let's finish what we started this morning," she demands and she runs her hand over my crotch.

I don't even have the door closed before she's naked and hopping up on my bed. I trip over my pants trying to get to her and she laughs, but I quiet the giggling fast enough when I flip her over, cover her mouth, and slide deep into her. She arches her ass up toward me and bites down on my hand.

"You are fucking perfect, princess," I growl at her. And she really is. She's soft and sweet in all the right ways, but also wild and hungry in others. I feel like she'll never be fully satisfied and I love that her desire matches mine. I fuck her hard, which is a relief after the gentleness of last night, and it makes me crazy that she's so into it. I reach down with the hand she's not biting and rub her clit as I fuck her. She grows so wet that it's impossible to focus on anything else. I forget everything but Lily's cunt as I come, and then I flip her over to face me.

She grins. "I love your cock."

It's vulgar and dirty and, coming from a girl like her, it sounds ridiculous, but it's just as good as hearing her tell me she loves me.

"You're such a dirty slut," I tease her, and then I worry that she'll be offended. I'm only playing and I don't want to hurt her feelings, and I definitely don't want to discourage her slut-like behavior with me, but she just giggles.

"Yeah, but I'm *your* dirty slut."

I play with her tits and her nipples get hard under my touch; it doesn't take long before she's moaning and begging for more. I slide down the length of her body and slip between her legs. Her pussy is wet again and I lick along the length of it, loving the way she tastes.

"Oh, God, Jack. More," she begs, and I swirl my tongue over her, writing her a little love letter with my tongue. I imagine she has no idea, since she's losing control, bucking wildly and slamming herself against me. I flick her clit and she screams. It's loud and desperate and almost painful. I feel her come. I don't know if she's ever come like this, the wetness spilling down her legs and onto the bed. She looks mortified when I look at her face and I smile, licking along her thighs and around her cunt until she's clean. Then I sit up and meet her eyes.

"I'm so sorry," she says.

"For what?"

"That was, um…"

"Fucking fantastic," I tell her. "Princess, you are a fucking dream come true."

She still looks sheepish, but I gather her into my arms and hold her, our naked bodies fitted together perfectly, and this time I do fall asleep. Although the nagging voice is still trying to ruin my mood, I silence it.

Chapter 16

We both have exams and we agreed to a mutual, albeit forced, exile, so we could work on papers. It seems like my entire day is gone and I haven't seen Lily at all. I still have band practice, too, but she promised to come by later so we could at least sleep together. I miss her and I feel embarrassed that I do. I also have to fight not to listen to the voice reminding me how dangerous this is, and how badly it will go when it ends. I know it will have to end, but the delusion is too pleasant to give up. And so I stumble along, like an ignorant fool, and I derive great joy just from looking at her.

At practice, I decide to share a few of the songs I've been writing, and when they're done playing, Neil just stares at me. Eric and Devon smirk and I don't know what they're thinking.

"Really, dude?" Neil finally says.

"What?" I ask.

"Did you just come in here and play fucking power ballads?"

"I-" But there's nothing I can say, because yes, I did write fucking power ballads. I close my mouth and look at the three of them and suddenly everyone is laughing.

"Hey," I whine.

"Fucking power ballads," Neil says and I laugh, too. Because who the fuck writes power ballads?

I don't mention Lily, because the next thing you know, I'll be writing shit for a boy band and I know they'll never let me live it down. Neil shakes his head and we go back to our moody rage songs. I need to stop writing music with Lily around.

There's still enough buried in me to put into the band. Lily makes me happy when I'm not thinking obsessively about how it will end, but she isn't everything. There's still my dad, my mom, my own hatred of things, Alana...

I play and try to lose the thoughts as they swirl around me, darkening the once bright light of being with Lily. I push them into the bass, telling myself that I won't leave here burdened with them, but when everyone else is tired, the thoughts are still there. The blackness is starting to settle over me again and I try to shake it. Band practice is over and I'm afraid to go back to Lily like this, so I walk. I have no destination and no plan.

I light a cigarette and I realize after I've been walking a while that I'm heading toward the bar. Since I met Lily, I've felt the need less, but it's back and it's destructive. I don't want to feel; I don't want to be alive.

I take out my phone and I think about texting her, but I can't. She thinks she can handle me; she thinks we'll be okay. How can I tell her that sometimes her eyes aren't enough to stop me? That sometimes all I can think about is dying? No one has ever really understood it, except Alana, and that's what drives me to text her instead.

I need you, I type. *I'm a fucking wreck.*

What about Lily?

She won't understand. Please?

Sure. Give me an hour.

And so I tell her to meet me at the bar and I walk slowly, smoking half my pack of cigarettes and wondering why the darkness is so heavy. It feels like whenever I think I've moved past it, it finds me again and obliterates all that is good.

The night I gave into it, I stood in my bathroom for an hour, just staring at myself in the mirror. I could have called someone, could have yelled to my grandmother, but I didn't. I just stood, silent, trying to come up with one reason to stay. After an hour, I had nothing – and so I gathered the rope. My grandmother told me later that she found me in the morning. I fucked it up, so I was still half-conscious, and she got me to the hospital. When I woke up, all I could think about was the fact that I couldn't even die right.

I hate these nights. I hate the way it comes from nowhere. Everything was good. It was so fucking good and now, here I am, spiraling.

I dig in my pack for the last cigarette. How the fuck did I smoke more than half a pack in such a short time? The self-destructive voices are back, telling me everything I already know. *You're worthless. You'll only ruin her life. Just kill yourself. You will never matter.* For what was both the flicker of a moment and the wonder of a lifetime, Lily drowned them out. She was hope. She was release from pain. I don't know what I was to her, if anything other than an enjoyable distraction, but in a short span of time, I thought she *could* be part of me. But now, the voices are laughing. Because why would a girl like that ever want to be included in my world?

Alana is already at the bar. She's anxious and I see her before she sees me. She's biting her nails and tapping her foot. I hate doing this to her. I can't give her anything of myself. For whatever reason, I close myself off to her, yet I demand her attention and affection when I want it. And she always comes running. I'm not even a good friend.

"Hey," I say from behind her.

She spins quickly, nearly falling off the stool.

"Are you okay?"

That's the question of my life, isn't it? Everyone always wants to know if I'm "okay." What is okay? Is it the same as happy? Is it hopeful and willing to fight? I'm none of those things. Is it being able to talk it out, rather than running to the nearest bridge and throwing myself from it? Because I guess I'm there. I reached out to someone for help, so does that mean I'm better?

"I don't know," I tell her honestly.

"What happened? Is it Lily?"

"No. That's just it. She's perfect. It's nothing. There is no reason for me to feel like this. Well, no *new* reason."

"So what happened?"

"I was happy. I was fucking soaring, Alana. I fell for her so hard and it felt *good*. It felt real. I looked at her and I saw a version of me I could tolerate reflected back. But then, she wasn't there and I was playing with the band and it just ... I can't give her anything. How do I fit into her picture perfect world? Just imagine. Her parents would probably take her out of school if they met me."

"Maybe they're not like everyone else. *She* wasn't."

I shake my head and order a beer. I have to walk back and I don't want to be out of my fucking head. Besides, I told Lily I'd see her tonight.

"She's a fucking enigma. But she isn't a representation of the world. Percentages dictate-"

"Percentages don't mean a fucking thing," Alana says. "You tell yourself these things so you can hide when it gets too fucking hard. You tell yourself you deserve to be treated like shit, so that when you are, it hurts a little less. But without the pain, you'll never find what's worth staying alive for. And Jesus. I just need to know you found something."

"What the fuck is worth it?" I demand.

"I don't know. But I keep going. Dave kept going. Your grandmother kept fucking going. And it's bullshit that you think you have the goddamn right to leave us behind to pick up the fucking pieces."

I don't respond. How can I?

"Look, Jack, I dropped everything tonight to come here. But for what? If you want to sink into this fucking place, you're going to sink and I can't stop you. I can call Lily. I can go to her and ask her to fix you. But next week, next month, next year, maybe things won't work out. And then what? Are you going to put your fucking life in her hands? Or in mine? Because we're just two people. If *you* don't love you, it means nothing for either of us to."

"She doesn't love me."

"You haven't even given her a chance. You quit before you even got started. Like you always do. But hell. I'll always be standing around, waiting to pick up the mess."

I can't believe how much it hurts. I'm not angry at her. Everything she says is true. It doesn't lighten the heaviness over me. In fact, it just adds to my burden, but she's still right. I reach out and take her hands. She looks up at me, her sad eyes sadder than I've ever seen them.

"I love you," she says. "If you were gone, it would leave me with nothing. No one ever cares about leaving me. You have your shit, I know, but please, stop thinking about leaving me, Jack. I can't survive it. I can't get that fucking call. If you're gonna do it, you better pick up the fucking phone and tell me where. Because you need to take me with you."

I get off the stool and take her by the hand out into the alley. Holding her against me, I sob into her hair. "I can't take you there," I tell her.

"Well, I can't live without you."

Alana is putting something on me no one ever has. Obligation. I've never been indebted to another person. I don't even know how to owe another person a part of me. But I will fucking die before I will let her hurt like this. The thought makes me chuckle in its irony and she looks at me, rage and misery giving way to confusion.

"Are you fucking laughing?"

I kiss her lightly on the lips. "It's just the ridiculous notion that I would rather die than break you. Which, given the circumstances-"

"I fucking hate you, you know."

I kiss her again. "I know."

"Fucking asshole. Go back to your fucking dorm and find that damn girl. And don't let her get away from you because you're too much of a pussy to love her."

"Can you give me a ride?" I ask sheepishly.

"You're a fucking asshole," she repeats.

Chapter 17

I can't tell Lily why I'm so late, and so I don't; I just tell her band practice ran long. She looks fucking adorable in her soft green pants and sweatshirt and I just want to hold her. She doesn't complain and we lie in my bed, cuddling. It's absurd; it's innocent and sweet and pure and everything I'm not, yet she makes me feel so complete. The depression still weighs on me, but I force myself to be present now, with her.

"I missed you," she says once I'm curled up around her.

"Me too."

"I wish you'd come back sooner. You could've helped me with my math homework. Aren't you like super math guy?"

I laugh. "Not exactly."

"Yeah, well it sucks. But I'm glad you're back."

I breathe in her permanently strawberry-scented hair. I don't have words. I don't want to reveal what she needs to hear. I know that eventually I need to tell her about my time in the hospital. However, I've seen the desperation in Alana's eyes when I make a casual comment about wishing I was dead or when I get quiet after an argument. I never want to see that in Lily's. I never want to doubt that her feelings are real. If she knew how desperate I am, how close to the precipice I've come, she'd love me out of some kind of debt. And while I may be able to face Alana's obligation, I can't demand it from Lily.

She falls asleep and it's what we said it would be – sleeping together, since we're both worn out from exams. I don't fall asleep, though. I listen to the soft sounds she makes as she sleeps and I think about killing myself. Not about actually killing myself, but of the existential nature of the desire. I don't know how to control it, but neither has any therapist I've seen. It appears without warning, like it did tonight. Sometimes there are triggers, even small ones. Triggers like facing the misery of the songs I wrote before Lily, now that I know what life is like after her. Sometimes there are no triggers.

What scares me most of all is that even if I could move on from my past, even if I learned to cope with my family, I can't see a life past the next few years. Even when I'm not actively suicidal, my mind always tells me that someday it will be too much, and I'll never be an adult. The concept of thirty feels impossible.

How do I reconcile these thoughts with holding Lily? She's soft, she fits perfectly in my arms, and she trusts me. She *trusts* me. Not the way Alana trusts me, because Alana knows I see a part of myself in her. Lily trusts me without reason, without logic, and without fear. How do I tell her that someday, possibly when neither of us expects it, I could snap and be so overwhelmed by my pain that nothing would stop me from dying? How do I say to this girl that, no matter what she does, I don't know that her face will appear in the mirror next time? That I could stand there for days and she may not register if the need to kill myself overpowers anything we've built? And how can I ask her to try anyway?

I can't do any of those things, so instead I edge closer to that precipice, and I will the light to come.

****

Exams and papers step in and take away the free time to think about dying or defining our relationship. We're both tired and busy and we spend the next night the same way, just cuddling and holding each other. The time will come when we'll face the demons that are waiting, but right now, school comes first. By Thursday afternoon, I'm ready to pass out, although my exams are done. I have one last paper to write and then work all weekend, but no more tests. Although my eyes ache as I force them to stay open, as soon as I see Lily waiting outside for me, I have a newfound energy.

"Hey," I say and take out a cigarette.

She looks sideways at me. "You know smoking is bad for you, right?"

I just laugh and light the cigarette. It's not a long walk back to the dorm, but it's a decent day and I feel better walking with Lily. Whatever shadow passed over me only a few days before has dissipated. Sure, it will be back, but it's not right now, and I try to focus on that. Try to focus on Lily. It's still early and there's time to go to dinner, but first, I want to drop off my bag.

"Do you want to go to dinner?" I ask her as we make our way to my room.

She's quiet and shrugs. "I don't know."

I don't know if she's being evasive. "I'm sure they'll have something resembling food," I joke.

She nods, but doesn't say anything or look at me. I open my door and I feel the lightness give way to the burden again, but before I turn around, Lily has shut the door.

"Did I do something wrong?" she asks.

I shake my head. "No. Of course not. Why?"

"You haven't touched me in a few days."

"Was that before or after you passed out from studying microbiology?"

"That class is a waste of my time," she says and sits on my bed.

"Listen, princess, I would be more than happy to forego dinner and spend the rest of the night touching you, if that's what you're so worried about."

She grins and pulls her shirt off, revealing her absolutely perfect breasts. Oh, fuck. If there was any exhaustion left, it's gone.

"You still amaze me," I tell her.

"Why don't you come over here and show me?"

I may not be able to make her happy for a long period of time, but I can make her happy in this moment and I determine to do that. I want her to lose herself with me, so that even if it isn't forever, it will always be a good memory.

I go to my drawer. I have a vibrator tucked away in an unopened package. I don't remember what possessed me to buy it, but it's been there a while and I'm happy to have it now. I want to make Lily the center of the universe and I want to be outside of her pleasure for once. I just want to see that look of bliss wash over her face.

She smiles when I take the toy out of the package. "For me?" she asks, and the innocent girl is gone. Lily is all sex, all desire, and I still can't get over how much she broke down everything I'd expected of her.

"It's *all* for you," I reply and she lies back, opening her legs. I want to be there, to be in her, to be with her. But I also want to be selfless, to give without taking, to show her what she means to me when I can't say it.

She's excited and I reach between her legs, readying the toy into position. I've never actually done this, which makes it both thrilling and terrifying. I've always expected my own satisfaction in the end. I don't even want Lily to touch me. Well, that's not totally true. I want her to touch me very badly, but I can last one night.

I slip the vibrator inside of her, holding her open to take the toy in, and my cock twitches at the wet heat of her pussy. Jesus, I want her, but the way she groans and the way her eyelids flitter make holding out worth it. I love being in this position, this force that gives her exactly what she craves, without needing her to focus any of her energy on me. She can just give herself over to the sensations with no worries at all, and she is eager to do that now. She grows wetter and I slide the toy in and out a few times to ensure that she's ready. I haven't turned on the vibrations yet, and I want to tease her a little.

"How does that feel?" I ask.

"Mmmm," she says, which I take as a good sign.

I push it in a little bit deeper and then I flip the switch to the lowest setting. Lily gasps and holds the sharp intake of breath.

"Your pussy is beautiful, princess."

She groans and I watch her writhe against the toy. I meet her movements with it and she balls up the sheet in her fists. "Oh, God," she groans.

Increasing the speed of the vibrations, I push the toy deeper within her and she cries out, before immediately biting her lip.

"Go ahead and scream," I tell her. "I love watching you come."

She's breathing in short, quick gasps and I know she's nearly there, but I also know she's holding back. Lily is still, somewhere in her mind, the good girl and she clearly worries about what other people will think. Not enough to turn down what I'm doing, but enough to make her orgasm lesser than I want it to be, so I slip the toy even deeper and tell her to hold her thighs together. I get up, turning on the radio – loud - and I return to the bed.

"Don't worry now. No one can hear you. You can enjoy yourself, Lily."

At the sound of her name, she jerks her hips up and the vibrator slips out of her. I push her legs apart and rub her clit for a few minutes. She opens one eye and I know she's looking for the toy again, but she can't say anything because her clit is swollen under my thumb and she's too excited. I am so fucking hard it hurts, but I don't move to undress or do anything but help Lily let go entirely.

"More," she cries.

"More what?" I tease.

"More," she repeats and she turns her legs to the side toward me. I push them back and kneel between them, sliding the vibrator back inside of her. I push it as far as it can go this time. It's still buzzing on its medium setting and Lily begins thrusting her hips up and down. I hold onto her thighs and watch her. Her tits rise and fall with her quick breathing and her face twists in absolute ecstasy. I lean over and kiss her, at which point she nearly bucks me right off the damn bed.

"Oh, princess," I whisper and lay my body over hers, still dressed. She reaches a hand up into my shirt and caresses my back as I fuck her with the toy.

She's moaning and desperate and I know she's close. I press the switch again and increase the speed to the highest setting and Lily fucking loses it.

"Oh, God, Oh, Jack, Oh, FUCK ME," she screams. I don't have the heart to tell her that she is way louder than the music could ever be. She just repeats the same combination of monosyllabic sounds, my name, and a desire to be fucked. I watch her writhe and then I can see it. The orgasm makes her entire body go stiff and she points her toes down toward the mattress, flattening her legs. I fuck her even harder with the vibrator and she clenches her thighs around my hand as I push. Suddenly, she holds her breath and then, as she tilts her head back, she opens her mouth and screams so loud that everyone in the entire dorm probably hears her. Hell, half the fucking school probably does.

"Oh, God, Jack," she cries and I feel her come as she drenches the toy, my hand, and the sheets. Her entire body jerks underneath me for a few seconds and then she is still. I turn the vibrator off and put it in the plastic package that I'd left on my dresser.

I lie next to her and she doesn't open her eyes for a few moments. Then she rolls over onto her side, props herself up on her elbow, and looks at me.

"Fuck you," she laughs.

"What?"

"That was so unfair. You're incredible, Jack."

"I love knowing how easily I can make you come, princess."

"Like no one else," she sighs.

Her tongue slides into my mouth and we slowly explore each other. I love that she just said that – that I make her come like no one else. I pretty much figured, but knowing it? It's the only thing I'm good at, but she seems perfectly content with that. She slips her hand down into my pants as I kiss her and I groan against her lips as her fingertips brush the head of my cock.

"No," I whisper. "It was supposed to be all about you."

"I don't mind," she says against my mouth.

"Hell, I'm not going to survive if you don't take those lovely fingers off my cock."

I move away from her and stand up.

Lily looks confused. "Don't you want to-"

I shake my head. "Fuck, yes, I want to. I want to disappear inside of you, but you have an exam tomorrow and we both have papers. And if we get started, I'm going to fuck you all night, and that would be bad."

"Bad?" She raises her eyebrow.

"Okay, well it would be *amazing*, but I have a scholarship to keep up. Some of us-" But I stop because her face falls and we both know what I was going to say. *Some of us don't have everything handed to us.* It slipped out before I could think it over and I want to punch myself. She's on scholarship, too. I know that but still I almost said it.

"Yeah," she says and reaches onto the floor to get her clothes. She dresses fast and I want to apologize, want to pretend I wasn't going to say it, but I don't want to lie to her. I do wish, however, that I didn't naturally feel inferior to her still when it came to certain things.

Instead of addressing it, I change the subject and we look over a pizza menu. Neither of us wants to go to the cafeteria now and, by the time we place the order, she's back to normal. I'm not, but hell – when am I?

I help her study while we wait and eventually we eat. By the time we're both done working, it's late and the moment never comes for me to say I'm sorry. We fall asleep with me still making excuses.

Chapter 18

I spend the morning in the library while Lily takes her exam, hoping our paths will cross later when she comes here to write her paper. I have to work, but it's finally the weekend and exam week is over. I get everything done before I have to leave and I'm feeling good. I'm still a little sexually frustrated from holding out last night and, although it was worth it, I'm ready to get crazy with her. I need to forget everything but the way she tastes and smells.

Sadly, we don't run into each other, but it's probably better that way anyway, given the horrible ache in my balls. I'd end up passing out from needing her.

I take my bike and enjoy the ride. It's just getting to be cold enough that it stings if you're outside long without gloves, but it's not yet cold enough to keep you from going outside. The air is fresh and crisp and the only thing that ruins it is how suddenly the trees were stripped bare. I feel like they were full of leaves just yesterday, but now the ground is a pile of reds and oranges and the trees all look broken. *Maybe it's a warning. Because your own breaking point is coming,* the nagging voice in my head says. I tell the voice to fuck off, because I'm mature like that.

I'm disappointed that both Sandee and Liz are on dinner tonight, because that leaves Nicole as wait staff. She's my age and she's probably the most annoying person who has ever graced planet Earth. Even if she wasn't plain irritating, she's still so inept that it makes you wonder if you're being pranked. A really, really long and pointless prank. Also, I barely work with her, but in the six months since she started here, she's developed a stupid fucking crush on me.

She smiles when I walk in.

"Hi Jack," she says and she drapes herself over the counter so her tits are barely in her shirt. If she never spoke, she might be hot. But trust me, her amazing tits are just not worth the price of listening to her.

"Hey."

"It's just us today." This declaration is made as if it's a profound statement about the future of our romantic entanglements. Of which there will be none.

"Cool."

"And it's really quiet."

I look around. There is one old dude drinking coffee. Right now, I would give anything for a crowd. "Yeah, looks it."

I try to make my way to the kitchen but she leans her body against mine. "That guy seems pretty much set, so maybe you need help getting some stuff from the walk in."

On one incredibly stupid night this past summer, a night just like this one, I was in the walk in getting food to put out to defrost for the morning and Nicole came in looking for something. She'd just started working here and I had no idea how annoying she was. Her shirt had been unbuttoned low and she'd been insistent when she went for my belt. I'm ashamed to admit it, but in a moment of weakness, I fucked her against the door for all of eight minutes. It was meaningless and stupid and actually pretty damn crappy for both of us, but she's been unable to take the hint since. It will never happen again and now, aching balls aside, it's definitely not happening with Lily in the picture.

"I don't think so," I tell her.

"Why not? It was fun," she whines.

I don't feel like rehashing the fact that, in reality, it wasn't. I just need to get through the lunch shift. *Someone* will be on in only a few hours.

"I'm gonna make sure everything's stocked," I tell her. "Why don't you roll some silverware for the dinner crew?"

"I don't like rolling silverware."

There's no comeback for someone this stupid so I ignore her and go into the back. I don't really need to check much since the morning shift left everything full for us and clearly no one's been around. However, I make it look like I'm stocking things and taking inventory. Nicole peeks her head through the door and I start counting aloud from the number 12, to make it look more realistic. She at least has the common sense not to interrupt my count, but as soon as she's through the door, there's an enormous crash. I sigh and go out to the floor.

An entire tray of glasses and silverware is now at my feet. Well, to be more accurate, a tray, a pile of silverware, and a fucking ocean of glass are at my feet.

"Get the broom," I sigh.

"Where is it?" She asks as if it's moved since the last ten times she knocked shit over.

I ignore her, get the broom and sweep up the glass, and return to the back to count fictitious items. Holy hell, the dinner shift crew cannot get here fast enough.

By the time Sandee strolls in a few hours later, I'm ready to tackle her in a hug.

"Hey, Jack," she says and follows me out back for a cigarette. I love my job, because it's one of the only jobs where you can sneak off for a cigarette immediately after punching in. Technically, we aren't supposed to, of course, but right now the only other people in the building are Nicole and the same old dude.

"Can you *please* ask Jordan to stop scheduling me with Nicole?" I ask as I light my cigarette.

"You're the idiot who thought it was a good idea to start something with her."

"Sandee, I fucked her for like eight minutes in the walk in. It's not like I broke her damn heart."

"Can you stop with that? You're young enough to be my kid."

"Yeah, if you were ten when you had me."

"Still."

"Hey, can I ask you a stupid question?"

She smokes her cigarette and nods.

"Ever been in love?"

She takes a really long drag and reaches into her jacket for her flask. She offers me some, but I decline. She takes a swig and answers me. "Of course. It didn't end well."

"What happened?"

"Our lives were just on two completely different tracks. I had big plans. I was gonna move away, go to school, and make something of myself. He was happy to stay around town and get hammered."

"But you loved him?"

"I did. I mean, at the beginning, it wasn't clear how he was. But a year or two later, after we were out of high school and I still hadn't left for college, I started to resent him. Then, I got pregnant. And so that's that."

"But he's not around," I say, not meaning to pry, but also curious.

"No. He was happy to stay around, until there was a *reason* to stay around. And then he was out the fucking door. But it's okay. I have Mikey and he's the only man I need in my life at this point."

It seems so unfair to me. Sandee's a nice person. She's still pretty, for someone her age, and she has so much love in her. Yet she's alone.

I try to imagine myself ten years from now. Will I still be working here? Will I be telling some college kid about my relationship failures? In my case, I'll be the one who fucked up. As I think about it, it's just a big void. There's no way I will live to see thirty. The darkness is always creeping behind me, ready to throw me over the edge. I simply can't take another decade of it.

"Listen, sweetie, I can only guess why you're asking," Sandee says and finishes her cigarette. "But if you have a chance at love, go for it."

"You know my only role models for relationships are my grandparents and parents, right?"

"Look, I know you've been through a lot. You told me about your mom and dad and you've hinted about your grandfather, but plenty of couples work. Just because you and I don't know them, it doesn't mean you give up."

"But is the hurt worth it? If it's guaranteed to end, why force yourself through that kind of pain?" It's an honest question and she looks at me seriously.

"Because otherwise, why bother?"

She goes in and the problem is that although she meant for the question to be inspiring – to give me something to hope for – all it does is remind me how little there is. I'm starting to feel the darkness coming back until my phone buzzes in my pocket. As if she knew, Lily's texted me saying, *I can't wait to see you in a couple hours. I have a surprise for you.*

Yeah? I text back. *What is it?*

You'll see. Don't worry. I'm keeping it safe in my pants. The little winky face emoticon is really the kicker. Her efforts at sexting are more cute than sexy, but the ache in my balls returns. She's so much more than that, but I can't pretend the physical isn't a significant part of it as well.

I text her back that I can't wait to see her either and put my phone back in my pocket. Breathing in the cool autumn air, I make a decision. Tonight I'm going to take the biggest step of my life so far and tell Lily that I love her. Because, like Sandee said, if you have a chance at it, why not try to take it?

Chapter 19

I take a shower before going to see Lily after I get back from work. It only registered on the way home that I didn't hesitate when Sandee offered me something to drink; I simply said no as if it was natural. I can't imagine Lily has any idea how much she's impacted me in such a short time. I wish I could rationalize it, but then again, if I could, she could as well. And there's no way she'd still be in my life if she could make any sense of it.

By the time I'm dry and dressed, I am anxious as hell. There are a million voices in my head telling me all the things that could go wrong, but I need to tell her. And then I need to tell her the rest of it. Although I don't think I can do both in the same night. Soon, though. Because if this is going to be a relationship, I need to be honest with her.

Knocking on her door, I'm shaking. The door swings open almost immediately and I smile, thinking she's as anxious as I am, but my brain can't process what's happening. Lily's sitting in her desk chair and the guy standing in front of me is big, blond, and angry. I don't know why he's angry, but he's growling in my face about something. A little voice tells me that this is the same guy Lily was with a while ago, at the café and then on campus before I went home for the long weekend. But that doesn't make sense, does it? They broke up. She's with me now. Isn't she?

"Who are you? Princess, what's going on?" I ask her but she won't stop staring at the floor. I try to will her to meet my gaze, but nothing works.

The big blond guy is yelling and then he pushes me. I don't see it coming and I'm across the hallway before I know it. My back hits the wall and a switch is flipped. All of the rage I've suppressed for years – since I started college really – explodes inside of me and I step forward, returning the shove. The guy has at least thirty pounds on me, but I can't see right now. All I can think about is hurting him, because somehow I know that everything I thought tonight would be is no longer possible. And it's all *his* fucking fault.

He reaches out one of his stupid giant hands and grabs me by the throat.

I see my mother writhing under my father's hands as he holds her down on the living room carpet. She's trying to breathe, making weak sounds asking me to get help, but I just watch. I don't understand it; it's surreal. It can't be happening. And then my father twists and she's silent. It's all I can see for a moment before the illusion shatters and I free myself from this asshole's fucking grip. I wind up and hit him, but his jaw is solid, unlike my memory.

I push him off balance for a second before he hits me, knocking me onto the hallway floor. I want to kill him, to hurt him, to make it as if he never existed so whatever he's doing here is not real. I love her. I really, truly fucking love her and the pain I feel as he slams the door, taking her from me, is so deep that I stay on the floor and try not to feel anything.

Only a couple minutes go by and then her door opens and she's running. I try to speak, to tell her I'm sorry, but she just says she wants to be alone and takes off down the emergency stairs. The guy follows her.

At first, I decide I'll stay here. Right here. I'll just pass out and hope I never wake up. Because I don't have any fight in me to chase them, only to see them reconcile and walk away into their perfect little world. What was I thinking? She could never love me. I was a distraction, a bandage to cover whatever temporary wound he'd left, but now that he's back...

No. The voice is adamant and loud, which is surprising. Usually the voices encourage me to give up, but this one continues to repeat only that one word. *No.* No, she won't walk away, at least not without an explanation. No, I won't just back down that easily. It may not have been much time, but whatever we had was real. Even if she was using me as a means to forget him, she felt something. I know she did. It wasn't just the sex, although there was definitely some intimacy the last few times that I've never experienced with anyone else.

There was something more, too. When we were studying for exams, I'd look up and catch her looking at me. When we fell asleep together, I waited until she was asleep and she sometimes whispered my name in her dreams. Even when we'd see each other after classes, she would smile in a way that made me feel like the entire world was just extra space – and that she and I were at the center of it.

No way. Fuck him. Whatever they had, it's not what they have anymore. And I am not walking away from her.

I run down the stairs and push out into the night. I can see her across the quad, but I can't see him. I don't slow down and I cross the grass as fast as I can. He shows up from out of fucking nowhere at the exact same time.

"Princess, what the hell is happening?" I ask.

The guy turns to me. "She's not your fucking princess," he spits and then turns his attention to Lily. I barely listen to him, but I make out the word "loser." Because that's all I will ever be to people like him. *People like Lily.* There's the asshole voice again. But it isn't true. She isn't that girl. She doesn't believe that. I know she doesn't.

"Shut up," she says. "You don't even know him. I fucked up, not him."

"Don't bother defending me," I tell her. "I don't care what some asshole thinks." He glares at me but it means nothing anymore. I've seen that same fucking glare a million times in my life. From my dad, from his lawyers, and from every fucking carbon copy of this asshole looking at me right now. I'm sure he's had it all. Fuck him for judging me.

"He's not an asshole. He's just hurt," Lily says and her face is heartbreaking. I don't understand.

"What is going on?" he asks and I want to know the same thing.

She looks at me and takes a deep breath. "I thought Derek and I were over. I guess it wasn't clear. He's my boyfriend."

"You still have a boyfriend?" *No. This can't be happening.* How can she possibly have a boyfriend? I picture her lips on mine, still feeling the way her hand would brush my cheek as she kissed me. I imagine lying on top of her, our bodies rocking together, as I was buried deep inside of her. I picture falling asleep with her cradled in my arms. All of these things – and she has a fucking boyfriend?

"I didn't know we were still together when you and I..." She lets her voice trail off and Derek, I guess his name is, looks between the two of us. Recognition flashes in his eyes.

"What did you do, Lily?"

"Jack and I have been together lately," she tries to explain.

"And what? You *love* him? It's been a week!" He's looking at her like she's a fool, but I'm the one who feels foolish right now.

"I know it's only been a week, but I have feelings for him," she says.

"Do you? Because you're telling me you have a boyfriend right now," I point out.

"It's complicated. I care about you both," she argues and looks at both of us with longing.

"Lily, I came up here to take you away for our anniversary. Let's just go and we can deal with this. Alone. It's been a week. There is nothing in a week that can make up for the past year." He takes her arm and I see the way they look at each other, the way he holds her next to him as if they fit together perfectly. A year? They were together a *year*? I can't win against that.

"Yeah, go, princess. I should have known I'd never be right for you," I tell her, but she stops me.

"No, don't go," she cries out.

"He's right. You have a history. Don't make this worse than it needs to be."

"Lily, what do you want? *Who* do you want?" Derek asks and she looks back and forth between us again several times, breaking free from his hold on her. She starts to sob and I want to hold her, to tell her it's okay, but it's not going to happen.

"I want you both to leave me alone. That's what I want," she snaps. "I don't even know who I am anymore. I can't do this right now."

Derek reminds her that he loves her, but she isn't listening. She turns to me and says, "You don't even know me yet. Derek and I weren't even done and I made a huge mistake rushing into something with you, Jack. Being with you wasn't a mistake. In fact, it was the best week I've had, but it's only a week and I need to face that. You don't even want a relationship."

"Right," I answer, because I can't tell her now. And the worst part is that I feel it deeper than I even thought I did. I can feel my pores crying out for her. I'm so in love with this girl that it could kill me, but I cannot tell her anymore. She keeps talking, about needing time, about figuring herself out, but I don't hear anything but pain. Why was I so fucking stupid? She could never love me. I'm a worthless piece of shit who's never earned love from anyone except for one stupid, equally broken girl.

I watch Lily walk away. I don't know if Derek follows, because I can't see anything but black. Miles of black reach out ahead of me and I somehow manage to text Alana, begging her to come see me, and then I make it up to my room. Digging out the first bottle I touch from under my bed, I drink half of it. I can't even place the taste and the label is swimming. There are tears, but I can barely feel them. I feel nothing but the crushing weight of hopelessness and I sink onto the floor, hugging the bottle to me and falling asleep.

Chapter 20

"Wake the fuck up," Alana says and kicks me. The light comes from behind her so she's nothing but a silhouetted ghost. I try to make her come into focus but my eyes are on fire. There are two shapes in the room and I squint, trying to distinguish whom they belong to.

"We'll be fine now. Thanks," Alana says and one of the shapes grows more distant. Suddenly the shape is gone and I hear the door close.

Alana leans down and shakes me. "Get up, get your shit together, and tell me what happened."

I vaguely remember a text telling her that I needed her, but why did I need her? Something about Lily. Princess...

And there it is. The entire shitstorm that was the evening bursts again around me, like fireworks that refuse to fucking die. I keep seeing Lily's sad eyes and then watching her walk away. I know that walk. People don't walk away like that and come back. I let out a huge sob that sounds more like a wheeze.

"Tell me, Jack."

"Princess. Derek. Boyfriend. Over." I'm slurring and I don't know how to feel. There is so much pain, but there's also an incredibly comforting numbness from how much it hurts.

She pushes me upward until I'm sitting against my desk. I lift my knees to my chest and bury my face in them. She can't see this. I can't breathe through the wracking agony that's stealing the air from my lungs. Alana just sits next to me, wraps her arm around my shoulders, and waits.

I reach into the drawer next to me and take out a plastic butter knife. I think it's from the takeout I got with Lily. Was that just yesterday? I bend it hard until it snaps and I take the sharper piece, digging it into the flesh of my palm. Alana watches me, but doesn't interfere. I can't kill myself with a plastic butter knife and things could be worse.

I dig and dig until a small drop of blood forms and then I drop the stupid fucking thing. The blood bubbles and I just stare at it.

"Feel better?" Alana asks. "That was dumb."

I don't say anything. I just keep staring at my palm. I had hoped that the physical pain would divert my focus from what is twisting inside, but now I'm heartbroken *and* my fucking hand stings. Great.

I picture Lily for a brief moment and my breathing picks back up until I can't see straight. I put my head down between my knees again, since I'm not getting enough oxygen. The heaving sobs have turned to hyperventilation. I punch the hard, cold floor of my dorm room over and over, but soon I have to stop in order to avoid passing out. Alana rubs slow circles along my back.

"Breathe, Jack. Just breathe."

It's easier said than done. What the fuck was I thinking? What kind of moron am I? The breathing gives way to laughter and I completely lose it, sliding down my desk until I'm prone on the floor, still laughing. How fucking stupid. As if I was going to go in there and declare my love for her and be welcomed in to her life. I'm a worthless waste of space; I don't belong in anyone's life.

I open my eyes fully and the overhead light glares as I scream, the sound echoing through my room. I need to do something, to run away, to hurt someone, to hurt myself. I'm barely present as I grab Alana's hand and lead her out of my room. The fucking freshman whose mother glared at me on move-in day pokes his head out of his room, probably to make sure I'm not dead or something, but I want to fucking punch him. I don't want his sympathy. I don't want anyone's sympathy. I just want Lily.

"Fuck you," I spit at him, and he shuts his door. It's childish and stupid, but fuck him. Let him go back to his room and call Mom and Dad. Let them talk about their happy fucking family. Let him go on Facebook and tell all his buddies from home about the fucking train wreck that lives across the hall.

I take the back way out of the dorm, down the fire stairs just like Lily did earlier tonight. The dark dankness of the stairwell mirrors my mood and I almost stop and toss myself down the last few flights. But then I picture that fucking freshman kid coming out here and seeing my dead bloody body. I wouldn't even feel bad if he did; I just don't want him telling someone on fucking Twitter about it or writing a blog about his feelings about the dead kid. Goddamn, I don't want to be a blog post.

Alana doesn't talk. She just follows me down the stairs, across the quad, and down to the parking lot. I didn't grab my helmet, but I don't care.

"I need to go for a ride," I say.

"Jack, you are in no condition to be driving. Get in my car. I'll take you wherever you want to go, but you're not driving."

I want to argue, because sitting in the car isn't the same. However, for a split second, before I processed it, Alana sounded like Lily when she said my name. I look up at the night sky and I whisper a soft prayer to anything that might exist that the sky opens up right now and takes me.

Alana pushes me to her car and opens the passenger door. I'm not used to being looked after like this, but my body won't move. If she walked away, I sincerely believe that I would sit here on the ground and wait to die. The idea of walking, of eating, of breathing – it all just feels hollow.

She gets in her side and turns on the heat. "Get your shit together," she says. "It's been a fucking week. You can't lose yourself like this over a fucking week. What if whatever you'd hoped would happen *had* happened, and then a year went by and we were here? How the fuck would you survive it?"

"It's not Lily," I try to explain. "I know what it looks like, but it isn't *just* her. I don't know how to explain it. A few hours ago, I stood in the shower and I could actually *feel* tomorrow. I wanted there to be a tomorrow, and a next week, and a next year. I wanted to be present. I wanted to be alive."

"And now you don't? You don't want to be alive because of a girl you fucked a few times?" She stops and looks at me. Her eyes are full of tears, but behind the tears is real, palpable anger. "Fuck you, Jack. Really. Fuck you."

"Why?"

"You're my best friend. You're my *only* fucking friend. You call me all the time, needing me, and I run to you. I told you what it felt like to think I was going to lose you. And you just sit here and tell me it doesn't fucking matter. That the last few years – all my sacrifices, all my putting you first – it means nothing because some girl fucked you a few times and got bored. You are such an asshole." The tears come out full force now. I wish I could take Alana's pain away, but like everything I do, I fucked this up. All I do is destroy and break.

"I *never* want to be alive," I tell her. "I've learned how to get by, except for once in a while like the other night. But I never want to be here; I just don't want to leave you behind. I don't want you to feel like I do all the time."

"What are you saying?"

I shake my head and give in to the pain that's been rising. I break down with Alana, both of us so damaged and so hurt and so fucking incapable of healing the other. "I love her. I fucking *love* her. And I was going to tell her tonight."

Alana holds me and lets me fall apart. I don't smoke, ask to go to the bar, or move to touch her. I want to show Lily. I want her to come back and I can say that I didn't hide from how she made me feel. I want to go to her and tell her that I can be whole with her, that I don't need to lose myself in dying. But then I realize that I can't do that. She has her perfect boyfriend. She has someone who doesn't need to make these kinds of declarations, because he's whole to begin with.

"Where do you wanna go?" Alana asks after a little while. I can't just sit here in her car forever and I swallow hard. My breathing has returned to a reasonably steady pace and I look out the window. The moon is low in the sky and I suddenly need to belong somewhere.

"Take me to see my mom," I tell her.

****

As far as I know, three people have been to my mother's grave since the funeral. My grandmother, who has since stopped, me, and Alana. I took her once when we were an actual couple and she's come back a few times with me.

She pulls the car up to the street near the grave and we walk to the area where my mom's tombstone is. Last time I was here, a week ago, I brought flowers. They're still there, but with the chill in the air, they're dead. Apparently the grounds crew hasn't been by to pick them up, so the little stone is almost dwarfed by a bouquet of crunchy near black roses. I reach down to pick them up and Alana takes them from me without speaking.

My mom's stone is small because we couldn't afford much. She left us nothing but debt and any savings was put into lawyers for my dad. The state suggested we skip the stone, but thankfully, my grandmother refused. It might be dumb and they might have spelled her name wrong, but I like knowing there's at least *something* commemorating her existence. The stones that surround hers almost make her memory invisible, which I suppose is some sort of metaphor.

I look at the place where my mom is. I know she's not *here*, but there's nowhere else she is anymore. So this has to do.

I sit on the ground across from the stone. Alana brings the flowers to the car, leaving me some privacy. The flowers could wait, but being here is hard. And it's much harder with someone else. She tried once to comfort me, and I ended up yelling at her. Now, when she comes with me, she keeps her distance.

I try to ignore the name and close my eyes. I wish I had memories of my mother. Memories that didn't involve her being high out of her fucking head. But there's only one. The same one I always go back to when I want to remember her well.

I was seven, I think. My first grade class was having a craft fair for the holidays and we were all supposed to invite our parents. I was really excited, because I'd made snowmen out of cotton balls. I guess I must have expected someone else to think cotton ball snowmen were amazing, but so far, no one had bought any. I remember feeling incredibly discouraged.

Looking down the tables, I saw other kids selling their crafts. One girl made barrettes out of paperclips and she'd nearly sold out of them. She'd invited everyone she knew and she had like twenty aunts show up in addition to her parents. My mom was running late and my dad was out of town for work, so I was just sitting with my snowmen, feeling sad.

Heather, the barrette girl, came over to my table and I beamed at her. Maybe she was going to use some of her earnings to buy one of my creations. She just glared, though.

"You'd sell more if you were happy," she said. "No one wants to talk to you if you're pouting." And then she turned back to her table. Marketing tips from a fucking first grader.

My stupid kid heart felt broken, but I tried to do what she said. I smiled and said hello to every single person who came in, but no one would buy my snowmen. By the time the craft fair was wrapping up, everyone else was down to almost nothing, but I still had a full table of cotton ball snowmen. Maybe I'd made too many.

I was ready to cry, but Heather told me people would like me more if I smiled, so I did.

My mom came rushing in with ten minutes left of the stupid fair. She took one look at me and knelt down next to me, taking my hand.

"Baby, what's wrong?"

"No one wants my snowmen," I told her and that was it. My mom was here and I could cry. She hugged me close to her and whispered several times that it would be okay. Almost all the other kids and their families were packing up, but my mom grabbed a tray from one of the kids who'd made cookies and loaded it with my snowmen. She left one with me and winked.

"You need to keep one. Someday, when they're in high demand, you'll have an original."

Then my mother, who would later that year lose all semblance of normalcy, took a tray of snowmen around to the other tables and parents and out into the school hallway. She came back just as the fair was ending and the tray was empty. She handed me the ten dollars, all ones and coins, that I'd earned and kissed my forehead.

"Sometimes you just need to know who to ask for help, Jack. But it's okay to ask." I had no idea in the first grade how ironic those words were. I was just so fucking happy to have sold all my snowmen. All except one. I carried my last creation proudly out of the school and felt like a hero. I loved my mother so much in that moment.

A few years later, after my home life had slipped off the rails, I overheard my first grade teacher telling another teacher the snowmen story.

Even with my mother now out of her mind, I listened, thinking that I still had the greatest mom in the world. Until I heard what the teacher said.

"She went around school begging teachers to give her change for a ten, so he would never know. Then she took the whole tray and dumped those snowmen into the dumpster out back. The poor kid was so happy when she came back. He thought everyone had bought them. I guess it was a nice thought, but after everything that's happened since, I wonder."

I walked away and never told anyone about the snowmen. Maybe the teacher was lying. Maybe she was mad at my mom and wanted to make her out to be a bad person. I don't know. But it changed the path of my life. Because the only good fucking memory of my childhood was like everything else – a façade for the hollowness that filled my world.

I stare at the tombstone now, remembering those stupid snowmen and how my mom told me it was okay to ask for help. Help she never told anyone that she needed.

"I need you, Mom. Goddammit, I fucking need you so bad," I say and the tears land in the dirt beneath me. "You told me to ask for help. Please, Mom. *Please* help me."

I don't hear Alana behind me until she sits and takes my hand. I bury my face in her shoulder and let go, crying about my mom, my dad, Lily… my entire fucking life. I hate being weak. I would rather be angry, but right now, it just fucking hurts like hell. And I want it to stop.

Chapter 21

Alana stays with me all night. She's worse than the nurses when I had to stay in the psycho ward. She keeps asking if I'm safe, as if when she gets up and goes to the bathroom, I might jump out the window. I don't have the energy to explain to her that my previous attempt was anything but impulsive. Whenever I talk about it, she gets miserable, and I can't take it back. So I just promise her that I'm fine.

I'm not fine. I don't want to die at this point, but I don't want to live, which is something Alana can't comprehend. She thinks they're the same thing, but they're not really. Not wanting to live is more of a passive reluctance to trying, whereas wanting to die is definitely an active state. I'm passive. Weak, pathetic, and passive.

"I just want to be whole. Why do I have to exist in so many pieces?" I ask her.

She sighs. "Because life is a shitty fucking lottery. And we drew the shortest fucking straws."

"She made me think I was worth it to someone. Really, really worth it."

"You're worth it to me."

"We feed off each other. When I fall apart, you pick me up because you know that when the time comes, I'll do the same for you. That's not the same as being worth it. She made me believe that I could be something else. Something other than this."

"Someday, Jack? Someday you'll realize that *this* is pretty damn amazing. Even with all the cracks." She smiles sadly at me and we fall asleep. I'm exhausted.

No one tells you about pain. They tell you that it hurts, that sometimes it's consuming. What they don't tell you is that it's not the pain that can kill you. It's the uncomfortable numbness that follows, the weakness in your body when you realize your lungs may stop taking in air and you just can't exert enough energy to care. It's the way taste and color and smell fade from the world and all you're left with is a sepia print of misery. That's when the shift starts – the movement from passive to active. I fall asleep, hoping that the morning will bring back the pain. At least the pain is a thing.

****

The morning brings something, that's for sure. When I wake up, it takes a little bit to remember and my sense of smell is restored. As I breathe in the scent of strawberries, I roll over to embrace Lily, to kiss her, only to see Alana sleeping next to me. My brain is shocked back into reality – and then the numbness returns. It's over. It's really over. It hadn't even fucking started yet.

I have to work and Alana's in a panic, as if I'm going to kill myself in the kitchen of the café.

"I'll be back after work. I swear."

"I'm staying with you for the weekend," she says.

"Fine. But I need to go to work," I tell her.

She nods and I change, feeling somehow weird about getting undressed in front of her. It still feels wrong, like I'm cheating on Lily. I laugh, a bitter biting laugh, and Alana looks up at me. I just shake my head. I'm sure she hates Lily, but I can't. It's not her fault; it's mine for thinking that I had the right to want her.

I leave an hour before I need to, because Alana is bugging me. She's never been suicidal. I kind of don't understand how, given what she's been through, but she never has. She's been depressed and angry and she's certainly self-destructive, but in all the years I've known her, Alana has maintained hope. It's kind of amazing, but it's also depressing because I wonder what's broken in me that makes me incapable of that kind of optimism.

It's too cold to drive around aimlessly, so I end up at work early. Sandee pours me a coffee, because it's dead and the morning shift is all still here. Normally I'd offer to relieve the cook, but I don't feel like it right now. I don't really feel like *anything* right now, but I try to pretend. I warm my hands on the coffee mug. For as numb as I am, I seem to be able to register temperature just fine. Everything is awash in browns and blacks, like something out of a Wyeth painting, but hot and cold still reach me.

"How are you?" Sandee asks.

It's funny. I just saw her yesterday. Yesterday, I made the decision to give myself over to Lily. It hasn't even been twenty-four hours, although it feels like forever. What's stranger is that Sandee doesn't know. The customers in the back booth don't know. My grandmother doesn't even know. The entire world has ended – and it's like a secret that only Alana and I share.

It reminds me of the days following my mother's murder and the funeral. When I went back to school, before I moved here, the teachers all knew, as did a few kids. But the story hadn't really broken yet. All around me, people were talking about dances and algebra and class rings. It almost made no sense. How could the world be spinning? How could everyone exist so separately from me?

Of course, months later, once the trial started, I would have given everything to go back to that isolation. Because as much as I thought I wanted them to share in my misery when it happened, I quickly discovered that misery is not a shared experience. Instead, it's what makes other people think that they know you – and it makes you vulnerable. Once the world knows where you're fragile, it will set out to break you every day. My classmates didn't feel guilty or sad about my suffering; they embraced it as the anomaly it was and made sure that I knew it made me a freak. Changing schools didn't help, either. All it took was one Facebook message and the right people on the receiving end.

"Jack?"

I realize Sandee's been talking. "Sorry, I was just thinking," I reply.

"Still wondering about love?"

She's being nice, but the question claws at me. "You got a minute before I punch in? Wanna come outside with me?"

Sandee calls to Mal to watch the front so she can go on break. He yells something back, which is probably a no, but the one table will be fine. I follow her out back. The pallet pile is low today and I sit on it, resting against the wall of the café. Taking out my cigarettes, I borrow Sandee's lighter.

"I love this girl," I say.

"Alana?"

I shake my head. "No. Lily. She's a freshman on my floor. I brought her in here once, but you weren't on."

"Well, good for you," she says and sits next to me on the pallet.

I breathe in from my cigarette and try not to start hyperventilating again now that I'm thinking about it. I mean, I haven't *stopped* thinking about it, but to put it into words...

"I was ready to tell her last night. And then I found out that she still has a boyfriend."

"Oh, Jack." She takes my hand.

"She's not a bitch, if that's what you're thinking. I think it's complicated. But they have a history. And Sandee... he's right for her, in so many ways that I could never be."

"You don't know that. These things aren't always how they seem, you know."

"In this case, it's true. She's just so... good. She's the kind of girl who deserves it all. She's the kind of girl who makes me want to believe in something beautiful."

I close my eyes, inhaling the smoke and trying to feel nothing else. As soon as I close my eyes, I see her. Her blue and green eyes, her nervous smile that's half frowning, and her stunning body. It isn't sexual desire that I feel when the images flash across the back of my eyelids; it's the desire to be the guy I am with her.

I open my eyes and gasp, dropping my cigarette onto my thigh. I could move, but I don't. I just watch as it burns a hole through my pants and stings like a motherfucker when it comes in contact with my flesh. *Huh. That's good. You felt it.*

"Sandee, can I tell you something?" I ask as the cigarette rolls onto the pavement.

She hands me another and I thank her. She doesn't reply, which I assume means I can go ahead.

"When I was senior, I tried to kill myself. Lately, it's been on my mind again a lot."

"I *never* want to hear those words again, Jack," she says and she pulls me into a hug.

It feels weird to be hugged. I don't get a ton of physical affection and it's strange to have someone touch me with no sexual intent. It's so... soft. Not like physically soft, but soft in a way that I can't explain. My life is hard, my thoughts are hard, and sex is hard. I self-destruct slowly each day. I don't live for small pleasures. I don't think about anything beyond, at most, my next practice or show, my work schedule, or exams. The idea of things like next year, graduation, a real job – these are unreal. But when Sandee hugs me, it's almost like I get a glimpse into what people who see those things feel. As if they comfort one another so that they can keep looking forward. When there is nothing on the horizon, you just stop looking up.

"I won't, but it's not because I want to live."

I haven't tried to explain it to anyone except once with Alana, who freaked out and got so drunk she couldn't remember the conversation the next day, and one therapist who seemed nice for three sessions – until she suggested Lithium.

"When the feelings came that first time," I continue, "I had no idea what they were. But after that attempt, I realized I would keep fucking it up. So I stopped. Later, I found ways that were less – definitive."

"How so?" Sandee asks.

"The first time, I tried to hang myself. Clearly, if it had worked, I would be dead. The second time, I took off on my bike. I went up to the mountain and I took the roads up there fast. It was barely spring and they were still slippery in places. I didn't bring a helmet and I just flew. I decided that if the cosmos wanted me dead, I would die. If they didn't, I would be alive."

"That's incredibly stupid," she says. "What if you'd died?"

I laugh, because the question is so sweet, but I also feel so weak. Sandee is another one like Alana. She has every reason to do the same things I do, but she doesn't. "That was kinda the idea."

"I understand sadness, Jack. I understand the kind of sadness that crushes you and makes you think the next breath will be the one that kills you. I know how it feels to wake up in the morning and think you just can't handle one more day of this. I've woken on a Tuesday and the idea of Thursday was impossible. I couldn't make it that far."

"So how did you?" I really want to know. Because medication, therapy, alcohol – none of it has worked.

"I love my son. My life may be bad but he's in it. When I wake up and feel like that, I picture him waking up without me. And I drag my ass out of bed. Because when you love someone that much, you just have to."

"I'm not selfish," I argue.

"I didn't say you were. I don't believe suicide is selfish. I do, however, believe that you of all people know how it feels to be the one left standing. Do you want other people to feel like you did? Like you still do?"

"No one would."

"Alana would. *I* would. And I bet that Lily girl would."

I shake my head. "She wouldn't even know."

"Let me ask you something. What if she is in fact with her boyfriend? How would she feel if she found out you killed yourself? Don't you think she'd see herself as the cause? How do you think she'd live after that? You said she made you believe in something beautiful. Even if she isn't it, do you think there's nothing else that's beautiful? And do you want to take away whatever it is that makes her that kind of person? Because the girl you love? If you kill yourself, that girl dies with you."

"I won't do it. I won't hurt her. I won't be any more of a burden on people than I am," I say.

"It's never a burden to love someone, honey. Do you think it's easy putting up with what I do with Mikey and the school? Or his father, who doesn't help us? Of course not. It's hard and some days, it's almost impossible. I wanted to go to college. I wanted a life. But my son *is* my life. And he will *never* be a burden."

I wish I could tell her how much it hurts me to hear her say these things. Not because I don't believe her or because they aren't wonderful things. But because my own mother never saw it that way. Maybe it was because my grandparents were always fighting and she was never taught how to be a parent. I know my grandmother is full of regret about letting things get out of control with both my grandfather and my mom, but it's how she is. She just wants everyone to be happy, even if the happiness is found at the bottom of a bottle or at the end of a needle. I could resent her, but I don't. She came from her own abusive family and she swung to the opposite end of the pendulum.

It's so depressing to think of my family, because it just reminds me that I'm not the kind of guy who wins in the end. I don't get to be with girls like Lily.

"I really love her, Sandee. But she's so much better off this way. And I won't ruin her chance at happiness, just because it destroys me that I'm not a part of it. I refuse to be the reason the light in her eyes goes out."

Sandee stands up and I look at my watch. Shit. I have to be on the clock in like two minutes. "Jack," she says quietly, "I really hope that somehow or other things work out with this girl."

"Thanks, but they won't," I say.

"You never know."

I nod. "I do. But she gave me a glimpse of something. And who knows? Maybe someday I can be even a small part of what I was with her. Because it was good with her. *I* was good with her."

"It sounds to me like you have something worth hanging onto if the chance comes up. Anyone who can make you love yourself, even a little, is worth fighting for."

I have nothing to say to that. Lily walked away from me last night. I would fight for her, but she doesn't want me. I just need to be thankful that she was even in my life for the breath of an instant.

Chapter 22

I force myself to get through each day that follows. I throw myself into school and into practice. We got another gig for the weekend after Thanksgiving and this time we headline. It's a big fucking deal and the band really helps me to drown all the thoughts.

At first, I look for Lily everywhere. I think I see her a few times, but each time, I feel pieces of me shatter again, and soon I stop looking because it hurts too much.

I have a huge programming project coming up for my design class and I work on that for days, barely sleeping, and it makes me feel more human again. It isn't a replacement for anything, but it's a distraction and I probably put together the best project I have in my entire academic career.

Sober and celibate, I don't have a fucking clue how to be alive. But some stupid voice in my head continues to tell me that someday, maybe she'll come back. And I want to show her that I'm worth it. I know it's delusion, but it gets me from day to day.

Alana comes up to visit a few days before Thanksgiving. She's been trying to give me my space, which after a week of her constant attention, I demanded. When she arrives, I have to fight my own damn body. As always, she looks fucking fantastic and she's wearing a short ass skirt. My mind may still be living in a dream world where Lily is present, but my cock is happy to take what it can get. I don't move to touch her though and she sits on my bed, crossing her legs.

"I have no intention of fucking you," she says and her eyes go to my ridiculous erection. Girls have no idea how much it sucks to be a guy sometimes. I'm still heartbroken but my body is totally ready to move on.

"My body's dumb. I can't stop thinking about her. But yet, your legs look fucking great in that skirt."

She smiles. "Well, I'm happy at least part of you is ready to rejoin the living. But control it. I have some big news."

"Yeah?"

She nods and takes out her cell. She passes it over to me and I look at the text she has open.

We miss you. When are you coming home?

I miss you, too. I'm actually getting a short leave for the holidays. I have to spend most of it with my family, but maybe...

It's a date.

She signed off with a smiley face. I don't understand. He hasn't spoken to us in years.

"But how?" I ask.

"I got his number from his mom. You know, neither of us asked. For two years. We just dwelled on the fact that he left us. I wonder how many times he came back for leave, and how many times we could've gone back. Made it right again."

"It'll never be the same, Alana. You can't make it the same," I argue.

"Maybe not, but I can fucking make it something. Which is more than you're doing, I might add."

"Not cool. She doesn't want me."

"We thought Dave didn't want us either. Maybe you need to try."

"It's been almost a month."

She shrugs and holds up her phone. "It's been two fucking years."

"Let's just drop it," I say, because it's different with Lily. She's not in some country across the globe; she's down the hall. If she wants to come back into my life, she knows where I am. "Anyway, you coming over for our big Thanksgiving feast?" I ask.

"Wild Turkey and Smirnoff Cranberry?"

I sigh. It's been our Thanksgiving tradition for nearly five years now. Since the first time, when Alana broke into her stepdad's liquor cabinet and snuck over after he passed out. For a few years, Dave was also a part of it.

I've been trying to behave, trying to be the kind of person Lily would want, but Alana's my friend. It might be a stupid and self-destructive tradition, but it's still a tradition. "Yeah," I reply.

"Awesome. I'll be there as soon as my mom's new boyfriend stops trying to pretend we're a family."

She gets up and goes to my Xbox and grabs one of the controllers, tossing the other one to me. We spend the rest of the night shooting zombies and I almost forget.

****

On Thanksgiving, Alana does come over, but she's pissed when she arrives. And she's sans alcohol. I'm a little relieved, because my pointless oath to Lily will be upheld now, but I'm also sad, because Alana and I don't come from homes with traditions. Even if it was a stupid, fucked up one, it was still ours.

"What's wrong?" I ask her.

"My mother's new boyfriend. He's fucking intolerable," she complains and throws herself onto my bed. I sit on the end next to her.

"He didn't try any shit, did he?"

She rolls her eyes. "No. Not Owen. Fucking goddamn *Donna Reed* shit. He cooked an entire fucking Thanksgiving dinner. With stuffing. The homemade shit. Not even that stuff in a bag."

I laugh. "And?"

"And then he wanted us to fucking talk about being thankful. He even thought I was going to stay in tonight. He brought board games, Jack. Fucking board games."

I shrug. "I like board games."

She rolls over and kicks me. "I'm twenty fucking years old. The only guys in my life have been assholes, drunks, pedophiles, or fucking train wrecks."

"And me," I remind her.

"You're included in train wrecks, my friend. Right at the top of the fucking list."

"Nice. At least I'm good at something," I say.

"Jack, you need to save me. He wants us to go out tomorrow, all three of us, to buy a Christmas tree. And to decorate it. The last time I think I saw a fucking Christmas ornament was when my stepdad threw one across the room at my mom because she bought the wrong eggnog. We don't *do* Christmas."

"Maybe you should," I say and it's said before I even realize it. I say it like it's obvious, as if I wouldn't be packing my shit and getting the fuck out were the situations reversed. I relent. "You can stay here for the weekend if you need to. I didn't even see my grandmother today. She spent all day at the prison helping with the meal."

"That sucks. Weren't you invited?"

"Yeah. Have I ever gone?"

She sits up. "I don't know. I thought you were all about being normal now or something."

"That seems to be your current dilemma," I tease. "But seriously, if you need a place to stay..."

She shakes her head. "No, it's okay. I'll go buy a tree. But if the word caroling even leaves his mouth, I swear to God..."

"Alana, it's the 21st century. No one carols anymore. They send singing ecards."

"Yeah, you tell Owen that. I bet he fucking carols."

She's complaining, but I know a part of her loves it. Because as much as it's easier to hate everything and everyone, Alana isn't all that different from me. And we both still have an inherent need to belong to someone. Her mother has always been so worried about her boyfriends that Alana learned a long time ago to be alone. But I can tell that she secretly loves the idea of buying a tree with a family, even if it is a dysfunctional one.

I don't even remember the last time we had a tree. Or Christmas for that matter. Usually my grandmother buys me a couple things and we have something to eat, before she takes off to see my dad – and I go see my mom. But it isn't Christmas. Other than the fact that I get up at the ass crack of dawn, it could be any other day. Last year, my presents were wrapped in baby shower paper. I teased my grandmother that she was going senile and she played along, but later, I saw the receipt and realized it was half off – and Christmas paper was too expensive. There's something really sad about knowing that you're so poor you can't buy wrapping paper. Meanwhile, I'm off at school, living off a scholarship. These are the things that motivate me to do well in classes.

"I didn't get any booze," I tell Alana, changing the subject and feeling a little empty.

She shrugs. "It's okay. I probably shouldn't be hung-over tomorrow. Owen mentioned pancakes. Do people eat pancakes after noon?"

I lie down next to her and hold her hand.

"Are you all right?" She rolls onto her side and looks at me.

"I'm fine. It hurts a tiny bit less every day."

"You know, Jack, if it's meant to be..."

"No, don't give me that shit. Because I know what is 'meant to be,' and Lily and me? We're not it. But I like thinking maybe that's a stupid cliché and there is no meant to be."

"Come with us tomorrow?" Alana asks. "Buy the tree. Have some cider or whatever shit you drink when you have a tree. Hang that silver shit with me."

"It's called tinsel."

"Yeah, tinsel. Come over tomorrow. Please?"

I wonder if I can. I wonder if being at her house with her mother and Owen acting like normal people, doing normal things, will hurt too much. I can't even picture these things. As far as I knew, they only happen in movies. But I don't have to work and my grandmother will probably be tired from spending the day serving Thanksgiving dinner at the prison. What the fuck else am I going to do?

"Sure. I'll come over and buy a tree," I say.

****

Owen's a nice guy. Like a genuinely *nice* guy. He talks to me like we've known each other for years, showing real interest in my major and telling me about his friend who works for a game studio. It's surreal. I knew theoretically that people like Owen existed – people who are optimistic because they have a reason to be, people life has been easy for but who feel apologetic that it has. But I've never met one. I know nice people at the café, but most have been through their own shitty stories. Owen's an only child, his parents are still alive and married, and he has always had good things happen to him. And yet, he is so excited to share with Alana, her mom, and me. As if he doesn't see how far out of our realm of experience his whole life is.

They'd already had the infamous pancakes by the time I got there and now we're out looking for a tree. I have no memory of ever buying a tree. Does one just go out into the woods with an axe? I know that's not the case because I've seen parking lots full of sad trees leaning on poles, but who gets these trees? Are they carried in a big fucking tree truck? I imagine it's not worth it to ask, so I stay silent as Owen drives the four of us around town looking for "the right lot." It's grown dark by the time we find it.

The right one is on the edge of town and it looks like no one comes here. A guy dressed in a Metallica t-shirt and jeans is the only person around and he glances at us once while we make our way through the trees. However, as soon as I walk into the aisles between the rows of trees, I get it. I'm overwhelmed by the smell of pine, the crisp coolness in the air, and the undeniable sensation that this is both normal and important. People do this. People are happy here. The trees are just trees, but because they're *here*, they change everything.

I keep to myself while the three of them pick out their tree. Although I was invited, I'm still an outsider. Instead, I walk the rows and I think of Lily. Is she buying a tree tonight? Is Derek with her? Do her parents bring him with them when they have holidays? I picture being here with her. Just us, me holding her hand, and smelling strawberries mixing with pine as she gushes about ornaments and presents and Christmas and things that remain alien to me.

My heart is so fucking full of her and this fantasy, until I realize she will never be here with me. I'll never be a part of that with her. I look up between the tilting treetops and, even with the clip-on lights in my eyes, I can see a smattering of stars. How can a person be so crushed by misery and yet be able to dream of something so beautiful?

Alana comes to find me where I'm still standing and breathing in starlight.

"We're heading home now," she says.

I breathe deep one more time and follow her. As soon as I make it back out of the trees, the ghost of Lily fades and it hurts all over again. It's been a month. How fucking long is it going to take?

Chapter 23

I spend the night on Alana's couch after we decorate her tree. I suppose decorate is not the right word, since her mom owns three things that can pass as ornaments. Right now, there are a couple of lights and some tinsel Owen brought, the three ornaments, and one of Alana's old teddy bears as a tree topper. It's the most pathetic Christmas tree on Earth, but when we turned down the lights and sat by the colorful, albeit dim, illumination of the tree and ate Oreos her mom bought, it felt far more like a fucking family than anything else I've ever known.

Now, everyone's sleeping, but I have to work, so I leave a note and head home to shower and change before leaving for the café. My grandmother's asleep as well, but I trip over a plastic bag from Wal-Mart as I try to get into my room. There's a Post-It on the bag.

Bought you a few things for school during the big sales on my way home. Missed you, Jack. So did your dad.

I crumple the Post-It. I feel simultaneously guilty for spending no time with my grandmother and angry at her for mentioning my father. He's never going to cease to come between us.

I dump the contents of the bag on my bed. She bought me another set of sheets, which I shove in my closet behind a bunch of junk, where there are already four sheet sets. She seems to think I go through a fuckload of sheets, because she buys me sheets at least once every couple of months. I don't tell her, which I suppose I should since she spends the money for nothing, but it would crush her. The thing is, though, the washing machine on my floor isn't complicated. So I keep the sheets and every so often, I bring a set back to school, when the one set I have is starting to look old. I just can't keep up because, well, no one needs this many sheets.

There's also a small saucepan in the bag, which I toss onto my pile of stuff for school. I'll bring the pan back. My grandmother buys me four things: alcohol when I'm close to losing it, sheets for some imaginary bed that's always eating them, shoes because she doesn't know how to buy clothes for me, and pans. I have no fucking clue why she buys me the pans. I live in a dorm. I usually leave the pans in the shared kitchen on my floor, but no one really cooks in there. Because there's the cafeteria and we're all required to carry a mean plan. Maybe she thinks I love cooking since I drive so far to work at the café. I could never explain to her that it isn't because I have a passion for cooking, but because I have a passion for running away.

I get ready for work and leave a note on the board on the side of the fridge for my grandmother, remembering to thank her for the bag of stuff. It looks like it might snow, so I go back inside and add a PS telling her I borrowed the car. I don't have a long shift today and she'll probably be asleep for a while. She has my number if there's any kind of crisis, but I'm sure she'll just watch TV.

As much as I miss the freedom of my bike, the advantage of the car is that I can listen to music. I pull a CD from my bag, just a collection of songs I burned, and I turn it up as loud as it'll go. Of course, it isn't all that loud since it's my grandmother's car and she drives the kind of car a grandmother drives. Still, it's the release I need.

The car is full of the sounds of people as bitter as I am and I sit for a minute. I'm not angry – not really – at the moment, but the music makes me think of Lily. I go back to the last night we were together, running the vibrator along her pussy until she screamed so loud that no music could cover how much she enjoyed it. I wonder if Derek can make her come like that – and now I'm angry. I'm angry at the fact that I have nothing else to offer. I'm angry that he's probably fucking her right now and she's not even thinking about me. And I'm so fucking angry at her for walking away from me. I've cried, I've agonized, and I've longed, but I haven't raged. Now I'm fucking raging.

I grip the steering wheel tight and slam my head against it, which triggers the horn. I scream into the noise in the car and back out of the driveway before my grandmother comes outside to try to figure out why I'm honking the horn. It's a long enough ride on empty roads that I savor the seething fire in my blood. It's not healthy but it's better than numbness and it's better than wanting to die.

By the time I get to work, the anger has dissipated. I'm left with only the embers of the scorched memory of a girl who could've been everything.

****

After the long weekend, it's back to the chaos of school and projects and practice. I can't believe I still haven't seen Lily around campus, but it's probably better this way. The ache is still there, but I know seeing her will be like ripping a bandage off a seeping wound.

On Wednesday night, at band practice, when Neil breaks out a bottle of Jameson's, I take a shot, which makes me hate myself a little. But Lily is never coming back – and the whiskey helps to erase the past. I have no intention of getting drunk, but it's a concession to the person I am.

"You guys think this weekend will be something?" Neil asks.

He loves this band. He loves the music and he loves performing. I, on the other hand, have no long-term plans. Sure, it'd be nice in theory, but I can't truly imagine the life of a musician. I want to get away and leave no roots, but I don't know that I want to escape on an endless tour with people I barely know.

Music soothes me, but performing can suck. It can be a rush, but every show requires willpower I pull from a reserve that's slowly going dry. Once the initial high wears off, the high that comes from the playing itself, not from the performing, I'm left with something else. All those eyes looking at me, all those people judging me. And to get up there and play something I wrote? Sure, Neil is the voice of my pain, but it's still *my* pain on display. It's still *my* time in the hospital or watching *my* father kill my mom that Neil's singing about – and sometimes it's even worse, because I can't explain. I can only play my bass and stare at the faces of the people in the crowd, the empty eyes of people who live in a world where people don't hang themselves. Nothing makes you feel more like a freak than displaying your suffering for the world – and having them miss the fucking point of it all.

It's hypocritical and I can't explain it. I both love it and hate it at the same time. With each show, I suffer the anxiety, the fear of judgment, the agony of having a part of myself taken from me, taken by people who can never understand. And then every time they fucking clap, I get a rush from it. I hate them while I think of them, while I imagine sharing my songs with them, but when they like the music? I'm suddenly their best fucking friend.

Devon nods in response to Neil's question, excited because he still has the innocence of inexperience. He still revels in the applause alone. He doesn't yet hear the silence between the claps, the echoing condemnation of every note someone thinks you could play better. Devon only hears the immense satisfaction of respect. "It's gonna be fucking awesome. You realize how big this could be? Fucking headlining?"

Eric, the rational one, shrugs. "It's big, but it's a local club. I don't wanna get carried away. Although I still think it's pretty amazing for our fan base."

Neil nods. "It's like it all paid off for once. Yeah?" He looks at me directly this time. "Right, Jack?"

I grab the bottle of Jameson's and take a giant swig. How do I answer him without sounding like a dick? I prefer being the opening band. When no one expects anything of you, they don't judge you as harshly. With every success comes the need to do more, to be better.

"It'll be fucking sweet," I say, because in some situations, the easiest solution is to lie.

"It's insane," Neil continues. "A year ago, we couldn't even find a drummer."

The funny thing about people is the way they perceive things. There are four of us and we each see this show as something totally different. For Neil, it's recognition of his efforts and he doesn't care that the club only holds three hundred people. Because a year ago, there weren't *three* people who knew who we were. I don't really know how Eric and Devon feel, but I'm simply awed by Neil's acceptance of the small rewards. I always want it all. Not in this case, but Neil's the type who would look back at the short time I had with Lily and say it was better to have had it and lost it than never to have known her. I can't accept that. For me, there is only success or failure. There are no shades of either.

Devon smiles. "Well, you have one now. Speaking of which, let's get this shit down."

We pass around the whiskey one more time. I take two shots, because you don't fall off the wagon in small steps. And then we practice, letting our hopes about this weekend drive us. I don't know what I'm hoping for, but as I play, I see blue-green eyes under the stage lights and I give myself over to the music.

Hope is stupid, but I cling to it like a fucking life raft.

****

Neil is pacing. The club's packed. The opener is decent, but it's clear that everyone is here for us. They're wrapping up and then we'll be on after a short break. Neil runs a hand through his hair and continues walking back and forth before I kick my foot out and trip him.

"What the fuck, man?"

"Sit down. You're making me nervous as fuck," I say.

He sits, but he taps his foot, which isn't much better. Eric and Devon went to the bar to grab drinks and I hope like hell they get back here fast. Neil needs a fucking lobotomy, not a beer, but a beer will have to do.

"You realize this is everything? Like my entire life happens tonight," he says.

Neil's never come out and said so much, although I read it in him. Music is his way out. He doesn't talk about his life. He lives off campus, alone, in the shittiest house I've ever seen, but hell, he's twenty something and when he's on this side of the country, he lives in his own house. That's still pretty fucking sweet. But every so often, something in Neil's face tells me that he has plenty of experience with the things we write about. In the band, though, neither of us is our past. We're just a singer and a bassist with nothing but right now between us.

"Because I wasn't nervous enough, right?" I ask.

The joke doesn't cover the fact that I feel the same anxiety that Neil does, although for different reasons. For him, this is his shot. If tonight goes well, the road opens up for him. For me, it's a bigger crowd with more of my own songs. And there's that stupid voice that keeps hoping Lily saw a poster around school and will make her way to the show. I know Alana was here earlier, but when I check for Devon and Eric, she's gone. She wouldn't leave, so I assume she's in the bathroom.

"You're good. I sometimes wonder if you even know that," Neil says, but any chance of that being a conversation fades immediately as Eric and Devon come back. We each down a shot of tequila and chase it with a beer before it's time to get onstage. I didn't stick to my plan to stay sober, but as I walk out on the stage, I'm glad I drank enough to anesthetize the heartbreak that bursts within me.

She's here.

Lily looks fucking incredible. I don't know where she found the dress she's wearing, but she doesn't even look the same. The sweet girl I fell in love with is there, but this new Lily is somehow wilder and tougher. She's still beautiful, but now she looks as dangerous as she is. And it's unnerving, because if I thought I wanted her before, I had no idea what it felt like truly to want.

I look down at her face and her eyes meet mine. My body reacts instinctively and begins to play the notes, but my mind is lost in her. I love her; any doubt is gone. Her eyes look to me with a silent reverence and she opens her lips slightly. I want to lean over right now and kiss her, to feel her body against mine, to smell strawberries as I breathe her in, but I keep playing. I don't know what the story is with Derek, but I see in her that there's nothing except us now. I have a million questions, a million things I need to say. But first, we have a show to play, and I focus on that. My eyes don't leave hers for the entirety of our set.

The applause at the end is fucking deafening and Neil looks like he could cry. I want to celebrate with them, to enjoy this, but I can think of only Lily. Neil comes close to hugging me, but then we both stop and look at each other.

He laughs and shakes my hand instead. "I saw her, too. I get it, Jack. Go. We'll be around next week."

"I'm glad it was everything you hoped it would be," I tell him.

"It really fucking was. But there's one hell of a beautiful girl out there waiting for you."

I don't even gather my stuff. I just run back out onto the floor until she's only an inch away from me.

"I didn't expect to see you. It's been a while." I have to fight not to kiss her, but I need to know for sure that I didn't misread her eyes first.

"It's been too long. But I needed to know," she says. She doesn't move, either.

"And do you?" I ask.

"I do," Lily whispers and looks down at the floor. "I'm sorry it took this long, but I owed you that. I wanted to stand here and tell you that I was sure."

"I don't know what to say. I…"

I want her. I want to bring her home, to make love to her, to be with her in every possible way. I want to tell her what I meant to tell her the night that Derek appeared. I also want to tell her everything about me. The truth about my past and my own sadness. But first, I just want to hold her hand and listen to her voice.

"Can you give me a few minutes to pack up and then we can go for a ride?" I need to throw my stuff in the van and then I can spend the whole night with Lily. If she'll let me.

"Take as long as you need," she says.

I'm back in less than ten minutes and we go to my bike. I want to go home with her, but I want to talk to her first. I want her to know that she's so much more to me than a few wild nights. Sure, I've missed her body and I can't pretend I don't want her wrapped around me, but I've missed *her*. When I stood in a row of Christmas trees, it was Lily I yearned for, not sex.

There's a playground I pass all the time on my way to work. It's a little rundown and I've never seen kids there, but it wouldn't matter at this hour. No one's going to disturb us. I lead Lily to the swing set. The swings are full of fallen, dead leaves and rainwater, so I clear one for her before sitting beside her. I look down and draw shapes in the dirt with my Chucks.

"I'm really glad you came tonight," I tell her. "You look beautiful."

I'm afraid to look at her. She still hasn't said it and I can't ask. I think she was hinting that she wanted something with me, but what if I'm wrong? I've been hurting so much for her. I want these last few seconds of not knowing to matter, in case she plans to tell me there's nothing left.

She looks over at me. I can see her in my peripheral vision, playing with a strand of her hair. She twirls it around her fingers, sighs deeply, and speaks quickly in one breath. "I want you. If you'll have me."

I will take you completely, I think. "What about you? You said you needed to figure yourself out."

"I did. I probably still do. I'm not definitely sure who I am or what I want, but I care for you. In just a few days, I knew that I cared for you," she confesses.

It's what I wanted to hear. It's what I kept hoping would happen. I don't know if I should ask, but it means too much not to know. I turn and look at her, taking the strand of hair and pushing it behind her ear. My fingers brush against hers and I'm not surprised that the blazing spark is still there.

"When did you break up with your boyfriend?"

"That night after I asked you to leave me alone."

It's the most beautiful thing she could have said.

"Really?" I ask.

"Really. I almost went to your room after Derek left, but I wanted to come back to you like this instead. I wanted you to know that you weren't a backup plan. You're my choice."

"No one has ever chosen me, princess."

She takes my hand. "Until now."

The conviction with which she says it amazes me. She's so *sure* that I'm the right choice, that I'm what she wants. It's beautiful and scary and overwhelming.

We talk for a while about what happened, her own confusion between the two of us, her history with Derek, and her realization that she was ready to move on. However, it wasn't an easy choice and I can sense that instantly.

"You still care about him." I point out. "I can hear it when you say his name."

I try not to let jealousy factor into my thinking. I know exactly what it feels like to love someone so much, but in the wrong way. And I'd never give up Alana, even for someone like Lily. Because you can't do that to the people who matter in your life. I'm not going to be the guy who demands a girl give up her friends. Lily's who she is because of Derek and, although I may not want to hang out with him, I can't fault her for keeping him close. Admittedly, I kind of hate him and the thought of him touching her makes me want to break something, but she's worth too much to me to make an issue of it. I mean, as long as she's not still dating the asshole, I can let it go. Or at least I can keep my mouth shut.

She admits that she does still care for him, but I believe her when she says it's not the same. However, I don't want her to think that being with me will be like being with him. I adore her, but I'm still a train wreck, as Alana so kindly put it.

"Princess, you're not going to put me back together and make me right again. You know that, don't you?"

"Jack, I realized something that you never have."

"Yeah? What's that?"

"No one needs to put you back together and make you right. You're fine just like this. I want you exactly as you are."

"You've seen my life," I argue, shaking my head. "The shit I carry around with me. How can you say I don't need fixing?"

"Because that is what makes you the guy that I fell in love with."

I inhale slowly and try to focus on breathing. She said she loved me and, this time, she means it. This isn't one of those passionate declarations that you later regret. I didn't know something so good could hurt so fucking bad. But hearing it? It's like feeling all the broken pieces of my heart coming back together one at a time. I think it's healing, but it's excruciating.

"You really love me?"

"I do, Jack," she says and she starts to cry. They're not sad tears; they're the tears of carrying around so much fear and anxiety that you feel like you can't bear it anymore. And then the moment comes when you don't have to and the relief is so euphoric that crying is all you can do. I know those tears, because my own are threatening to match hers.

"For a month now," she continues, "I've avoided you, because I didn't want to say the words if they weren't true. I thought maybe it was just escape, something different from Derek, and that it would fade. I thought if I moved on and if I didn't miss you, if I didn't yearn to see you every time I took a corner, then I would know."

"And?"

"And it was your eyes I saw when I fell asleep at night. When I walked to the elevator every day before class and every afternoon after class, I waited for you to come through the doors, and every time you didn't, I ached for you. I had everything else and I was happy. But I still looked for you every night when I ate dinner. Every voice I heard sounded like yours. That can't be lust. I didn't even feel that way when I was with Derek and we've known each other since we were kids. Something about you, Jack, something in you just makes sense for me."

"Why me, Lily?" I worry. "What if I can't be what you need?"

"That's why I waited. I'm not looking for someone else to be what I need. I'm looking for someone I want," she says.

"It's weird to be wanted," I admit.

"I doubt that. I wanted you plenty before."

Oh, hell. This is a serious conversation, but I can almost hear the sounds she makes when she's underneath me, as she gives herself over to the ecstasy of it all. I haven't been with anyone since her and we didn't even have sex that last night together. It's taking a hell of a lot of willpower not to throw her onto the ground right now. Especially in that fucking dress.

I try to lighten the mood. "So that's what you're after?"

She grows serious again and tells me about her own emptiness. It's weird to hear words like that coming from her mouth. Lily is, to me, the epitome of everything good. But I believe her when she talks about emptiness, because although it may not be the same as mine, she feels it even as she talks about it.

"Lily," I say, trying to comfort her, "I know better than anyone what it feels like to be missing something. I don't want to rush you. I can wait. If you aren't ready."

She shakes her head. I can't believe she wants me in her life, but I'm not going to argue. I gave her the out, but she's holding my hand and she looks at me like she's scared of losing me. As if she could.

"Okay, but there's one condition," I tell her.

"What's that?"

I hate myself for saying it, because I want her so fucking bad. But I want her to know that I want *her* and I want a chance to prove how much she means to me. "I'm not fucking you," I tell her. My cock is ready to hurt me.

She laughs. "What?"

"I'm looking for a girlfriend," I tell her.

"Right, because you didn't fuck my brains out for days straight already," she teases. Which is really fucking unfair, because it's not like I don't remember how incredible she feels. I'm trying to be noble here and she's making it so damn difficult.

"Look, I'm serious," I say, but I'm still smiling, because she fucking loves me. "Do we have a deal? Do you want to be my girlfriend?"

"More than anything," she says.

I stare at her and I'm trying not to grab her and break every promise I just made. She reaches down and goes for my zipper. This girl is going to kill me.

I stand up quickly, which is no small feat, since my jeans are so tight that I'm going numb. I wrap my arms around her.

"For the first time, I want to love someone," I say. It's going to be difficult, but I want her to know. And I know eventually it'll happen – and I want to blow her fucking mind when it does.

She stands on her tiptoes and kisses me. It hurts not to take it further, but we don't. Loving Lily scares me to death, but for once in my life, I feel like I was made to do something right.

Chapter 24

We only have two weeks until break, which is like some kind of cosmic joke, but they're two wonderful weeks. We haven't done anything sexual and, although I have to take a little longer in the shower if I want to avoid having my cock actually explode, I haven't pushed. The way Lily looks at me every day is worth spending a lot of time jerking off. I don't know how to be in a relationship, but she makes it easy.

She's an English major, which I learn one night accidentally. Sometimes it seems so odd how little we really know about each other, but I love the moments when I discover something new about her. She's in my room going through my books while I'm trying ineffectually to study. My bookshelf is lower than my bed and I can't focus on programming languages when her ass looks so fucking good. She turns around with a book in her hand and I sigh. I am seriously going to die.

"Hemingway?" she asks.

"Yeah. I know, I know. It makes me a pretentious douchebag, right?"

"Not at all. He's my favorite. He was the first writer who made me want to major in English. I loved reading, but his books just cut me."

I think the universe likes fucking with me. She is so ridiculously perfect that I don't even know what to say. I just nod and mumble something about liking Hemingway, too.

"What are you majoring in?" she asks.

"Computer design. I want to make games."

"Cool."

"Really?" I raise an eyebrow. Most girls think it's stupid, like I only want to do it because I'm too lazy to work and I must just want to play video games all day. They have no fucking idea how hard the coursework is.

"Yeah. I'm a shitty gamer, but they're fun. Besides, I can barely use Google. I admire anyone who's that good with technology."

"I can teach you," I offer. "To play. I mean, I can teach you programming, but it's not all that interesting. But if you want to play…"

"Yeah, why not?"

She joins me on the bed and grabs the bag of Skittles I've been eating to keep up my energy. We still have exams before we leave.

"What are you doing?" I ask. She's taking the Skittles out of the bag and color-coding them on my bed.

"What?"

"You're insane. OCD much?"

She laughs. "No, it's just... well, it's dumb, but I only like the red ones."

"What?"

"I only like the red ones. The rest taste funny."

"Lily, they all taste like sugar, chemical compounds, and food dye." I shake my head. "Are you suggesting red dye is better than green dye?"

She shrugs. "I don't know. I only eat the red ones. It's like a thing. You think I'm weird?"

I lean over and kiss her long and hard on the mouth, but pull away when my body starts craving more. We've been good and we promised we'd wait until after break. She's sexy and sweet and perfect, but I want to give her this. I've never made these kinds of sacrifices for anyone. Maybe to normal people, it isn't a big deal, but I desperately want to prove that I can make someone else happy, not physically but entirely. And I want to show her that I can keep my word.

"I don't think you're weird," I tell her. "I think that's the cutest fucking thing anyone has ever told me." I scoop up all the non-red Skittles and eat them in one handful.

She leans over to my desk and picks up my Xbox controllers, handing me the black one and taking the white one for herself. "So you gonna teach me to play?"

"If you want to," I say, pushing my work aside.

"I warn you. I'm bad."

"No one is *that* bad," I laugh and turn on the console.

I spend the next three hours teaching her how to aim for an oncoming zombie's head. She is fucking God-awful. I have never seen someone so bad at video games. After three hours, she still can only hit one out of every ten zombies. I think there may be something wrong with her hand-eye coordination.

But I don't care. She took three hours of her life to do something that mattered to me. Because in this vortex that we're living in, I matter to her.

The darkness has been staying away, for which I'm grateful. I haven't told Lily about it yet. I fully plan to tell her, but I kind of want to wait until after the holidays. I don't need to put that worry on her when she goes home for break. She hasn't said as much but I get the impression she hasn't told her family about me. She's the kind of girl who comes from a good, stable family and I don't blame her. I have no interest in forcing the issue. I'm happy with her. I don't need approval from anyone else.

****

A few days before break, I'm in Lily's room with her, her roommate, and her roommate's boyfriend. They've been friendly, but it's still weird being a part of someone's life like this. I've talked to both Alana and Sandee about it and their answers are strikingly similar. They tell me to shut the fuck up and be happy for once. So I'm trying.

Lily gets a call and goes out into the hallway to answer it. I feel a little stab of fear, but I trust her completely. I focus on the conversation I'm having with Lyle about gaming and try not to listen for Lily's footsteps coming back into the room. She'll tell me what it's about when she's ready. I still have my own secrets, and I'm not going to be a hypocrite. However, I can't say I'm not relieved when she comes back and asks if we can go to my room. She keeps saying she left something, which makes no sense, but Lyle and Kristen keep looking at us like they're hoping we'll leave anyway. I don't doubt that they enjoy our company, but none of us are looking forward to break. When you get used to spending so much time with someone, even the smallest breaks feel endless.

"What did you leave?" I ask Lily when we get back to my room.

"That was my brother who called," she says. "He wants to meet you over break. Like at my house. With my parents."

I sit down. "When?" I want to meet them, if she wants me to, but I need time to prepare. I can guarantee I will not be what they're expecting.

"Are you sure you want to? I can make up an excuse." She seems evasive, as if she's thinking of something else, and I wonder if she's trying to hint at the fact that she doesn't want me to meet her family.

"Do you not want me to come over? Are you ashamed of me, princess?"

"No, it's not that," she insists. "It's just that my family is… I mean, we're…"

"Normal. Not a dysfunctional mess of a dead mother and a killer father," I finish.

"I didn't mean it like that. I'm sorry, Jack. It wasn't what I meant."

I can tell she feels terrible and I know it's not what she meant, but someone needs to say it. Because it's not like it will never come up. Sooner or later, we need to accept the fact that we don't belong together, no matter how much we want to. I'm not ending things and I'm happy with her, but I understand that there are some things working against us.

"It scares the hell out of me, but if you want me to come over, just say when," I tell her.

"After the holidays." She says it without thinking, as if the "holidays" are a given. I don't have the energy to tell her what holidays are like for me. I'm thinking about Alana's Christmas tree and wondering if they added anything to it, when Lily walks closer and runs her hand down my chest. And I forget all about Christmas trees.

She leans in to me. "I think there are certain things that have been neglected for way too long."

"But we agreed-" I try to argue.

"There is no way I can wait until after break. I need you," she says. Her hand reaches between my legs. Well, she'll know exactly how difficult it has been now. She runs her hand over my cock and my entire body leaps off the chair toward her touch.

"Oh, Lily. I don't want you to think-"

I don't get to finish, because she kisses me. She bites down on my lower lip and I have to think about my programming final project to avoid coming right now. Oh, fuck, I want her.

She breaks from the kiss but she doesn't move away. Instead, with her lips still against mine, she slips her hand into my pants and purrs, "I don't think anything except that you need to take that enormous cock out and fuck me like I know you can."

Well, there's no stopping it now.

"Okay, princess. You asked for it," I say and rip her shirt off. I stare at her tits as I toss her onto the bed and Lily works fast to get her pants off. Kneeling in front of her, I go for her clit. She's already wet and I tease her until she's moaning and bucking underneath me. I can't believe how long it's been since I've touched her. Our bodies respond to each other as if it's been both seconds and years. I'm so hungry for her, but there's no awkward rediscovery of what works. I run my tongue up and down her pussy and she cries my name.

"I'm gonna make my girlfriend come," I say, looking up at her.

She moans as I go back to her cunt and she clutches my head between her legs with her thighs. As she comes for me, I wonder what the fuck I was thinking being so noble. Lily and I are phenomenal together.

"I want you," she says. I want her too, but I just love how she looks when I make her come. I'm dying a little but it's so worth it to make her this happy. I run my hands along her naked body, enjoying every curve. I've yearned to touch her like this again and I'm taking my time. Sliding my fingers into her, I almost lose it. Her pussy is so wet and so fucking warm and I want nothing more than to slip myself into her. But the teasing will make it even better in the end.

"Jack, I need you to fuck me like you used to," she begs.

"Are you sure? I don't want to ruin us," I tell her. Once it happens, there is no going back. If she thinks that's all there is between us, then there's no way I can convince her otherwise. The longer we wait, the more I can be sure she knows how I feel.

She unzips my jeans in response and that's it. I can't say no to her.

I roll her on top of me and she pauses for a moment over my cock. The smile that spreads across her face makes me wild and I lift my hips, pushing the head against her. She doesn't break eye contact and then, the world disappears. She's wrapped around me, her pussy tight as she slides all the way down on me, and we both inhale sharply. It's fucking staggering. People use drugs to get even a hint of this kind of pleasure.

Lily begins to ride me and she links her fingers with mine as she does. She doesn't look away and I wonder if anyone has ever died from delirium.

"Hey, boyfriend," she teases and I lose my fucking mind.

"Princess, I fucking love you," I attempt to say but I don't know if it's coherent. She lays herself against me, her tits against my chest, and her face against mine. I let out a noise from the back of my throat. She comes while she rides me slowly and all I can say is her name over and over. It's the only thought that I have.

I move under her, pulling my hands away, and I bring her body even closer. I push all the way into her, thrusting with months of need, and she screams in rapture. I feel her orgasm as it runs the length of her body. She leans back and I fight not to come yet, not until she falls against me again, fully satisfied. I let go, caressing her hair, and the orgasm is entirely new. It's not only the months, but all the years of being incomplete. With Lily, I belong for the first time. She kisses my neck and I explode into her.

I can barely breathe, but I whisper, "I love you." She says it at the exact same time.

Chapter 25

It's been obvious that Lily doesn't want me to meet her family for the holidays, and I'm not surprised. Still, I'd love to do something for her for Christmas. I don't know what, since I can't afford much. And I certainly don't know why, since I can't remember buying anyone presents. However, it becomes an obsession over the few days leading up to break. I drive Sandee crazy at work asking her opinion and I text Alana relentlessly. I don't want to go through this big process only to give her something stupid, but I can't afford things like jewelry.

I'm starting to give up the entire plan, but Alana agrees to come over to help me brainstorm. It's Saturday and Lily's leaving later this afternoon. Alana's only planning on staying for a little while anyway, since Dave's back already and they picked things up fast. I can't wait to see him, but she's kept him locked away for a couple days. Today, he's being forced to spend time with his parents, which is the only reason I'm seeing her.

"So, let's run through ideas," Alana says after settling on my desk. She's as beautiful as always, but there's something new in her. Something softer. I'm glad things with Dave are going like they should; it just makes sense.

"I have none," I complain.

"How much do you have to spend?"

"Fifty bucks? Maybe. I just got next semester's schedule. The books are fucking ridiculous."

Alana grabs a legal pad from my desk and readies herself to take notes, but I reach into the top drawer and hand her the thirty similar lists I've made over the last week. Nothing works. Nothing says Lily. I could buy her a book or a CD or something pretty, but those are *things*. I want to give her something that says us, not something I could buy for a fucking Secret Santa gift.

"I thought you had no ideas," she teases.

"I don't. These are all the bad ideas."

"Okay, what does she like?"

"I don't know," I say. "I mean, she likes lots of things, but nothing she can't get herself or that will feel personal. Nothing her friends wouldn't buy her. And I don't want to buy her a friend gift."

"Get her a dildo," Alana says.

"What?" I laugh.

"For real. I know you want to go sweet, but hell, Jack. I was there that night. She'd be all over that."

"That isn't very romantic," I point out.

"So buy her a dildo and write her a poem." Alana hands me my pile of lists and my legal pad. "Honestly? The last gift I got was a box of pencils. That was when my mom bought me presents. What about you?"

"Sheets."

"Or pans?" Alana knows me well and it's comfortable, especially now that we've moved past our history.

"So seriously? A dildo?" I ask.

She shrugs, but I consider the suggestion. The night before things fell apart, when we used the vibrator I still have in my drawer, was fucking hot. Maybe it's not a bad idea.

"Here," Alana says and hands me her phone. She has a web page up with suggestions for sex toys to please women. I look at her and she raises her eyebrow. "It's better than sheets, pans, *and* pencils combined."

I sigh and add the website info to the lists. I want to ask Alana for more ideas, but there's a knock on the door. I know it's Lily. I shove the papers in my desk.

She comes in and the entire world stops. It's like living in a fishbowl, where the edges of the universe span outward, but the only thing in focus is the area right in front of you. Lily is the little plastic castle, and I feel like the fish, surprised every time I see her, but so fucking happy when I do.

"Hey, Lily," Alana says.

They talk, but I hear nothing. Lily is all I can think about and she looks so good. It's rude to rush Alana out of here, but I need her to go. I need Lily and my body can't wait. I have to be close to her, at least one more time before she leaves today. I don't know when I'll see her again, but it could be a full week. In normal time, a full week is nothing, but without her eyes, it's a lifetime.

"We're doing gifts?" Lily asks. *Damnit, Alana,* I think. Now I *have* to get her something and she's going to be all hopeful, only for it to suck.

"Just something small," I tell her.

"So, what is it?"

Alana laughs. "Presents are supposed to be surprises."

"I liked my birthday present. Is it that kind of surprise?"

The soda I'm drinking burns as I nearly choke on it. What happened to the innocent girl I thought she was? "Christ, Lily."

Alana tells her about Dave and then gets up. "I'll let you guys have some privacy. Jack, when are you heading back?"

"Probably tonight," I tell her, although it might be late and I know she and Dave are still "reconnecting" or whatever. I get up to walk her out and close the door behind her, turning to Lily and bringing her body to mine.

Her lips are so soft and I disappear in kissing her. This means more to me than anything with her, because when Lily returns my kisses, they're honest and meaningful and vulnerable. She trusts me, which is evident as her body opens up and she lets me guide the kiss. I don't know how to be trusted like this. I've never trusted many people and I certainly don't think I deserve to hold such fragile trust from Lily. But the fact that she believes in me, the fact that she *does* trust me, despite all rational reason not to, makes me feel like the entire world is both upside down and finally right.

She moans against me, but I move away, smiling at her.

"I didn't realize how much you liked that present, you know. I think I'm a little jealous."

Seeing her with Alana was hot, but things have changed now. I don't want to share Lily with anyone. It's not a possessive kind of control, but a simple need to be enough for her. Hell, I'm jealous of the damn dildo I'm thinking of buying her. I want to be the only one to drive her wild.

She presses herself against me. "Nothing to be jealous of," she whispers against my cheek and then she kisses down my neck.

"You're so damn hot, Lily. You could make a guy crazy."

"Mmm. Like this?" She rubs her hand against my crotch.

I can't believe she's leaving and I need to burn her memory into my body.

"You're leaving soon?" I ask, which makes her rub against me harder.

She moves away from me and my body jerks involuntarily toward her. I need to feel her, to touch her, to lose myself inside of her. She reaches into my dresser and turns around, holding out her perfect, soft hand. Resting in the center are the handcuffs and ball gag we played with when things first started.

"Oh, hell," I moan and I picture her that night, at my mercy and so sexy. Now, Lily is so much more than an incredible lover. Now, that kind of vulnerability is unbelievable to me, because she's emotionally at my mercy as well.

She doesn't speak as she slowly strips out of her clothes. Her entire body amazes me, no matter how many times I see her. I push her onto the bed and handcuff her, but this time she's facing me. I'm tentative as I put the gag into her mouth, but she nods fervently. There is something so wrong about this. I should want to protect her, to hold her and caress her, not to do the things my body and mind are screaming to do to her. I can't resist the desire to be rough and to feel her out of control along with me, but I also don't ever want her to think I'd give her up for this.

She spreads her legs and I look at her eyes. I'm scared of pushing it, but her eyes are gleaming. She's excited and I realize just how right it is with her. Again, she trusts me, enough to allow me to explore her darkest desires with her. She's willing to share things of herself that she's probably kept hidden from everyone until now.

There's a slight twinge of guilt as I think about the secrets I'm still keeping from her, but she kicks me in the thigh and nods her head to address the fact that she's naked beneath me. Now isn't the time to talk, and as I slip inside of her, I give myself to her fully. I don't need words to tell her what she means to me.

Lily is losing herself underneath me and I play along.

"Do you like it like this, princess? Do you like it when I'm rough?"

Oh, God, she does. She tightens herself around me and it's no longer a game. I close my eyes as she pushes against me with all of her. Digging my thumbs into her arms, I feel her come under me and that's all I need. I release too, and uncuff her, falling against her and breathing her in.

She reaches down and takes out the gag and then wiggles out from beneath me, turning onto her side so her back is to me.

"Fuck me again, Jack," she begs.

I roll over onto my side and rest my cock between her legs. I've never had much difficulty going several times, but with Lily, it's a guarantee. If she wants to, I can keep going, because making her happy is the single reason I want to wake up every day. I thrust slowly against her until I'm hard and then I move into her one more time, feeling her rock back and forth against me.

I run my hands along her soft body until I reach the curve of her hip. Brushing my fingertips against her ass cheek, I slide my hand between our bodies and tease her asshole with my finger.

Lily cries out and begs for more. I fuck her harder and slip my finger inside of her as well. She makes soft, moaning pleas for even more, again and again. Every thrust is met with increased desire. I kiss her everywhere; I can't stop kissing her. I want to consume her. My cock is wrapped in her, my finger is teasing her ass, and my lips are caressing her skin. Yet I feel like I need to fold myself into her somehow.

"Lily," I whisper. The feeling of her name on my lips makes me so hot. The sound of it is as beautiful as she is. I nibble on her ear and beg her, "Come for me, baby."

"Oh, fuck, Jack. Fuck."

She writhes and twists against me and I keep my arm wrapped tight around her so she can't move far. My thrusts are insistent and rhythmic, but her body is all over the place. She feels like she's melting, but I hold on tight, guiding her to orgasm.

She's both begging me to stop and begging me to continue and I just keep pounding into her, until she's limp against me, and soaking wet between her legs. I touch and kiss her everywhere. By the time I come along her ass, she is quivering and she can't say a complete word.

"I'm gonna miss you," I tell her and I slowly rock her back down by playing with her clit until the swelling subsides. She has one more soft orgasm against my hand. "I love you, Lily."

I get up to go to the bathroom, to clean up and get some tissues. When I come back, she's still lying naked on my bed, but she's no longer shaking.

"You're incredible," she says and her face is glowing.

"Only with you, princess. You make me incredible," I tell her and gather her in my arms. I want to fall asleep holding her, but she has to go soon, so we lie there silently until it's time.

"I'll call you as soon as I get home," she says, running her hand through my hair and kissing me softly. Her eyes are wet, and I'll miss her, but for once, I have no doubt that it's only temporary.

Chapter 26

I end up heading back after Lily leaves. I need to figure out her gift and the dorm is almost silent. She was one of the last ones to go and it just feels eerie being here alone. I already have enough trouble belonging. There's something about an empty college dorm that really doesn't help those feelings of isolation.

I don't go home right away, swinging by the café to see Sandee, Liz, and Mal. Nicole's on too, though, so I don't stay long. I have two weeks off as a "Christmas bonus." When you're a short order cook at a café that gets no real business, you don't get a cash bonus. You get a turkey. Since I didn't want to eat a 15-pound turkey by myself, they took pity on me and gave me time off.

Alana texts me while I'm at the café; she wants me to meet up with her and Dave for dinner. He was planning to wait to see me, but after she told him she'd seen me earlier in the day, he decided he wanted to get together. It's a little terrifying. It's been a long time and I'm afraid it will be awkward, but as soon as I meet them, the time is gone. Dave grabs me in a hug, which is not really like him.

"Dude, I fucking missed you," he says.

I shake off the hug, because even after two years and even though he's my best friend, it feels weird. People just don't touch me.

"You never wrote," I remind him.

"I just didn't know. I figured you hated me."

"Why would I hate you? You were my only friend."

Alana clears her throat.

"You and Alana, obviously."

Dave shakes his head. "It was tough, man. I knew I needed out. I needed to get the fuck away from my dad. But going there, dealing with that shit... It's just not real what happens over there, you know? I felt like I was split into two people. This guy you knew – and then this guy who's seen some really, really fucked up shit. And I didn't want you there with me. You've been through enough. That was my burden to face."

I think of Sandee and what she told me. "It's never a burden to love someone," I say.

"What the fuck? Are you gay now?"

Alana laughs. "Hell, no. Jack wouldn't know what to do without a girl."

"Not *a* girl anymore," I say. "*The* girl."

She rolls her eyes, but it's teasing. I know she's happy about it. There's been a shift in everything. A lightness in our friendship, a lessening of the need we have and the demands we put on each other. It's not all Lily or all Dave, but a combination of them as well as growing up and realizing some things about the way we are.

"So I hear," Dave says. "When do I get to meet her?"

I shrug. "Sometime after the holidays."

"You're not seeing her for Christmas?" He seems surprised.

"Now you're doing holidays too?" I ask.

Alana speaks up. "Owen invited Dave. We're having things. Like Christmas Eve. And food. And stockings. He even bought one of those calendar things. With the chocolate in it?"

"No idea," I say.

"Well, it's this like cheap ass calendar with a countdown or whatever to Christmas and every day, there's a Christmas-y chocolate when you open the little window for the day. There's a fucking picture that I think is supposed to be the same as the chocolate. Today it was a picture of a bell, but the chocolate was just a round piece of chocolate."

"Nice." What the fuck do you say to that? People have chocolate countdown calendars for Christmas; I have pans.

"Eh. Don't worry about it," she says. "The chocolate tastes like ass."

I don't resent Alana or Dave for having plans for the holidays, just as I don't resent Lily for not inviting me for hers, but I do feel a little left out. I wonder, if things had turned out differently, if I would've had Christmas with my parents. Or would my mom still be a junkie and my dad still be running away to work?

At home after dinner, I unpack and run a load of laundry. It's always weird coming back for break. My grandmother and I don't know how to coexist, because we just have different goals. She wants to visit my dad and watch TV and enjoy quiet for the first time in her life; I tend to want to disappear. I love her, but I've never felt *home* here; I've always felt like a guest. Even with the basement to myself, I don't usually leave my room except when I have to do chores or something. I know she tries and I kind of wish things were different, but it's habit now.

I'm sitting in my room, reading over my lists for ideas for Lily. I followed Alana's suggestion and ordered the dildo, because at least I know Lily likes sex with me and I know that's not something she'll be sharing with anyone else. But I don't want to give her a dildo for Christmas. At least not for real. My phone buzzes and I pick up without even checking. No one calls me when I'm home unless it's someone I want to talk to.

It's Lily and I settle back on my bed, surprised by how relieved and overwhelmed I feel to hear her voice.

"I miss you," she says. "What are you up to?"

"Nothing much. I went out for dinner with Alana and Dave, but now I'm just sitting in my room, reading. My grandmother wants to take me shopping tomorrow for shoes."

"Shoes?"

"She doesn't know what to do, Lily. So she buys me shoes and sheets and pans. Because it's the only way she can deal with things."

She's quiet for a minute and I realize I probably ruined her night. Her parents probably have tinsel and chocolate countdown calendars, too.

When she speaks, her voice is nervous. "What are you doing for Christmas?"

"I'll probably open a few things in the morning and have lunch with my grandmother. She'll go to the prison in the afternoon. I'll probably ride out to see my mom. And then I'll come home and drink a shit ton of eggnog. And eventually, I'll just drink the rum."

She laughs but it's a sad laugh. I don't know what she expected, though.

"Can I come up for Christmas?"

"What about your family?" I don't want to get my hopes up, but hearing the word Christmas from

Lily like that makes me feel like I'm part of something.

"I'll see them Christmas Eve," she says. "I mean, unless you have other plans?"

I laugh. "Yeah, you can come up for Christmas."

"I want to go with you. To see your mom, I mean."

"Are you sure?" What's strange is that there is no hesitation in me. I'll bring her if she wants to go and it's then that I realize exactly how much I love her. Because it took a long time to bring Alana, and she's it. But Lily asks once and I am ready.

"Positive."

"I don't know what to say to that," I admit.

"Don't say anything. Just let me in."

Her parents need her, so she has to go, but she tells me she loves me and we make plans for Christmas. I hang up, feeling completely overwhelmed. Christmas. With Lily. And then I go into overdrive, because I need to make this perfect. I need to plan something that will show her just how much she means to me. And it starts by reading through these damn gift ideas.

****

On Christmas morning, I get up early not only to open the shoes I bought with my grandmother just days before, but also to see Lily. She said she'd be here by ten and I'm pacing by nine. My grandmother and I decided to skip lunch today, so I could have the time with Lily. She's getting ready to go see my dad while I stare out the window, waiting for my girlfriend. I'm not upset at all, because seeing Lily is better than anything else. I bought her gift the same day I got the shoes. Her real gift. When I bought it, I thought it was perfect. I pictured giving it to her and I imagined she'd understand how much I feel for her. But now, thinking about the bag sitting on my bed, it seems so fucking stupid. It's the kind of gift a little kid gives his friend in first grade – and I'm planning to give it to the goddamn love of my life. I am a fucking moron.

I almost decide to throw the whole thing out, but I don't have a backup plan. Except a dildo and that's not what you give the girl who changes you. I know she's giving up so much to be with me today. For the first time in my sad life, someone cares more about me than anyone else. And it's an amazing feeling that I want to reciprocate. I just wish my gift was less lame.

At five of ten, there's a soft knock on the door. I open it and Lily's standing in the doorway. Her blonde hair is down, but she has a bright red scarf wrapped around most of it. She's bundled up in about eighty layers of fleece.

"Merry Christmas," I say.

She almost forces me down the stairs and into my room. It's kind of sweet that she already feels comfortable enough to walk right in. As soon as I shut my bedroom door, she takes the scarf off and rushes me, kissing me all over my face and neck. "Merry Christmas, Jack. I love you. I love you so much."

I step away from her, not because I don't want to touch her, because believe me, I really, really do. But I want to give her the gift. I lead her to my bed by her hand and she takes off some of her layers. She lays each on the floor as she gets it off and I can't help but think of that fairy tale of the princess and the pea. Except this time, the princess *is* the damn pea.

After what seems like thirty layers later, Lily lies back on the bed and smiles. "Have I told you how much I love you?"

I sit next to her. "You have, but you can tell me again if you want."

She looks up at me and her blue green eyes are sparkling. "I love you."

"I love you, too. And I have a present for you."

"You didn't need to get me anything," she says. "I didn't get anything for you yet and, honestly? You're all I could ever want."

"I feel the same way, but I wanted to. I've never done this," I tell her. "I'm worried it won't be right."

"It's just a present. You're overthinking it."

She reaches out her hand and runs her fingers through my hair. It still takes me by surprise that the smallest touch, the slightest sign of affection can not only set my pulse racing, but can also make me feel so many varied emotions at the same time. Her fingertips have a power in them to pull out all of my deepest secrets. And I want to share them with her. I want to lay myself and my life at her feet and give myself over to this magic she holds. I want to be complete with her, because she makes me feel like I deserve completeness.

"I'll never get over your eyes," I say as she rolls over and kisses me on my forehead.

She flushes. "You make me feel like the only girl in the world."

I sit up and bring her to my chest, stroking her hair and breathing in her familiar and still overpowering strawberry scent. "You are, Lily."

There's something frightening about loving someone this much and I move away from her after a moment. It's still only been a short time and I can't deny that I'm scared of what could happen. I smile, though, and reach into my nightstand for the first part of her gift. Turning around, I see her playing with the tissue paper in the bag for her and I playfully swat her hand.

"Not yet."

She grins. "Stop teasing me."

"If I recall correctly, you love to be teased."

I can't resist her and I push the bag off the bed, moving over her body and kissing her everywhere. She moans and arches her back, calling my name, and I don't care about gifts or holidays or anything but hearing the noises she's making. She undresses me, but I just look at her, still wearing a few layers of fleece. She reaches between my legs and strokes my cock. I tilt my head back and give in to the way she fists her hand around me and makes me feel so fucking good. How on Earth did I find her? It's impossible to stop her, but I don't want just her hand. I want every part of Lily, my girlfriend, my princess. I reach down and take her hand away, focusing on removing her clothes.

When she's naked on my bed, I kiss up along her body, starting at her feet. There is nothing about Lily that I don't worship. Reaching her stomach, I kiss her and she digs her fingers into the back of my head.

"Oh, please, Jack."

There's no way I could say no to her and I make the rest of the trek up her body quickly, until I'm positioned to enter her. Before I do, I touch her lips with my fingers. "You're beautiful. You are so fucking beautiful."

"Merry Christmas," she says and I slide into her. She brings her legs up to wrap them around my waist and this is better than a million presents under a tree. I might not have chocolate calendars or stockings or a normal family, but I have Lily.

Chapter 27

We fall asleep together after. When I wake, I realize it'll never get old to roll over and find her tucked beside me, her slow breathing tickling my side, and her hair draped across a pillow. I kiss her softly until she wakes up and she smiles at me as she opens her eyes.

"I'm sorry," she says. "I was so tired."

"It's okay. It's only noon."

She moves closer and runs her hand along my chest. I have to fight all the urges in my body to touch her everywhere again. There are several things we need to face today. I grab my boxers and slip them on, reaching into my nightstand and taking out part of her present again. Sitting down, I toss the box next to her.

"Open it," I say.

She isn't one of those girls who takes her time with gifts. She tears off the paper instantly, and I kind of understand why my grandmother wraps my stuff in baby shower paper. I spent twenty dollars on a roll of paper, a small bag, and tissue paper. I don't even think I used the tissue paper right. I just shoved the mass of it on top of the present in the bag. It looks kind of stupid, but apparently Lily doesn't focus much on what's on the outside anyway.

"Seriously?"

She laughs and holds up the dildo Alana helped me pick out. It's really ridiculous looking. It's supposed to be flesh-colored, but it's some kind of weird orangey pink, and I don't even know what shape it is. Lily puts the box down between us and reaches over, pulling the elastic of my boxers back. She goes back to the box and holds it up. "Shaped like a real penis," she reads aloud. "Jack, I hate to break it to you, but you don't have a real penis."

"You want to test that theory, princess," I ask her and push her back onto my bed. She's still naked and God, do I want to test that theory. I want her and I know she's feeling the same way.

"We're never going to get out of bed," she says.

"And?"

She moves away from me and grabs her shirt, throwing it over herself, and then she steps into her panties. "I hate doing this. God, I really hate doing this, but I want to go with you today. I want to be a part of that, too. I want you to trust me with everything you are. Not just this." She must see the mood shift in me, because she finishes her thought. "Not that *this* is not a wonderful way to spend my Christmas."

"I don't want you to feel bad," I tell her. The moment is gone and the mood has changed. I sit up and find my clothes, dressing, because I can't just spend all day with her in bed, pretending everything else doesn't exist. "And once we go..."

"Jack, I don't love you because you're fucking amazing in bed. I love you because when I finish classes at the end of the day and leave the building, I can count on you to be standing by that same oak tree, looking lost and confused that there's someone counting on you. I love you because when you think I'm sleeping, you whisper your fears to me, and I love that you have fears. I love you because you bought me a dildo for Christmas, which is both so wrong and yet so ridiculously *you*. And I love you because when you look at me, I love *me*. Not in an arrogant and selfish way, but in a way that makes me feel like I deserve to be looked at like that."

"You deserve everything, Lily. But I have so little to give you."

"I told you," she says, as she brushes my cheek with the back of her hand, "I only want you. That's more than everything else combined."

It's quiet for a minute and I don't know what to say to her. I feel like I need to preface going to see my mom with some explanation, some story. I need Lily to know everything.

"There are so many things I still haven't told you," I remind her.

She takes my hand. "So tell me. And then we'll go see your mom."

I take a deep breath and then I tell her everything. I tell her about the snowmen. I tell her about the fighting and what my mom was like outside of that one instance at the craft fair. I tell her what I heard from that teacher. I even tell her what it was like, what happened daily and how I felt. Lily doesn't move; she just keeps holding my hand. When it starts to hurt too much to keep talking, she holds me, and then the words finish spilling out. I describe watching my father kill my mom, how scared I was, but how I didn't understand. How I *still* don't understand.

"And there's this unspoken obligation," I explain. "That I owe him forgiveness. That sooner or later, I have to let go and move on. As if he owes me nothing in return. As if he didn't owe me a fucking mother."

Talking about it brings too much back and I don't want Lily to see me this way. On the night when I called Alana because the darkness was enveloping me, I realized how much I love Lily, but I also realized that there are parts of me I don't want her to see. I don't want her to know that I'm this person.

"I don't know what to say," she says, her voice shy and sad.

"Can we just forget it? Maybe I'm not ready." I pull my hand away from her and turn around, bringing my knees up to the bed and trying to quell the shaking in my body.

I feel her behind me, reaching her arms around me, under my arms, and across my chest. She doesn't talk, just lays her head against my back and holds me.

"I want to be real with you," I tell her. "But I'm afraid you'll hate me."

She speaks into my back. "I'll never hate you. Please trust me. I might not know what to do or what to say, but I'm not going anywhere, Jack."

I don't turn around, but I continue speaking. "I can't move on. I can't be someone else. My grandmother has been pushing me to help my dad, to encourage this rehabilitation program the state wants to try with him. And I go, because she wants me to go. But if he died in there? If I never saw him again? It'd be okay. I don't think I can forgive him. I don't think it will ever be understandable. My mom wasn't perfect. She wasn't a good person; I know that. I'm not stupid and I know so many things now that I didn't know as a kid. But she was a person, Lily. And she was my mom. I didn't get to pick her."

"I know," she whispers. She doesn't know and she knows she doesn't know, but the words are comforting nonetheless. They tell me that she's listening, that she's trying to understand.

"I wish he'd left. Just walked out. But he killed her. He choked her to death in our fucking living room while I watched. I just can't forgive that. I'll never forgive that."

"You don't need to forgive anyone. Except yourself."

I move so that she's on my side instead of behind me. Her eyes are wet with tears, but she's not scared of me. All that's present in her face is sadness.

"What do you mean?" I ask her.

"You act like his actions define you. I'm not you and I'm not going to speak about your family. I won't offer my opinions on what kind of people your parents were or are. And I won't tell you whether you should or shouldn't forgive him. What I will tell you is that you're more than them, Jack. You're not your past."

"But people-" I start.

She shrugs. "People can fuck themselves."

I can't help but laugh.

"I'm serious," she says. "Any person who judges you because of your father is not only an asshole, but they're stupid, too. Because anyone would be lucky to know you."

"I just don't know how to let it go," I admit.

"Sometimes the things we hold onto are the things that hold us back."

"That's pretty fucking wise."

She smiles, still sad. "*You* taught me that. I might not know what you're feeling, but I know that I want to know. I know that I want you to be a part of my life, to be my future. But you're always looking behind you. Turn around. Look forward."

"The future is terrifying," I whisper.

"It is. But it's easier together."

I think about her words. I've never seen the future. All I've ever seen is darkness and misery and suffering and the countdown of my life. But she's right. Whenever there was hope, whenever something seemed good, I ran away. I convinced myself that it was going to end and I lost myself. I let the darkness win, because it was easier than hoping for the light. Because what if the light didn't come? Or worse, what if it did? The absence of it was easier to face than its loss.

"There's more," I tell her. This part is going to be the hardest and I'm worried about bringing her into this. Because it's not the kind of thing you can unknow – and it could change us completely.

"Go ahead," she says. "I'm right here."

I try to find the words, try to explain what it felt like, how helpless I was and yet how sure. I describe the mirror and the distortions that stared back at me. I tell her about the way that there was nothing ahead of me but black emptiness. I even tell her about how aware I truly was in the moments leading up to it, how I could feel the chair against my feet as if all of my nerves were pressed against the smooth wood of it. Even as I speak, I can feel the rope in my hands. I can hear the sound of the chair falling over and I remember how it was. There was no white light. There was no sudden regret, no moment when I would have given it all for more time to appreciate the little things. There was just more misery, more sadness, and more darkness that stretched on endlessly. Until the darkness was all.

"And then I woke up in a hospital bed, with a bunch of assholes standing around me, trying to label what was in my head. They had their go-to list of chemicals that would make me normal, their scientific names of disorders to explain why, when I pictured life, I saw nothing. I was there for months. When I left, I wasn't any different. They just titled me chronic and told me to keep telling someone my problems and popping my pills."

Lily's silent when I'm done speaking. She won't even look at me. It was too much; I knew it was too much.

So this is how it ends... Christmas Day. I still haven't even given her the real gift. I should have known this would happen. A fucking holiday? Like I would ever have the right to a holiday. And of all holidays, Christmas. Isn't it the "most wonderful time of the year" or some bullshit?

She has her back to me. I don't know when she turned away. At some point while I was talking, I guess. I keep my fists at my sides. I want to punch the wall. I want to hurt. I want to get so drunk that today never happened. But most of all, I want her to say something. I want to kiss her one last time. I want to tell her that I still love her, no matter what she thinks of me. I want to have a normal fucking life.

"I can't," she says and her voice is choked with sorrow.

"I know." I've already resigned myself to it.

She turns to look at me. Her cheeks are spotted white and red and her eyes are swimming in tears. She tries to talk, but it's just sounds of pain as the words refuse to come.

"No. I can't," she repeats, but she doesn't continue or move. She just stares at me. I don't know what to say or do.

"It's okay. I figured."

She leans into me and hits me hard in the chest, her little soft hands making the weakest fists and it's an out of body experience. She's punching me and crying and saying the word no, but all I can think about is how she's gorgeous even when she cries. How her punches don't hurt, but she's putting so much into them and it's kind of perfect. Finally, she stops and pulls my face down to hers, kissing my forehead, cheeks, and lips. She repeats my name over and over.

"I love you so much," she says. "You can't fucking leave me like that, Jack."

"It's in the past," I tell her.

She pauses. "Entirely?"

I can't lie to her. "No. Not entirely. But I want it to be."

"I was there as you said it. I felt what you were feeling. *You* felt what you felt back then, because it's not gone. You still feel like that, don't you?"

"Sometimes," I admit.

"How often?"

I sigh. "I don't know. It comes and goes. I can have good months. Sometimes even a few in a row. I also have bad months. And sometimes those are in a row, too."

"Have you... have you felt that way recently?" She looks so scared and I wish I could say what she wants to hear. I wish I could deny that the pain is still coursing through me, that the darkness is an endless tangible presence in my life, but I can't. And it wouldn't be fair to lie to her. I know now that I need her in my life, but I also need her to know me.

I nod. "Right before things went down with Derek. The night I was late from band practice. I called Alana and-"

She looks into my eyes. "Why not me?"

"I didn't think you could handle it."

"That's not fair."

"I didn't want you to see this. I didn't want to ruin whatever we were starting, to have you think of me as this guy. I just didn't want to change things."

"You need to call me. You need to let me in," she says.

"I'm trying. That's all of me. I have nothing else to hide." It's an incredible vulnerability that I've given her.

She hugs me and runs her hand along the back of my head. "I need you. Please, don't even think about leaving me that way. If you need to walk away, I'll cry and I'll miss you. But I can't survive *that*. I can't survive the empty place in the world where you used to be. Promise me, Jack."

I hold her and I promise her, because she makes me want to promise. She makes me believe there is something worth promising to hold onto. As she cries against me, scared of losing me, I feel what it's like to be needed, to be wanted. And it's the most beautiful feeling in the world.

Chapter 28

"You still haven't opened your real present," I tell Lily after we've both calmed ourselves. I can't get over the fact that she's still here, but she is. However, we have to see my mom and there's one more thing I want to do. It's already getting so late, but I want to give her the gift before we head out.

"Another dildo?" she smirks.

"Let's not pretend you don't love your toys, princess. I can name several instances when you have been more than happy to-"

She blushes and cuts me off. "I didn't say I *didn't* want it. Besides, there are almost three full weeks left of break. And we won't be able to see each other much. So..." Her voice trails off and I try not to think of her using it, of her unbelievable body and the sounds she makes when she comes. I'm fucking jealous of a pile of plastic.

"Don't get too attached," I grumble.

"Oh, Jack. Give me a break. Nothing is going to replace you."

I feel better although I'm tempted to remind her just how good it is with us, but I know we won't stop if I start. So instead I reach down and pick up the bag with the tissue paper shoved on the top. It's such a stupid gift and I almost change my mind. I bought my girlfriend a dildo and this dumb thing for Christmas. Some guys buy bracelets and rings. I'm really a terrible boyfriend.

"I thought this was a good idea, but I'm realizing how lame it is," I say. I don't even want to give it to her anymore.

"I'm sure it's lovely," she says.

"I'm sorry." I give it to her, because obviously I have to now that she knows it exists, but I try not to blush when she pulls out the giant wad of tissue paper from the bag. "And I don't know how that shit works."

"No one does," she laughs.

She reaches into the bag and pulls out the present. I put it in a tin that says "princess," which is probably for like three-year-old girls, but my resources were limited. Lily smiles and opens the tin. She stares at the contents inside and her eyes fill up. She doesn't look up, but I see the tears start to hit my bed.

"Why are you crying?" I ask.

She turns around and pushes me down on the bed, tearing my clothes off, and kissing me everywhere. Her agony about my revelations about my life, about my family, and about my fears is present in the feral way she touches me. She lifts her shirt over her head and kicks off her panties, before kissing me hard as she moves herself over my cock. I don't have time to think of anything else, because I'm inside of her and she's riding me hard before I even fully process what's happening. When she's like this, I can't think of anything but her and what she does to my body.

"Jack, I love you. I love you so much. Do you get that?"

I just nod, trying to ease the burning inside of me. I want to come. I want to explode already, but I don't want her to stop either. She's wild, moving fast, and her hands are rough as they claw along my chest and torso. I lift my legs up and she leans back, crying out so loud I almost forget that we're in my house and that this is supposed to be a holiday. Fortunately, no one's home.

I push up into her, lifting myself from the bed and hanging onto her hips. I love watching her from this angle, as her hair cascades around her and her tits are on full view. She's going crazy, touching herself as I rock her, and she tilts her head back, crying my name. Fuck, I love hearing her say my name.

It doesn't take long for her to come and she's desperate for it. She reaches back and digs her fingers into my thighs, tightening her cunt and pushing herself down onto me harder. I keep thrusting and I watch her as her whole body succumbs to the tremors. It's a beautiful, beautiful sight.

As soon as she's done, I let go and it's only seconds before my own orgasm rushes through my body. I grab onto Lily and push deeper until I feel it in my balls and then I release into her. "Fuck," I groan and she falls onto me. I wrap my arms around her and hold her while we both try to catch our breath.

After the sensations slow and we're both coherent again, Lily sits up on my chest and teases me with her fingertips. I swore we would not spend all day in bed, but look at us.

"Thank you," she says.

"For what?" I don't honestly know what at this point.

"The present. It's the sweetest thing anyone has ever done for me."

"Really? It's kind of stupid, isn't it?"

"Are you kidding? Did it just *look* like I thought it was stupid?"

She gets off of me and dresses, lifting the tin and placing it on my nightstand.

It was silly. On a whim, the idea came to me, but I can't believe this is all I did for her. I went to the grocery store, to the candy aisle. I bought every single kind of candy I could think of with multiple colors. And then I threw away anything that wasn't red, placing only the red ones in the tin. It was such a ridiculous gift now that I think about it.

"I should've bought you a necklace or something."

"This is the most thoughtful present I've ever received. Let other girls have jewelry. *Anyone* can buy jewelry. Anyone can't make something so personal."

"I love you. You know that?"

"Yeah. I'm pretty sure I really do."

****

I didn't tell Lily, but something she said really stuck with me, so when we were dressing, I took something from my desk and shoved it in my pocket. We're heading to the cemetery now and it's a big deal, but it no longer seems like a turning point. Lily knows me now. She's heard the worst and not only is she still here, she seems *more* attached to me as well. I wonder how long it'll take before that makes even the slightest bit of sense.

Because of the snow, the cemetery is mostly empty. Sure, it's Christmas, but it's cold and it's getting dark and most people are spending the evening with their living family. Since my only living family is at the prison, I come here. Every year. Because someone needs to. I can't imagine my mother being left alone on Christmas. But tonight is different. Tonight, I'm ready to say goodbye.

I don't expect never to return, to put my mother away for good. However, I'm ready to accept that she isn't here. That this is for me more than it's for her.

"This is her," I tell Lily.

The tiny tombstone looks even smaller with the snow on the ground. I reach down and brush some snow away from her name. *Evelyn Connelly*. That's it. No years, no details. Certainly no phrases like "loving wife and mother."

"Evelyn? That's a pretty name," Lily says.

"They spelled it wrong. Her name was Eveline."

"Oh. I'm sorry."

I take her hand. "It's okay. It's just a stone. She doesn't care what some person carving a memorial calls her. She's long gone."

Lily squeezes my hand and I step closer. I let go of her and bend down by my mom's grave.

"Hey, Mom," I say.

Lily kneels down next to me and puts her hand on my back. It's weird. No one has ever been here with me when I've talked with my mom – and I've never wanted anyone here. Alana always keeps her distance, but with Lily, it feels good. Because Lily is my moving on.

"Mom, do you remember the craft fair? I've been thinking about that lately. You told me it was okay to ask for help. Do you remember? Last time I was here, I did. I asked for your help, but nothing happened. I thought you'd left me. I thought you didn't care." I take a deep breath, trying not to let the hurt interfere with what I want to say. "But you know what? It took a little longer than I'd hoped, but there's this girl, Mom. Lily. She's right here. Do you see her?"

"Hi Eveline," Lily whispers. Her voice disappears on the wind.

"I needed you, Mom. I needed you so many times growing up. You were never there. After you died, I needed you even more. Sometimes I was angry, but mostly I just wanted to know why. I wanted to know why I wasn't important enough to you. Why you wanted to be high more than you wanted to be my mom. It really hurt."

The weakness and the darkness are both crushing me, but I focus on Lily's hand on my back and the words I need to say. Tears land in the snow and sizzle as I speak.

"I came here every weekend. Every holiday. Just wanting an answer. Why didn't I matter? Would I *ever* matter? And I know you can't tell me, but I believe you regret it, Mom. I do. I believe you would do it differently this time around. Because I have to believe that. I have to think it so I can get up every day, so I can put one foot in front of the other.

'I asked you for help. I don't know if you had anything to do with Lily coming back. But she did. And she told me something earlier today. She said sometimes the things we hang onto are the things that hold us back.

'I'm tired, Mom. I am so fucking tired. I'm tired of the anger and the resentment and the doubt and the fear. I love you. I can't help loving you and I'll always love you. But I'm going away. I know you're not really here anymore anyway, but I wanted to tell you. Just in case. I'll still come by when I can, but I'm looking ahead of me now. I'm going to live my life. I hope it's a life you'd be proud of, but even if it isn't, it will be mine."

I stand up and brush myself off. Lily joins me; she's crying, but she hasn't spoken or moved. I look at my mother's tombstone one more time and breathe in the night. I've never been an active participant in a goodbye. People usually just leave me and it feels surreal to be doing the leaving. It also feels liberating.

Reaching into my pocket, I find what I took out of my desk. I bend down one more time and place the cotton ball snowman on the grave. It's worn after more than a decade. I never got rid of it, always keeping that memory as the one thing my mom did for me and the one thing she taught me. But now, I realize she taught me plenty and the snowman is just a thing. Besides, I'd rather give it to her, to show her that, regardless of what that teacher said, she's still my mom. And no matter how much she fucked things up, I will always love her just the same.

"I love you, Mom. Goodbye."

****

After the cemetery, there's just one last thing I want to share with Lily. She's been far more than I ever expected and I can't believe how much I love her. Still, it's frightening to me, because she can't be this *right*. Nothing has ever been this easy and this right – and I just keep waiting for the other shoe to drop. But until it does, I want to savor everything about her.

"Hey. Would you mind doing one more thing?" I ask.

"Sure. What is it?"

"It's just something I want to show you. I'm not sure I can explain it."

"Lead on. Anything that matters to you matters to me."

From the cemetery, it's a short drive to where I want to take her. On the edge of town, by the old railroad tracks, there's a small cliff edge that hides behind a group of trees. Growing up, I came out here a lot, because it was the one place that was all mine. I never shared it with anyone. Not Alana, not my grandmother. I needed a place for me alone. It's strange that I've never seen another person here, but

I'm glad I haven't. Maybe the trees deter them, although when they're bare in winter as they are now, the cliffside is more evident. Whatever the reason, though, it's a small piece of the world that belongs only to me and I love it.

The snowstorm we had a few days ago has blanketed the ground in a soft white. There are only a few inches, but it muffles our footsteps. As we get out of the car, Lily looks around, but doesn't ask any questions. I take her mittened hand, the rough yarn between her soft skin and my own. Something about her mittens, blue and old fashioned, makes me fall more in love with her. She's such a perfect girl, but she's so happy to be a part of my life. I can't get it over it, but I'll fight to keep her in it.

I lead her through the trees. A small clump of snow falls from a branch overhead and hits her in the face. She brushes it off.

"Sorry," I say.

"Why?"

"I'm sure that was unpleasant."

I clear the remnants of snow from her face and she smiles at me.

"It was fine. Woke me up a little."

We keep walking and, when we break through the trees, I stop. There is little room to move, but the view still stuns me. In the valley under the cliff, the river runs cold, but the soft sounds of it echo up here. I look up and the moon is glowing, a giant orb of light shining over the snowy landscape. Dark clouds swirl around it, making it look like something fresh off an oil painting, but the moon is too bright to be swayed by a few wisps of cloud cover. Breathing deep, I can smell the freshness of the fallen snow along with the old pine that permeates the forest.

I say nothing as I sit down, knowing the snow is going to soak through my jeans, but I don't mind. Lily doesn't react – she just sits beside me. She pulls her knees up to her chest, hugging them close to her with her mittened hands.

Nearly twenty minutes pass in silence. It's a beautiful silence, the kind of silence that you only share with someone who knows you and who gets you. At one point, Lily takes off one of her mittens and holds my hand between her knees. She doesn't look at me, she doesn't speak, and she doesn't move otherwise. Instead, we just sit, listening to the river and looking at the moon. I feel so much love for her in this moment, although as we approach the twenty minute mark, I'm worried about what she'll say, what she'll think. What if she says the wrong thing? Will it break the power this place has over me? Will I feel disappointed that she doesn't understand empathically why it's important? Should I have told her something about it before I brought her here?

I squeeze her hand and break the silence by kissing her. She lowers her knees and wraps her arms around my neck. She grows more passionate in the kiss and pulls me down on top of her. I don't want anything more from her. Not here. This isn't the place. She seems to get that and her hands don't move from my neck. I imagine the ground must be cold and I break away from the kiss, lifting her to me, so her back won't get cold.

"The ground is freezing," I say.

"And wet," she replies.

"I'm sorry."

"Don't be. It's beautiful. Thank you so much for bringing me here."

"Are you sure?"

"Absolutely. This secretive little part of the world, tucked away here, undiscovered? It's like our own little square of the universe, a square reserved for no one else. I'm honored you felt I was worthy of it."

She gets it.

"I love it here. I first found it in a fit of depression, thinking I would throw myself into the river, let it wash me away and no one would ever find me. But the silence and the beauty of it just seemed too pure to be corrupted like that."

"Was that before or after-"

"Before. Usually, this place was enough to stop me, but I can't deny that sometimes, the darkness is too much to bear."

She takes my hand again. "Jack, promise me something?"

"I promise."

"You don't even know what it is."

I look at her, meeting those stunning eyes. Everything about her is beautiful. "I will do anything for you, princess. I love you. Truly."

"Fine, but promise me that if the darkness comes back-"

"It won't." I'm lying, but I still feel ashamed of it and I don't want her to feel obligated to love me.

"Okay, but if it does, remember this moment? Remember the moon. Remember the whisper of the river. Remember the way that the snow felt against your skin and how there is so much hope in this place. Remember that – and come back if you must. But remember how beautiful life can be – and remember that I love you and I want to experience life with you, in all its beauty and darkness equally."

"You're perfect, you know."

She shakes her head. "No. I'm not. But you make me feel like I am. And I love you for it."

"You really love it here?" I ask.

She nods. "I *really* love it here. It's the perfect place for you. And for us."

I kiss her again, because she knows exactly what to say. We begin getting a little more energetic in our embrace and I worry about sleeping with her here. I don't want to change this place and what it means, and I don't want to change tonight for her. If, someday, things fall apart between us, I would hate for a night like this to have a heavy sadness over it.

"It's so hard not to touch you," I tell her.

She stands and brushes herself off. "I know."

Lily walks to the edge of the cliff and looks down. "The river is speaking."

I walk over to her and wrap my arms around her. "Yeah? What's it saying?"

"That I'm the luckiest girl alive."

I lean down and breathe her in. She still smells like strawberries and, after all this time, it still both breaks my heart and makes me believe in a future. I want her bad, but I want to leave here first. I want this place to remain pure like this. I whisper in her ear, "Want to head back? I need all of you."

She turns around. "I'm happy to give it," she says and smiles. She slips her mitten back on and takes my hand. We walk to the tree line, but she stops before we leave the cliff for good. She doesn't say anything, just closes her eyes and breathes deep for a few seconds. Then, without a word, she steps forward into the trees and the magic slowly fades. Soon, we're back at the car.

Lily gives me the keys and climbs into the passenger seat. I get in and wait for the heat to kick on. She shivers, her breath fogging the windows. She takes off her mitten again and draws a giant heart in the glazed glass.

"I love you," I say, mostly to myself.

She writes in the heart. *I love you, Jack. For always.* Then she puts on the mitten, puts her hand on my knee, and faces me.

"Now show me," she says.

I start the car and we head back to my house, still quiet and remembering the evening. Something stands out and, in the driveway, I turn again to Lily.

"You didn't even take a picture," I say.

"Did you think I should?"

"No. I mean, it's just … everyone always takes pictures. Of everything."

"Why do you always assume I'll do whatever everyone else does?" She's not mad, just curious.

"I don't know, honestly. You haven't yet. You surprise me every single time."

"So stop doubting me, okay? I trust you. I trust you fully and I have complete faith in us. You should, too."

I look down and think about it. She's right. I've been looking for a problem, wanting her to be wrong somehow, because the month I spent without her was harder than anything since losing my mom. It's like I've been attempting to insulate myself in case it happens again, but there is no us if I can't let it go. And I want there to be an us with every ounce of myself.

"Okay," I tell her, "but if you want to take a picture next time we go, I won't judge you."

"I don't take pictures very often. They don't mean anything, really. They're just more things."

"They can be mementos," I say.

"Sure, but memories work just as well."

"I'm glad, but sometimes people like to remember."

"I'll remember tonight for the rest of my life. Fondly. And no picture could ever do it justice.

Besides, taking a photo would have removed me from the moment – and I wanted to be as present as I could. Is that weird?"

I hug her and kiss the top of her head. I cannot believe, even still, just how much she gets of me. "No. It isn't weird. It's like everything else with you. Perfect."

"You put a lot of pressure on me, you know," she says. "It's not possible to be perfect."

I see it in her. There's fear. This girl is the world for me and she's afraid she won't be enough. It's amazing to see that doubt in her eyes, not because I want her to doubt herself or us, but because she is so incredible – and yet she makes me feel normal. Right.

"Perfect to me?" I correct. "Because I can't lie to you, Lily. Everything about you is everything I could ever want. I know we'll change, grow up, learn new things about each other. But you make me want to share it all with you."

She leans in to me and puts her mittened hand in mine. "I love you, Jack." I kiss the top of her head, which smells, of course, like strawberries. Hell. This beautiful, perfect girl. I will never have enough of her.

Tonight, I want to make love to her in a way I haven't yet. Because now she has all of me – and the fact that I trust her with it is something both new and thrilling. The anger I feel, the hatred of my father, the misery at many of the things that have happened in my life? Well, they aren't gone. Life isn't that simple. But with Lily, the road ahead arcs toward the horizon and, at the end of it, I see myself growing older, being a man, being someone I can feel proud of being. I don't want to pretend that there won't be nights when I won't be able to break free of the sudden onsets of depression that don't fade just because you fall in love. However, I look to them now no longer as a guarantee that life is nothing but darkness, but instead as small obstacles in the way.

I hold Lily close to me in the car and the heater whirs as we embrace. It's not salvation to love her, but it's pretty damn close.

The End

CPSIA information can be obtained at www.ICGtesting.com
Printed in the USA
BVOW07s2235271013

334812BV00001B/11/P